Andrew has a PhD in environmental and marine science, Grad. Cert. in strategic studies and a Grad. Dip. Ed. He has published in peer-reviewed science journals and co-founded the New Zealand Aquaculture Magazine. Andrew has served as a watchkeeping officer in the navy. He has lectured and taught statistics, marine and maritime studies at a technical institute. During this period, he consulted to the fisheries and aquaculture industry. Subsequently, Andrew contracted to the offshore oil and gas industry in environmental management. He then taught secondary school science and mathematics and is a future schools STEM industry focus advocate.

To my family I dedicate a story of youthful resilience and triumph against the odds. To my daughters, Abigail and Eliza, never stop dreaming; my partner, Belinda, who never stops believing; and my mother-in-law, Jilly, who never stops hoping. For Garth and Ro whose generosity has carried us forward in life. For my father who taught me to always 'give it a go' no matter what. Lastly, for my mother who lost her battle with cancer and commented that 'you just have to soldier on and get through it'.

A.D. Morgan

SKIMMER – DEEP SEA

AUSTIN MACAULEY PUBLISHERS™

LONDON * CAMBRIDGE * NEW YORK * SHARJAH

Copyright © A.D. Morgan 2022

The right of A.D. Morgan to be identified as author of this work has been asserted by the author in accordance with sections 77 and 78 of the Copyright, Designs and Patents Act 1988.

All rights reserved. No part of this publication may be reproduced, stored in a retrieval system, or transmitted in any form or by any means, electronic, mechanical, photocopying, recording, or otherwise, without the prior permission of the publishers.

Any person who commits any unauthorised act in relation to this publication may be liable to criminal prosecution and civil claims for damages.

A CIP catalogue record for this title is available from the British Library.

ISBN 9781398409163 (Paperback)
ISBN 9781398409170 (Hardback)
ISBN 9781398409187 (ePub e-book)

www.austinmacauley.com

First Published 2022
Austin Macauley Publishers Ltd®
1 Canada Square
Canary Wharf
London
E14 5AA

No people, in particular, have contributed to the telling of this story. However, I would like to acknowledge life's circumstances and all those that have passed through my life. In doing so, the experiences and insight gained over many years have bought this story into existence.

Table of Contents

Synopsis	11
Chapter 1	13
Chapter 2	23
Chapter 3	28
Chapter 4	36
Chapter 5	41
Chapter 6	53
Chapter 7	62
Chapter 8	69
Chapter 9	78
Chapter 10	91
Chapter 11	98
Chapter 12	105
Chapter 13	115
Chapter 14	121
Chapter 15	129
Chapter 16	138
Chapter 17	145
Chapter 18	153
Chapter 19	161

Chapter 20	169
Chapter 21	174
Chapter 22	181
Chapter 23	191
Chapter 24	204

Synopsis

In the middle of high seas of the Southern tropical Pacific a young brother and sister from China are caught up in a plot to secure a technology that has the potential to revolutionise deep sea mining. Chang's sister is a successful robotics and artificial intelligence engineer in her father's company. Their father is the Chief Operations Officer of GlobeCorpMining, a Chinese-owned global mining corporation that runs the Pacific Harvester ship mining programme. Chang is a member of a crew of seven on a contractor sub-surface mining skiff or "Skimmer" collecting and supplying manganese nodules.

Skimmers are run by an artificial intelligence system called SAI and constructed in Australia. Contractor's lease or buy Skimmers and use them to mine manganese nodules for tenure holders operating in "the Area" regulated by "the Authority" and transport them to the Harvester. Attached to the Skimmers, mining drones called Xtracts travel up and down to the seabed 4000m below collecting manganese nodules. A laser signal communication streamer deployed to the depths below allows SAI and the crew to monitor and control mining operations.

One of the crew, an autistic youth from Australia named Connor thinks he has found a way make Xtracts learn autonomous group behaviour. With the help of SAI, he finds a way to make Xtracts learn to respond as a group to anything that may stop them carrying out their mining task. Chang becomes jealous and does not care much for Connor. He has a confrontation with Jonny the Skimmer pilot over his attitude. Jonny is a laidback Tongan-Maori who doesn't take lightly to Chang's attitude.

Chang is angry at the world and in the eyes of his family he sees himself as a failure. He wants to prove himself to his father. As Chang's anger grows, Stella the Xtract technician tries to be a calming influence. Her fun-loving personality and careless nature often get her into trouble. Ngarra, an indigenous Australian and the Skimmer operator in charge tries to keep them working together. Jesse is always on hand to help smooth things over. Being the Skimmer Communications and Security Officer, she is the most senior and mature person on the Skimmer.

Meanwhile on another Skimmer, the crew's families have been threatened if they do not help get hold of the technology Connor has started to develop. They are no longer able to communicate with other Skimmers and the shore-based crew monitoring centre at the Academy. They are off the grid and try to distract Chang's crew while others look to secure the technology. Ngarra's crew is tasked by the Academy to try and find the off-grid Skimmer and its rogue crew and return them to the Academy.

Max, the operator of the Sea Hunter vessels which carry out monitoring, compliance and enforcement in "the Area" and his off-sider Alex are looking for the off-grid Skimmer. Their contact at the Ocean Academy makes them aware of the potential value of the technology being developed by Connor on Ngarra's Skimmer. They use the off-grid Skimmer as a distraction to try and get close to, disable and board Ngarra's Skimmer and get hold of Connor and the technology.

Jonah, a founding member of Xed and the Ocean Academy becomes aware that Academy security has been compromised and that somehow the Sea Hunters and GlobeCorpMining are involved. She tries to protect Ngarra's crew and the information they have while also getting the off-grid Skimmer crew back safely. She also has a close relationship with Chang's father and despite her suspicions asks for his help to avoid the authorities and get her crew and the information safely back to the Academy.

In the meantime, Chang seeing an opportunity to win his father's favour and help his mother's situation is coerced into stealing Connor's work. He is told it will secure a place for him in his father's company. The crew on both Skimmers get caught up in the plot to secure the technology but no one seems to know who is behind it all. Is it Chang's father himself, the Harvester operators, the Sea Hunters, someone at the Academy, or is it someone else entirely and what's so important about a seemingly innocuous technology anyway?

Chapter 1

It was late in the day during the tropical Pacific cyclone season. At the ocean's surface a super weather cell had unleashed a raging cyclone. Beneath the ocean surface amongst the silence of the blue-green void such storms were not an issue.

Suspended a hundred metres below in an endless void a subsurface mining skiff; a Skimmer as they were called was waiting. Ngarra at just twenty years old was the operator.

He looked out and down each side from the Skimmer Artificial Intelligence console, or SAI console for short.

The remaining semi-autonomous mining drones were returning from the muddy depths four thousand metres below. Called Xtracts, they were placing their final loads of manganese nodules into Skimmer trays.

Along each Skimmer wing moving across the top of the trays, they disappeared into an adjacent recess. Docking clamps opened and the Xtracts moved forward locking into place.

The Xtract laser communication signal streamer was being retrieved. It was slowly wound in onto a large drum at the rear of the Skimmer, bought up from the depths below.

Xtracts were semi-autonomous. Hovering just above the deep ocean floor they used an array of sensors to identify manganese nodules on the seabed beneath them. They had large mesh scoops, robotic arms for picking and a mesh collection bin.

The configuration acted like a sieve, leaving mostly nodules in the bins. It also minimised the formation of sediment plumes and reduced the amount of sediment transported up to the Skimmer with the nodules.

As a result, at the Skimmer only small subsurface plumes of mud and silt drifted back to the seabed four thousand metres below along with the ever-present marine snow.

Other Skimmers operating across "the Area" were also collecting nodules. Ngarra's Skimmer had been in position a hundred metres below sea level for three days while nodules were bought up from the seabed four thousand metres below.

As Ngarra looked out he could see the sea life that had gathered; more than usual he thought to himself. Probably seeking shelter from the super cell of weather raging at the surface above them.

'I certainly wouldn't want to surface in that weather,' he said out loud looking at a reflection of himself.

Surfacing was prohibited due to the increased risk to safety of the crew posed by changes in weather over the last few decades in the region. Furthermore, with the advent of Piracy in the region, being at the surface for any length of time was risky. Small, cheap hybrid submarines now roamed the shallower depths raiding and stealing nodules.

While in position Skimmers were unable to move and were easy targets. A Skimmers defensive weapons array when underway was a great deterrent against such piracy but could not be used during mining operations.

The ever-present Sea Hunters gave Ngarra some level of comfort though. It was a great deterrent and so far, they had managed to avoid being raided and having their load stolen. From the SAI console at the front of the Skimmer Ngarra continued to watch as the last of the Xtracts disappeared into the recess along each side and docked.

To him the recess looked like a half pipe on its side; one along each side of the Skimmer. The lower leading edge of this half pipe extended outwards along the Skimmer wing. The mesh trays were positioned along it. Ngarra was getting impatient and after several days was looking forward to getting underway and delivering the latest load to the Harvester.

'It is all so concise and coordinated; almost surreal,' he thought to himself out loud.

Skimmers did not look like the sub-surface military manta drone developed by the USA. Military manta drones were developed by the American Naval Undersea Warfare Centre in the 2020's. They were semi-autonomous and could detach from submarines and seek out or hunt down targets.

Skimmers did not even look like the more traditional long black cylindrical shape of military submarines. Ever present, in the depths below they quietly went about their business along with other nations defence force assets in the resource rich region.

Skimmers looked radically different. They had a flattened shape. They looked like a chiton, a small invertebrate that you would find clamped onto rocks in the intertidal zone. They glided through the water at depths of up to two hundred metres. A crew of up to ten but usually six lived onboard and monitored the semi-autonomous Xtract mining operations run by the Skimmer Artificial Intelligence or SAI.

Skimmers had a self-sustaining power and propulsion system. It had two rim driven propellers at the rear powered by an integrated electrical propulsion system. No mechanical output was needed to drive a shaft. All the output of the engines was converted to electricity. It powered the drive system, weapons, the mining Xtracts, and life support systems. No separate generators were needed. A backup power system used the flow of seawater through a ram chamber along the bottom of the hull while underway. It drove an array of small turbines that generated and stored power. The ram opened at the front, low on the underside of the flattened hull.

Communication at sea had also changed. Eel drones released by large surface buoys linked sub surface Skimmer communication systems to satellites and the internet. It was called "the grid" and used a combination of sonar and laser communication signals. Laser light technology used rapid flash sequences of photons from a laser. It allowed for rapid communication at speed underwater, to the surface and ashore including live video and messages. Called Quantum Key Distribution, Eel drones and Skimmers communicated by emitting single polarised photons in rapid sequence.

A global communications corporation installed and maintained the network gateway, or "the grid" as it was called. The grid was funded through the International Seabed Authority by levies from State sponsors. As part of the conditions of being a deep-sea mining contractor, being "off the grid" was considered a rogue act that had serious consequences. It was considered a breach of "the Authority" Regulations and in contradiction of international requirements for maintaining good order at sea.

Ngarra's Skimmer was working in the Penrhyn Basin South of Samoa and the Cook Islands at about 10 degrees south and 165 degrees west. They were approximately eight hundred nautical miles due north of the Chinese owned

GlobeCorpMining mineral Harvester. The Harvester was positioned near the Tropic of Capricorn in international waters.

It was massive, about ten times the size of the Shell Prelude anchored off North-western Australia. It was a feat of Chinese engineering and automation. It was designed and built to remain at sea for the duration of its lifespan. With a small crew for monitoring AI systems, robots and drones it could maintain and repair itself and withstand the harsh conditions and super weather cells that now occurred in the region.

The Harvester sorted and processed nodules that the Skimmers delivered. The Chinese led Harvester programme had provided financial and technical support to Australia to develop the Skimmers. Along with adaptation of the technology developed during the future submarine programme rolled out in Australia through the 2020's and 2030's the Skimmer programme had proved very successful. Rising through the row of moon pools along the hull of the ship, Skimmers arrived. Robotic arms on each side of a moon pool offloaded the nodules onto conveyor belts.

By 2040 the South Pacific tropics had become a hive of contractor Skimmer activity. The Chinese owned Global Mining Corporation or GlobeCorpMining as they were called had a monopoly on deep sea minerals. Contractors leased or purchased these Skimmers to mine and deliver manganese nodules to the Harvester. They had secured significant rights and tenure in "the Area" in international waters and were a key partner in developing Pacific Island nation Exclusive Economic Zone resource access.

Ngarra was still looking out at the mineral trays that were now full of nodules. He loved being a Skimmer operator and was proud of his Australian indigenous heritage. Across the various dialects of the native language, from east to Western Australia one of the meanings of his name was "together with you". Tall and slim and with olive coloured skin and piercing brown eyes he had a commanding presence and demeanour.

He reflected on how he ended up in the Skimmer crew programme. He was fifteen when he started at Xed, which stood for Excellence in Education. It was a hybrid educational institute, a cross between a trade training institute and a high school. Xed linked applied vocational training and academic education with the world of automation. Xed focussed on working with youth in their final three years of high school for jobs in industry sectors that now relied on automation, robotics and drone technology. It was also a feeder into the Ocean Academy and its Skimmer crew programme.

'That was the great thing about Xed and the Ocean Academy.' Ngarra thought to himself out loud. He was still looking at his reflection in the viewing screen and talking to himself out loud.

'Counselling myself,' he said as he chuckled and thought that if the others saw him talking to himself, they might think he was losing it.

'They get involved in your life from every angle,' he said to his reflection. 'A lifelong journey if you choose to stay with them and enter the Skimmer crew programme.'

Ngarra thought he had better stop talking to his reflection. The others would come up shortly. Silently, he continued to reminisce.

Spread between Xed and the Academy, the campus housed some six thousand students at any one time from all over the world. There were no year groups or traditional classrooms at Xed or the Ocean Academy. A personal AI guided an individual's progress from level to level. Learning facilitators monitored progress and provided advice and direction where needed.

Ngarra snapped out of his thoughts and looked through his reflection and outside. He watched the sea life and thought about nature. The small plume of muddy silty sediment had attracted a variety of species. He often came up to the SAI console and looked out and thought about the marine life that had gathered while they were in position.

Deep ocean pelagic ecosystems near the South Pacific convergence zone had altered somewhat. The changing climate and the extended periods of El Nino contributed to warmer than average waters. Extreme weather events were also now much more extreme, one of which was raging above them now.

A seasonal intensification of bottom-up biomass production from upwelling had evolved over the last few decades. Combined with the redistribution of deep ocean sediment from all those small Skimmer plumes in the photic zone, there was now a source of bio-available iron in a traditionally iron deficient deep ocean region.

Ngarra thought out loud, 'it's like fertilising soil and turning it over.' Silent again he thought about the implications that had for the open ocean.

It had facilitated resurgence of photic zone plankton growth in a region that had otherwise become devoid of it. A resurgence in the large yellow fin tuna industry had followed.

Ngarra watched on as a small school of them swam around the Skimmer. The resurgence in the yellow fin tuna fishery was now substantial. It had become a great offshore asset for the small Island nations that had suffered enormously from the impact of accelerating climate change and the increasing extremes of weather.

While he pondered this, in his reflection he could see Jonny walk in behind him and over to the SAI console. He thought to himself, Stella would be at the Xtract console two levels below checking over operating systems.

'Hey Ngarra,' said Stella as her image appeared on screen at the SAI console.

Ngarra's mind came back to reality and what was going on around him. Time to get on with things, he thought to himself as Stella's voice penetrated his thoughts.

'One of the Xtracts malfunctioned and lost its load down there,' said Stella.

'We really need a better way of getting more of this stuff. I need to get the Xtract inside so SAI can get a maintenance drone to repair it. Look at me, between working on Xtracts and running maintenance drones, I need some new clothes.'

'You are stuck out here for a month at time,' said Jonny as he walked in and looked over at Ngarra and winked. 'Your vogue can wait sister,' he said laughing at himself.

Ngarra smiled at their antics. Typical, he thought. Jonny and Stella were always hassling each other.

'Says the dude that wears the same long pants and top day after day,' said Stella sarcastically. 'No wonder there is no woman in your life.'

'I have a woman,' said Jonny. 'She's hard but fair,' he said patting the Skimmer SAI console and smiling.

'Jonny stop, you're killing me,' said Ngarra chuckling.

'Whatever,' said Stella as she watched Jonny from the Xtract bay console screen pat the SAI console.

Stella was from Australia and at nineteen years old had a bubbly personality. She wasn't overly tall, but with blue-grey eyes, long brunette hair tied back and chiselled features she had an imposing presence about her. Stella loved hassling Jonny, or Jonny-boy as she so affectionately called him. She saw the best in everyone despite their short comings and Jonny certainly had a few of those.

'Cut it out you two,' said Ngarra having a chuckle himself. They were always hassling each other but it did lighten the mood somewhat. 'Hurry up and get that

Xtract inside. Oh, and check with SAI that our communication streamer is secure and intact.'

'What do you need clothes for down here anyway,' said Jonny. 'Nothing we have not already seen.'

Ngarra had to smile and chuckle at the comment. 'Jesse might have something to say about that.'

Jonny proceeded to laugh at himself some more. Being from New Zealand he had what could only be described as a typical Tongan-Maori vocabulary. He was solid and at over six foot you didn't want to mess with him. He had dark hair cut very short and brown eyes with deeply tanned skin. One of his arms had a tattoo sleeve down it showing his cultural heritage. At twenty years old he had grown up in New Zealand. He liked hassling people and having a laugh with them. It got him in trouble sometimes as he often spoke before thinking. He got along well with Stella.

'We still have to wait for SAI to finish preparations to leave for the Harvester,' said Jonny yawning. 'I'm off to get some food.'

Jonny walked off having a chuckle about Stella and signalling with his hand to Ngarra that he thought she was crazy.

'Great, I saw that,' said Stella sarcastically. She watched Jonny from the Xtract bay on her console screen as he moved off from the SAI console. 'I'll see you shortly Jonny boy.'

'Not much I can do here for now either,' said Ngarra as he swiped the screen clear and Stella's image disappeared, leaving just the audio link active.

Ngarra was a great Skimmer operator, but he was no match for Stella's skill and knowledge of the Xtract mining drones or Jonny's Skimmer piloting skills.

Stella had a natural flare for coding, which made her a great asset when monitoring SAI's operation of the Xtracts.

Once the Xtracts disappeared into the depths of the ocean, she made sure that SAI had no issues with control of them through the deployed laser signal communication streamer. Nodes along the streamer suspended to the seabed four thousand metres below received and sent a constant stream of data and information back and forwards.

Ngarra was about to leave the SAI console and join them for something to eat in the recreation area on the level below or rec area as they called it when the message board activated.

'Laser communication signal from Xed Academy crew monitoring,' said SAI. 'Eel drone proximity and grid buoy link nominal, live feed available.'

'SAI open message board,' said Ngarra.

In the centre of the SAI console images, virtual displays and holograms could be projected.

It was Jonah.

'Hi Ngarra, how is your Skimmer crew?' she asked.

Jonah always checked in on the crews. She was one of the founding members of Xed and instrumental in getting the academy started and securing funding for the Skimmer crew programme. Jonah had short blonde shoulder length hair, blue eyes and lightly tanned skin. She dressed casually and wore glasses. Her outwardly calm demeanour masked the intensity and passion she had for her life's work.

Originally from France, she gained Australian citizenship and a degree in education before working with the defence force as an Education Officer. After that she worked for the Department of Education before leaving and consulting back to the defence force.

It was in the early 2020's that she moved to New Caledonia and worked at the Oceans Centre. Based in Noumea the community-based Oceans Centre was funded by Australia as part of a technology and innovation initiative partnership agreement with Pacific Island nations. From there Jonah founded Xed and subsequently set up the Ocean Academy.

In the Xtract bay Stella heard Jonah over the comms link between the SAI console and Xtract console. Ngarra had left the voice comms open. She was going to tell Ngarra that SAI had recovered the malfunctioning Xtract.

'Hi Jonah,' she innocently remarked. 'These Xtracts can be a pain. Without the communication streamer we would lose them. Another one has malfunctioned.'

Jonah heard Stella and said, 'unless you have any brilliant ideas it's all we have. Every Skimmer is fitted out the same. All we can do is add more Xtract mining drones to each Skimmer.'

Stella moaned. 'Wouldn't it be great if by working with one you were working with them all.'

'Good point,' said Ngarra. 'A swarm of bees could gather more nodules than we do. Perhaps the solution is simple, who knows. Like a swarm of bees?'

He thought about it and what that might mean for mining.

'The dance of the Queen bee,' said Stella as she pranced around in the Xtract console.

Luckily no one could see her antics, Ngarra had swiped the video link clear.

'I just wanted to say hi Jonah,' said Stella. 'Ngarra, that Xtract is now in the service bay so I'm off to get some food in the rec area. Bye Jonah.'

She left the Xtract Bay and headed up to the level above and towards the rec area. Ngarra thought to himself, Stella could be painful sometimes, but you could always rely on her and SAI to keep the Xtracts running.

'Such a bright woman,' said Jonah.

'Yes, I would say bubbly bright,' said Ngarra. 'Anyway, we have twelve tonnes of nodules to offload at the Harvester.'

'Do we know where the Sea Hunters are,' said Jonah. 'Try not to give them an excuse to board you for an inspection!' she exclaimed.

The Sea Hunters regularly carried out sub-surface monitoring, compliance and enforcement and could hold up a Skimmer for quite some time if needed. Time was money and being held up disrupted the crew's ability to meet extraction targets set by the contractor. Funding of the Skimmer crew programme by GlobeCorpMining was based on meeting these targets.

'SAI where are the Sea Hunters currently located?' asked Ngarra.

'The Sea Hunters are South of Tonga inspecting another Skimmer,' said SAI.

'Good,' said Ngarra. 'Nothing but a pain they are.'

Jonah interrupted, 'You and the Sea Hunters Ngarra!' she said with a smile. 'You need to keep them on side, not annoy them. Anyway, I wanted to let you know that when you get to the Harvester you along with the other Skimmers will each be welcoming a new crew member aboard.'

'A new crew member!' exclaimed Ngarra. 'We already have one. Chang has been with us for over a year now. Now we have another to keep busy.'

'You will be fine,' said Jonah. 'Anyway, got to go. Will be in touch with the details of your new crew member.' Her image faded.

Ngarra sighed and walked out of the SAI console, through the watertight bulkhead entrance and down the stairs to the rec area. It was hard enough mentoring Chang. He was such a grumpy person. Now he would have another one to deal with. It had been a long day and he was looking forward to some sleep. He always got impatient at the end of a mining run. SAI had to run a full system check before they left. Early in the morning SAI would get them underway and heading to the Harvester.

Walking into the rec area he bumped into Jesse.

'How was your day?' she said. 'I've been catching up with security stuff.'

'Long and boring,' said Ngarra. 'How's the rest of the crew, Chang and Connor?'

'Fine, I think. Connor has been in the information hub all day and Chang; well, I think he is with him. Not sure what they are up to.'

With mining operations finished and SAI doing system and maintenance checks there was no need to have anyone on watch. They grabbed some food and sat down to chat with Stella and Jonny.

Chapter 2

Jonah arrived at Xed early the next morning. She was at the Skimmer simulation centre, or sim centre as it was called, going over crew placements that Rick had sent her.

'We have quite a number of new crew members to place on Skimmers,' her secretary said.

'Given the number of nodules being mined,' said Jonah, 'the demand for crews to monitor contractor Skimmers is high. I am expecting trouble though,' she said with a grim look on her face.

'Trouble, trouble from where?' her secretary said raising her eyebrows. 'Has there been a piracy incident?'

'Not recently,' said Jonah. 'It's been unusually quiet on that front. But a crew has gone rogue and taken a Skimmer off the grid. They are in breach of mining regulations in "the Area" and international maritime law. The contractor is demanding we locate and return their property. If not, they will request that the International Seabed Authority issue emergency administration orders. That means the Sea Hunters will track them down.'

'If the Sea Hunters find that Skimmer, they will disable it and board it,' said Jonah sighing.

Jonah had become very animated, waving her arms in the air as if to fend off some invisible enemy. Her secretary walked over to the coffee machine, asked for a long black and bought it back to her.

'Here you go,' she said walking back with it in her hand.

'Just what I need,' said Jonah.

She liked her coffee and was often seen walking around campus with one in hand. Her secretary walked off and left her alone for a while.

Jonah looked out through the instructor viewing screens in the sim centre at the two large Skimmers immersed in massive tanks, one either side of her thinking about the Sea Hunters.

The International Seabed Authority was able to use administrative orders to give prescriptive directions that had legal consequences for noncompliance. Such emergency orders were issued in response to breaches of regulations in "the Area".

The Sea Hunters as a contracted monitoring, compliance and enforcement agency could then locate, disable and board a Skimmer. Skimmers were disabled using Acoustic Remote Cavitation or ARC arrays. These arrays used sound generated and triangulated from three-point sources. A location specific cavitation bubble was created that disrupted propulsion systems. At longer ranges it could also be deployed from a torpedo array.

To board a Skimmer a Sea Hunter vessel carried a sub-surface interceptor drone. A breaching pod with a small boarding party was released and docked with the topside hatch of a Skimmer. It meant they did not have to force Skimmers to the surface for inspection, interrupt mining operations and risk exposure to super cells of weather or to piracy.

With a coffee in hand and thinking about the Sea Hunters and her Skimmer crews Jonah had calmed down. She had seen the opportunity to turn the Xed Ocean Academy into a centre for training crews to monitor Skimmers. It provided hundreds of students coming out of Xed with another option. It was something they could pour their hearts and minds into long term if they chose to.

Even those with learning difficulties such as dyslexia, autism, attention deficit disorder and literacy problems could be trained as monitoring crew on these Skimmers. What Jonah found was a common solution in Skimmers for those with learning difficulties. That solution was for students to work with a personal AI and to learn by doing.

It had taken some ingenuity but in collaboration with the Skimmer construction industry and GlobeCorpMining they had modified a Skimmer AI to become the Xed and Ocean Academy AI. With advances in quantum computing, it was essentially one SAI that ran all the education and training systems and simultaneously monitored all of the students' progress. It adapted individual learning programmes according to progress. It used the information to determine when they were ready to progress to the next level at Xed and graduate. They either got a job in industry or moved on to the Academy and crew training programme.

As Jonah sipped her coffee, she walked through the instructor area between the massive water tanks either side within which each Skimmer was positioned.

Her secretary followed.

At the rear they went through security and entered the crew monitoring and communications complex.

They walked out onto the soundproof mezzanine overlooking all the monitoring stations. The staff on duty looked up from the floor below and waved at her and returned to their work.

Jonah looked out over the displays, thinking about her students. By 2030 many of the more traditional manual jobs for high school leavers had disappeared. Youth were not engaged in the dawn of a new age, the age of machines. Senior high school leavers had to be proficient in the languages of coding or understand their use and application in artificial intelligence systems, drones, robotics, machine learning and data analytics. Without these skills' youth had found it increasingly hard to transition into work.

Jonah was snapped out of her thoughts by her secretary reminding her of the days schedule. Her thoughts turned quickly to the current situation and how to deal with it; a rogue crew and an off-grid Skimmer.

'Shall I organise an Xed Council meeting,' said her secretary reading her mind.

'Yes,' said Jonah. 'I am really worried about our rogue crew. Sorting this out is going to give me one giant headache. We need to locate the off-grid Skimmer and figure out why the crew has gone rogue.'

Jonah walked out of the mezzanine and down the steps to the main floor below. She stopped in front of one of the crew status and vitals screens. To the front and across the entire wall on one side she could see the location of every Skimmer crew on the grid, their status and vitals.

The duty officer came up to her and briefed her on any updates.

Clusters of crew monitoring stations were positioned around the complex. Staff were assigned to these stations.

Faces of crew members, their status and vital signs were all displayed. It was a fascinating place that very few got to see.

Jonah looked at the one blacked out status and vitals screen. She wondered where they were and how long they had been off grid before she was notified. Rick should have told her earlier, as soon as it happened. She wondered why he didn't.

Her Smartwatch activated. With a swipe of her hand, an image of Rick appeared. Rick oversaw the sim centre crew training and placement programme.

'Hi Jonah,' said Rick. 'I'm sending through the profiles of our Ocean Academy students that we should place with Skimmer crews. Have you got a moment to look?'

Jonah nodded her head and browsed the profiles. She spent a few minutes swiping through and studying the student profiles.

'I think some of them need longer at the Academy before coming through the Skimmer crew placement programme,' she said with interest. 'A number are still not up to speed with all the monitoring systems and emergency protocols. Some of them could even have done with more time in the Skimmer simulation programme.'

'That shouldn't stop us from placing them on Skimmers,' said Rick.

'Their AI gave them high scores in the Simulators when it came to work and living together. Feedback from learning facilitators is that in terms of social cohesion and emotional intelligence they are ready.'

'True,' said Jonah. 'We do put a lot of work in at the Academy when it comes to developing emotional intelligence, critical thinking, creativity, collaboration and communication.'

'Well,' said Rick, 'something the education sector should have been more proactive about. They should have seen what was coming, linking all this technology and automation with social upheaval and a lack of the more traditional jobs and roles.'

Jonah finished looking at the profiles and swiped them clear. She worried about sending Academy crew graduates out to the Skimmers. It was like letting her babies go out into the world. She often came over to the crew monitoring and communications complex to see how they were all doing.

'Tell me something I don't know,' said Jonah in reply to Rick's comment. 'Besides, that is why we have Xed. We have, and continue to, accept a lot of youth into Xed in their last three years of high school. I wish we could reach out to more.'

Jonah briefly thought about how education had changed. An education system that in previous decades had failed to consider the impact of the development of machine learning and artificial intelligence on the proliferation of automation, robots and drones that took over most traditional jobs and roles. A siloed subject orientated use of curriculum that focussed on dated and somewhat irrelevant content had left students struggling to adapt to this new world. But Xed was different, very different and it worked.

'Let's get the Xed Council together to consider the timing of placement of all these people on the Skimmers,' she said to Rick. 'I want them all placed with the more experienced crews out there as soon as possible. Also, we need to discuss with Council what to do about that rogue crew!'

'Right, sounds good,' said Rick. 'I have to go. I will see you at the Council meeting.'

Rick's image disappeared and Jonah's secretary went off to organise the meeting. Jonah stayed for a while, pondering over the crews and faces she had seen pass through Xed and the Academy over the years.

The timing of Xed, growth of the Academy and the advent of the Skimmer crew programme had been just right. Skimmers provided a way of staying at sea for long periods of time to collect nodules and return them to a "mother ship", the Chinese owned GlobeCorpMining Harvester. The development and construction of the Skimmers resulted in a constant supply of nodules being transported to the Harvester.

Through the 2020's Australia had become renowned for building submarines for its future military submarine programme. The large government contract was successful even if long overdue and with significant additional cost. All the additional infrastructure was available to use for other projects.

It was not hard for industry to win another large contract to build these sub-surface mining Skiffs, the Skimmers. However, a lot of concern was expressed by the United States of America, the United Kingdom and other defence partners about using advanced submarine technology to build Skimmers for a subsidiary of a Chinese owned global mining corporation that were then bought or leased by contractors.

Chapter 3

On the Skimmer Stella was at the Xtract bay console. It was forward of the watertight bulkhead and entrance to the maintenance bay. To the rear was the airlock and moonpool.

From the Xtract bay console off to each side was a watertight entrance to a passage that ran down each side of the maintenance bay to the rear of the Skimmer. Outside attached to the Skimmer the Xtracts were docked on their clamps.

SAI had released the Xtract that had malfunctioned the day before from its docking clamp and recovered it through the moonpool. It was in the maintenance bay where SAI had got a repair drone to fix the problem.

Two levels above, at the SAI console Ngarra and Jonny were checking Skimmer systems.

'SAI,' said Ngarra. 'Confirm load is secure and preparations complete for Harvester transit.'

'Confirmed,' said SAI. 'Load is secure, all systems nominal, completing hull integrity checks and securing Skimmer for transit to Harvester.'

Ngarra knew everything would be in order, but they had to follow protocol. It was their job to monitor SAI and cross check everything. That way if something did go wrong and SAI was compromised, they could respond quickly. Highly unlikely, but you just never knew when the need might arise.

Chang walked into the SAI console and looked outside. He was of medium build, had brown eyes and tanned skin. His hair was dark and combined over to one side. He always had this intense look about him, as if the world was on his shoulders.

The outer hull shields were still retracted. He could see the maintenance drones had finished checking over the Skimmers superstructure.

Seeing Chang, Jonny turned towards Ngarra and asked, 'Hey, have we got some downtime while at the Harvester?'

'Sure,' said Ngarra. 'A day or so.'

Ngarra had a mild form of attention deficit disorder and found it hard to keep occupied during mining operations. He always felt like he had to be doing something.

Luckily for Ngarra, Skimmers had a gaming room that could simulate a variety of role-playing games for the crew. They could also keep in regular touch with family and friends and had access to a variety of digital gaming devices, media and a gym to keep them entertained.

'Great,' said Jonny. 'Can't wait.'

Jonny slapped them both on the shoulder and joked about having a bit of fun. Ngarra smiled and Chang grimaced as Jonny imitated a playful boxer.

'I've got some me time to catch up on,' said Jonny playfully. 'Let's get out of here folks, time to go SAI.'

Chang brushed Jonny's hand off his shoulder.

'I just want to get to the Harvester and ask about my older sister,' he said. 'It's been a few years since I saw her last. I didn't even know she had started working with GlobeCorpMining. My father never said anything to me. Mind you why would he, I am a disappointment compared to my sister!'

Chang frowned and clenched his fists in anger and walked off. Ngarra looked at Jonny who just shrugged his shoulders. He thought to himself, I must find out why Chang is always so angry and what it has to do with his family.

Stella's voice came over comms from the Xtract bay and startled Ngarra out of his thoughts.

'SAI's repair drone has just about finished down here, and the maintenance drones have been recovered,' she said. 'We are watertight.'

She swiped her hand across the schematics loaded onto the screen of the Xtract bay monitoring console.

'Where is Chang,' said Stella. 'Ngarra, can you get him to come down here?'

In Chinese Chang meant "unhindered spirit". He was certainly unhindered, thought Stella to herself.

'Chang is on his way now,' said Ngarra.

Ngarra got SAI to locate Chang and request that he go to the Xtract bay. A moment later Chang returned to the SAI console and grunted something about doing another person's work for them and not wanting to go and help Stella.

'Say something did you Chang,' said Jonny with a smile.

Chang made a face at him as he walked out and Ngarra chuckled. Chang left the SAI console and headed down to the Xtract Bay. Jonny and Chang did not get along that well but tolerated each other's company. Jonny turned and looked at Ngarra, shrugging his shoulders again about Chang.

'Looks like we are ready to get underway,' he said to Ngarra. 'SAI has completed all system checks, our load is secure, the maintenance drones are back onboard, the Xtracts are locked down and we are watertight.'

'SAI, commence transit to Harvester,' said Ngarra as he nodded at Jonny.

'Announce when we are two hours from arriving at the Harvester.'

'Confirmed,' said SAI. 'Begin transit to Harvester and announce when two hours from arrival.'

'Right,' said Ngarra. 'Let's get out of here. Jonny are you up for some down time?'

Jonny turned and made a warrior face before racing off. Ngarra followed quickly behind as they went through the watertight bulkhead, bounded down the stairs to the rec area.

The rim driven propellers started spinning and gaining speed. The marine life that had gathered around the Skimmer including a school of yellow fin tuna parted and fell away. It turned level and in a wide arch, gaining speed as the power feed to the bladeless propulsion system increased pressure to the jets of water.

The outer hull shields around the SAI console and forward of the rec area below closed over the viewing screens. The camera system activated, showing the view outside. The ocean slid by as the Skimmer straightened up and gathered speed.

During ocean transits there was no need to have someone on watch continuously. Skimmer AIs were so efficient that there was rarely any need to intervene in their ability to self-repair or adjust navigation, propulsion and life support systems in transit to and from the Harvester.

As he made his way to the Xtract bay Chang felt the Skimmer move off. He wanted to do his own thing for a while, just like Jonny. To Chang they didn't really need to monitor anything. SAI could do it all anyway.

'Wish I was running this show,' he said out loud.

He entered the Xtract bay and saw Stella.

He hurried over to her.

'Why do we have to do this now,' he said angrily. 'Do this do that, get a life people. SAI does it all anyway.'

'Come on Chang,' said Stella. 'It's no big deal and besides you know these Xtracts and repair drones are controlled by SAI. We are just doing some standard crosschecks. Remember, these SAI's are like children, they still needed to be guided to learn. That's the whole point of us interfacing with SAI. It allows SAI to continuously refine its AI system to align with and make choices that are the choices we want.'

'Whatever,' said Chang. 'Guided machine learning, deep learning, whatever you want to call it. It's just another name for babysitting these Skimmers.'

'Well,' said Stella, 'I'm actually finished here so while you are contemplating how boring life is, let's go and catch up with Ngarra and Jonny in the recreation area. I could do with some more positive company,' she said with a sarcastic look and a smirk on her face.

Chang frowned at her, shrugged his shoulders and said, 'OK, well anything's better than checking SAI does the job it is meant to do.'

Chang made a face at the SAI monitoring screens. If SAI had even the slightest bit of emotional intelligence it would probably have given him a shock just for being annoyingly grumpy. Stella and Chang walked up the stairs and through the watertight entrance which closed behind them. They entered the rec area. Chang was still babbling on and telling Stella about why he thought Skimmers did not need crews.

'I just don't understand it,' Chang said. 'If more effort was put into monitoring from ashore then Skimmers would not need crews.'

'It's not that straight forward Chang,' said Stella. 'There are regulatory issues that have to be considered. Then there is the funding of the crew programme to consider.'

'That may be so, but you have to start somewhere,' said Chang. 'It's not as if all the Skimmers are going to band together and become some sort of sentient, self-aware entity that decides it doesn't need humans. That's paranoia at its worst.'

They looked around. Jonny and Ngarra were already seated and having some food. Jesse also came in, got some food and sat down with them. Jonny got on well with Jesse and he figured that it was because Jesse was a little older. At twenty-four years old, Jesse oversaw Skimmer communications and security. She had dark hair, green eyes and lightly coloured skin. She was quite slim compared to Stella. She was almost gothic in appearance and had a quiet and calm demander.

On every Skimmer there was one older person in this role. Other crew members either got promoted to this position or employed directly from the Academy if their aptitude for leadership was identified early. Part of a communications and security officer role was to keep everyone on task and working together. They had a calming influence on the team and were trained extensively in emotional intelligence, organisational psychology and conflict resolution as well as communications and security.

On a Skimmer the crew helped themselves to food. Orders were placed from set menus using the automated dining server. Skimmers did not need Chefs or designated cooks since food was all preprepared then cooked and served using automated machines. For some foods there was even a bit of protein manipulation. In other words, the meat was cultured using precision fermentation of plant-based proteins.

'Hey Stella,' said Ngarra. 'One of the mounts for the ARC array was not aligned when SAI checked it the other day. Can you confirm SAI has got a maintenance drone to repair it?'

'Sure,' said Stella as she sat down to eat.

Ngarra had a sudden thought.

He jumped up and took his food with him. 'Got to go. I'm off to see Connor in the information hub.'

Ngarra just couldn't sit still. The crew entertained his constant enthusiasm and need to be doing something, but it was tiring. He disappeared, walking up to the SAI console and then back to the rear of the Skimmer between the propulsion systems to where the information hub was located.

***

Connor was there looking at a set of algorithms that SAI was running. The hub was designed as a digital laboratory workspace. It had a large central circular console with touch screens at waist height. These could be swiped to project a virtual screen in front of you. In the middle of the console holograms could be generated as well. Around the sides of the circular space were several workstations.

Connor had information up on some of the displays. He had found a lot of data from his research on group behaviour patterning in animals. Other screens showed code for running related algorithms while others presented data analytics on the subject matter.

Connor at nineteen years old was on the autism spectrum. He had strawberry blonde hair, straight and hanging just below his ears. It often dropped across one side of his face, and he was constantly pushing it back behind his ear.

He loved his role as their science and technology information officer. He found anything to do with turning patterns in nature into numbers and algorithms interesting and could get obsessively focussed on it.

He was absorbed in finding out how to convert patterns of group behaviour in animals into algorithms for machine learning in Xtracts. He was trying with limited success to teach a simulated group of Xtracts to learn group behaviour during a deep-sea mining operation.

The subject was one of his passions and other Skimmer information officers envied his aptitude for such things. His excitement was contagious, and he was very charismatic about maths, patterns, living systems, the environment and earth.

However, if you didn't know him and tried to talk to him about anything else, he would not respond. Given his autism he would at times come across as quiet and withdrawn and was not good at reading or responding to other people's emotions and feelings.

Connor was deep in thought when Ngarra walked in to catch up with him. He saw him and ignored him for a short period, absorbed in his own thoughts. Ngarra watched as Connor talked out loud and walked around the hub. Connor often thought out loud. He got SAI to record and research everything he said.

'Schools of fish react together,' said Connor. 'Large flocks of birds react together, and ants react together, well sort of anyway. But ants also do more, even picking up their dead and removing them, or helping carry larger objects together, repairing nests, protecting and defending the colony. Much of this coordination is considered to happen through chemical communication.'

He turned and looked at Ngarra.

'What if we could get mining Xtracts to work as one unit,' he said to Ngarra. 'Like ants or a swarm of bees. They could all work together. But how would we ensure such a machine learning algorithm promoted development of the type of artificial intelligence that would mimic what is seen in nature and learn from it?'

Ngarra thought that any corporation or government agency that could solve the "autonomous group" learning problem would have a significant advantage when mining nodules at the bottom of the ocean. They would be able to move beyond SAI controlling and monitoring single semi-autonomous Xtracts through the communication streamer.

He remembered that during the 2020's a corporation had worked on bee drone technology. They tried to make them act and behave and learn as a fully autonomous swarm. It initially caused havoc with crop pollination. They had to revert to guided machine learning to control development of the swarm AI.

In the 2020's industry had also developed limited semi-autonomous group behaviour in small deep-sea pipeline inspection drones. Groups of these drones could work on subsea pipelines. They carried out inspections while monitoring each other's status and could repower or tow each other if damaged or shut down.

'Geeze,' said Ngarra as he shrugged his shoulders at what Connor had suggested and walked around. 'You know yesterday I was thinking about Xtracts and swarms of bees at the SAI console. Seems like great minds think alike, well not as great as yours though. I like it. We should get Stella in on this. She loves all this patterning stuff.'

'Yes fantastic,' said Connor. 'But it's not just animals behaving as a group in response to an event and moving around together. Any set of algorithms for learning autonomous group behaviour places the preservation of the group, or in our case preservation of the Xtract drones as a group above the individual. Like a Master switch.'

Chang and Stella walked past on their way to the rear of the Skimmer to check over the propulsion systems. As they passed the information hub, she caught sight of the large ocean bubble hologram Connor had got SAI to project.

Stella was chatting away to Chang about something she wanted to do when they got back to Xed. There was a beach on the coast of New Caledonia not far from Xed and the Ocean Academy. Chang was indifferent and pretended not to listen.

She could see Connor looking at Ngarra, well looking through him it seemed and pacing around waving his finger in the air and talking out loud. They were looking at a large floating virtual bubble of the ocean and within it was a group of simulated Xtracts.

She raced in and jumped around the ocean bubble hologram looking at the information projected everywhere.

'Thank god for simulations,' she said excitedly while looking at what Connor had got SAI to put together. 'This is great. I should work with SAI and track down some more scripts and algorithms for you to hack Connor.'

'Whatever turns you on,' Chang said. 'This is boring,' and walked gruffly off towards the propulsion system. He left Stella and the others behind and could hear them chatting away about the ocean bubble hologram.

Chang was actually quite impressed by the ocean bubble hologram and the set of algorithms controlling the large group of simulated Xtracts. Not that he would let anyone else know that.

Chapter 4

At Xed the Council had convened. They represented organisations from countries that had sponsored the original Xed initiative many years ago.

Jonah had seen the opportunity to link the Ocean Academy to a career pathway. Rolling out the Skimmer crew programme was that pathway. The only drawback was that the Academy crew programme was totally reliant on funding from the Chinese owned mining corporation.

Despite this, Xed, the Academy and the crew programme was a game changer in education. However, concerns were raised about the relationship with a Chinese owned mining corporation and the potential for compromising national security interests.

She wondered what if any personal agendas were afoot.

Rick had spent much of the day at the simulation centre. He had run over to the administration building to meet Jonah for the Council meeting, arriving just in time.

They looked around at the Council members. The Council member for the Australian-backed industry technology group that helped fund Xed spoke.

'This rogue crew and off-grid Skimmer are concerning!' he exclaimed. 'It could jeopardise our funding arrangement with GlobeCorpMining. We can't afford to jeopardise that arrangement. We have a constant stream of students from Australia, Oceania and the Asia-Pacific wanting to enrol at Xed. We now take a certain number from the Middle East as well.'

'Besides that,' said the industry representative for Pacific Island nations. 'Given we are down a Skimmer, we need to work out a way to increase the capacity of the Xtract mining drones to take more nodules. If we can't meet the nodule quota for the current level of funding for the crew programme from GlobeCorpMining they will reduce it.'

The Council members all nodded their heads in agreement. Jonah and Rick looked at each other and made a sign to talk later about it and not in front of the others. Jonah looked around the circle at each Council member. They were waiting for her to say something.

'It seems we are at a critical point then,' said Jonah swiping her hand across her smartwatch and projecting some figures on the number of crews, the Skimmers, their scheduling, and the number of nodules collected. Jonah pointed out some statistics on productivity.

'Despite the various issues,' she said carrying on. 'We are actually exceeding our targets. Contractors are just getting greedy.'

The Council members nodded in agreement. Jonah had got a little irritated with the negativity started to spread around the Council. Contractors would always push for more she thought to herself. Besides, without the crews they couldn't run them anyway. Rick could see her frustration and addressed the Council.

'We have sixty students in the Academy that are ready to move onto the sim centre crew programme,' he said.

He swiped his hand across his smartwatch and projected the student profiles onto the screens. The industry member for the United Arab Emirates spoke.

'Why don't we modify the Skimmer programme? GlobeCorpMining could take the last step and make Skimmers remotely controlled and monitored. We can train crews to do it here.'

'That's just not a workable solution,' said Jonah. 'It defeats the whole purpose of the programme; to give all those youth from the Academy a chance to make something of themselves in this new world.'

Jonah was getting frustrated with them all.

'I'm just pointing it out that's all,' he said.

Jonah quickly replied in a way that would ensure the member for the United Arab Emirates would save face.

'Of course,' she said. 'You may well be right. Ultimately the removal of humans from Skimmers altogether is where GlobeCorpMining may take it.'

The member for the UAE nodded his head slightly forward, in recognition of Jonah's reply.

'For now,' said Jonah. 'Let's focus on meeting the demand for crews on existing contractor Skimmers.'

She swiped her hand across her smartwatch and projected a range of 3D Pacific Ocean maps. The Council members seemed more positive and discussed the points made.

Over the previous two decades and using debt diplomacy industry representatives from China and China's government officials had slowly built-up business interests with Pacific Island nations. They had established trade agreements and invested in infrastructure projects.

As well as "the Area" on the high seas, GlobeCorpMining had secured rights over the seabeds within the nations of Tonga, Samoa, the Cook Islands and Tokelau Exclusive Economic Zones. This gave them access to a huge amount of deep ocean abyssal plains for mining operations. Tenures now extended from the South Pacific Basin in International waters to the northern reaches of the Tokelau Exclusive Economic Zone.

As China's reach and influence in trade moved across the Pacific, their military followed. A modern Navy and several small bases were now used to watch over and to protect and secure regional rights and interests. The Harvester programme followed the proliferation of island building in the South China Sea that had continued through the 2020's.

Jonah thought to herself, who could have seen what was to come? Changes in climate and the prevalence of Piracy that now plagued the region, the Chinese owned yellow fin tuna fleet, the Harvester, the Skimmers and deals with Pacific nations to secure fishing rights and deep-sea mining tenures? It all made sense now she thought but back in the 2020's it seemed as though the world was not looking in the right place.

Jonah got the attention of the Council again. They had continued to discuss how to ensure the ongoing financial viability of the Academy crew programme.

'All right, all right everyone' she said as they quietened down.

'What about this rogue crew? We have a Skimmer that has gone off-grid and I am getting grief from the contractor and from GlobeCorpMining about it.'

The Council member for Australia spoke.

'The breach of ISA regulations and international maritime law means emergency administration orders will be issued. The Sea Hunters will locate the Skimmer, disable and board it and detain the crew to hand over to State sponsor authorities.'

The Council member for the UAE spoke up.

'We also don't want the military intervening. It could cause an international incident.'

The Council erupted into conversation and argument about what to do and how to get the crew back.

The South Pacific Joint task force operated within most Pacific nations' EEZ's. They conducted anti-piracy operations, smuggling and drug operations as well as counter terrorism. Given all the mining activity, the military surveillance and rights to safe passage through territorial seas, there was a lot of surface and sub surface military activity. By 2040 half the world's new submarine fleet and support vessels built through the 2020's seemed to be operating in the wider Pacific Ocean.

Jonah thought about what the Council members for Australia and the UAE had said.

'I have an idea,' she said getting their attention.

'Let's get one of our most experienced Skimmer crews to track down our rogue crew. We can come to some arrangement with GlobeCorpMining to compensate the contractor. That way, we can bring them back to Xed and the contractor gets their Skimmer back.'

'What if they do not want to be found or bought back to Xed,' said the secretary.

'Then we have a big problem,' said the Council member for New Zealand.

'Perhaps a more direct approach?' said the Secretary.

'What do you mean by that?' said the Council member for Australia.

Jonah spoke up before they got off track.

'Let's not get ahead of ourselves and try my way first,' she said. 'Then we can decide what to do next. Are we all in agreement?'

The Council members all nodded in agreement and said yes.

'Let's meet again once we have more information on the whereabouts of this rogue crew and I will update you on progress,' said Jonah.

With that the Council member images disappeared leaving Jonah, Rick and the secretary standing alone. The day was getting on and Rick headed off quickly.

'I'm going to check in with duty staff monitoring the Skimmer crews then head home,' he said walking off and making his way through the building and across campus.

'See you in the morning,' said Jonah as she and her secretary headed off as well.

***

It had been a hectic day and Jonah and her secretary went to have a drink at the staff campus bar and get something to eat. She would then go to the drone port and fly home to her house overlooking the entire campus on the coastal hills behind them.

Once at the campus staff bar Jonah ordered a drink and sat down with her secretary. A few others were around, some she recognised and others not. The campus had grown significantly since the beginning and it was now difficult to keep up with people coming and going. Everyone knew her so she was constantly saying hi and catching up with people.

'I wish I could spend more time at home and less here,' she said. 'If it weren't for this rogue crew and off-grid Skimmer I wouldn't have to be here so much. Rick is quite capable of handling all this. I do wonder about his motives though as he seems a bit distant lately, like something is on his mind.'

'I hadn't noticed,' said her secretary. 'He seems fine to me but then again I don't see him as much as you do.'

'Well, I wonder what made this Skimmer go off-grid and what the crew has to do with it,' said Jonah. 'Contractors with support from their state sponsors either lease or buy these things for mining operations, we just provide crews.'

'True,' said her secretary. 'None of the contractors or us for that matter has to maintain them. They are maintained under agreement with the Australian company that built them for GlobeCorpMining.'

'It's a mystery,' said Jonah. 'It's anybody's guess as to why the Skimmer is off grid.'

They carried on talking for a while and chatting with others at the bar. Jonah then sent her secretary home before heading off to the drone Port and catching a flight home.

Chapter 5

Later that same day on the Skimmer Jonny and Jesse were in the rec area having something to eat. Jonny was explaining to Jesse how he had ended up in the Skimmer crew programme.

'I was not interested in Xed, the Academy or the crew programme. It just kind of happened that way. I really wanted to join the Australian Navy as a submariner. I was in Year ten at high school and some people came to visit. Next thing you know my parents said I had been accepted into Xed. Years have passed by and well, here I am.'

'I had a similar experience,' said Jesse. 'Some people came to our school. Quite suddenly a bunch of us were also informed by our parents that we had been accepted. We left in Year ten as well. I don't know how they choose us, but it all appeared to happen quite fast.'

They both pondered this a little more, looking blankly at the table while sitting across from each other.

'On that note,' said Jesse. 'I need to go to the SAI console.' Jesse got up and walked off leaving Jonny to contemplate how far they had all come.

'Well,' said Jonny to himself. 'Looks like I better make myself useful. Speaking of that where is Chang. I haven't seen him this morning.'

Jonny got up and placed his empty plate through the slider and walked off.

***

Jesse had made her way up to the SAI console. She was looking at the crew health monitoring status when a long-range sonar proximity alarm activated.

'Unidentified sub-surface vessel detected matching Skimmer course and speed,' said SAI.

'SAI,' said Jesse. 'Locate Ngarra and request him to come to the SAI console.'

Jesse thought quickly. Only Ngarra and herself could override SAI's mining protocols in an emergency. The only reason SAI would deviate from mining protocols was if there was a threat to human life.

Jesse swiped her hand across the SAI console navigation screen and projected a three-dimensional image of their current position into a hologram in the centre.

She thought to herself, nothing had come from Academy Skimmer crew monitoring and communications that any other Skimmers were in the immediate area. SAI had certainly not informed them of any change in Skimmer numbers conducting Xtract mining operations in the area. Besides, SAI had said it was unidentified.

Ngarra had heard the proximity alarm go off anyway and ran from the recreation area up to the SAI console.

'Ngarra,' said SAI as he raced to get there. 'Jesse requests that you come to the SAI console immediately.'

'Yes, I know,' said Ngarra. 'SAI, I am on my way.'

Irritating that SAI always knows where everyone is thought Ngarra to himself. It did not leave much room for privacy, but it was comforting to know that the Skimmers AI was always monitoring safety and wellbeing.

He raced into the SAI console. He looked straight at the navigation hologram that was projected into the centre of the console.

'Who or what is that?' he asked with a look of concern.

'Not sure,' said Jesse as she also walked around the SAI console. 'SAI cannot verify the signature. It's off the grid and has only been picked up by SAI on long range sonar.'

For some reason Ngarra's thought drifted to what he had seen Connor doing the day before.

'Have you looked into what Connor is developing in any detail,' he said. 'You should see what he is working on.'

'Not now Ngarra,' said Jesse. 'What do you think about this? We don't know who it is and there are no other planned Skimmer Xtract mining operations in our current location.'

They both looked at the unidentified sub-surface vessel matching their course and speed and wondered what was going on.

Stella and Connor had also heard SAI's request for Ngarra to come to the SAI console and were not far behind. They raced into the SAI console.

'What's going on,' said Stella. 'Looks like a party in here with this navigation hologram and all the chit chat. Anyone need a drink or something?' she said sarcastically and laughed and carried on in her usual sociable manner.

Jonny heard the commotion and walked in behind Stella saying loudly, 'what's up folks! Where's Chang?'

Stella jumped and playfully punched Jonny.

'Don't do that,' he said.

Stella's upbeat personality often irritated people.

Ngarra found it frustrating but amusing.

'Did you forget to take your chill pills,' said Stella laughing.

'Are you ever actually not happy and not jumping around,' said Ngarra. 'You are giving me a headache!'

Ngarra rolled his eyes and stretched his arms and neck backwards and looked up.

Connor had come in to see what was going on. All the hype had got him excited as well.

'Jesse, Jesse,' he exclaimed. 'You have to come to the hub and check out this idea I am working on regarding the Xtracts. It's great; I was showing Ngarra yesterday. Come and have a look.'

With everyone hassling each other and Connor jumping up and down about his work they had all got distracted from the situation at hand.

Ngarra got serious quickly, looking at Jesse who nodded back at him. He had better get this lot focussed.

'OK! OK! everyone quiet!' said Ngarra.

Jesse continued. 'We have an unidentified sub-surface vessel shadowing us. We have no idea what it is doing. I will contact Academy crew monitoring. Something isn't right about this. Ngarra you get this lot doing whatever needs to be done and where's Chang!'

Jesse had control in emergency situations or where events occurred outside of mining operations with the potential to threaten the crew's safety.

'Stella, get SAI to locate Chang and go and get him,' said Ngarra. 'Get to the Xtract bay and check with SAI that all watertight bulkheads are closed and secure, and the airlock pressurised. If something goes wrong, I don't want a flooded moon pool and airlock.'

'Roger that,' she said with a comical salute as she took off.

'Jonny, stay here and monitor SAI's progress tracking this vessel.'

Jonny made a little fist pump.

'Connor get back to the information hub. Get SAI to cross reference all known Skimmers and military submarines that might be operating in this area of the Pacific.'

Connor ran off to the hub.

Ngarra spun off actions for everyone to do.

He may have found it hard to focus for extended periods, but this had little impact on his quick thinking and reactions, and he was certainly good at that.

Meanwhile Jesse requested SAI to send a laser communication signal.

'SAI, do we have a message board or live feed,' she said.

'Eel drone proximity and grid node link is nominal,' said SAI. 'Live feed available.'

An image of an Academy crewing monitoring duty officer appeared. Jesse discussed the situation with them. During the conversation Rick's image appeared.

'Jesse,' said Rick. 'I just got here. What were you saying; an unidentified sub-surface vessel?'

'Yes,' she said. 'We think there is another Skimmer in our vicinity, but it is off grid. There is no signature, but our long-range sonar has detected it.'

Rick discussed the situation with the duty officer, and they looked over current Skimmer locations. Rick looked quickly at the blank crew monitoring screen and wondered if it could be the same one. It was still confidential.

'No other Skimmer has a scheduled mining run in your immediate location,' said Rick. 'It can't be an off-grid Skimmer. Crews only override their SAI and go off grid if it's a life-threatening emergency. Even then they must notify us. Only the Security and Communications Officer knows how to do it.'

Rick thought that he might keep this all quiet until he had more information. No need to get Jonah all worried about this little encounter at this stage. He asked the duty officer if they had any approved any other Skimmer deviations from scheduled mining runs near Ngarra's current their location. The duty officer said no.

'We have no record of any other Skimmer activity in your immediate location,' said Rick.

He looked anxiously around at the team in the monitoring and communications centre and carried on talking.

'Just carry on and reach the Harvester for offloading. It must be a military submarine.'

'It's not deep enough for that,' said Jesse. 'From its behaviour our SAI has calculated a high probability that it is a Skimmer. It's a Skimmer and it's off-grid. Now you tell me why a Skimmer is off-grid and following us!'

Jesse was getting very irritated.

'I don't know, I don't know!' said Rick a little nervously.

He tried to calm himself down and then carried on.

'Military submarines can come up shallower. I will get back to you; just maintain your current course and speed and do not use emergency protocols to override SAI and take control. SAI will get you to the Harvester regardless of what is going on around you. You need to offload that load of nodules.'

Rick had got quite aggressive, so Jesse got SAI to disconnect the live feed from the message board. She thought to herself, they were still some distance from the Harvester. Why an off-grid Skimmer would be shadowing them was a mystery. In fact, why was it even off-grid in the first place and why was Rick trying to convince her it was just a military submarine?

Jonny shouted out, 'It's changed course and speed. It's moving towards us.'

'SAI, plot course and intercept position,' said Ngarra. 'Project in hologram.'

An image appeared in front of them in the middle of the SAI console and showed an intercept position about thirty minutes ahead of them.

Connor came running back to the SAI console followed closely by Chang.

'Where have you been Chang!' said Ngarra aggressively. 'Get to the Xtract bay and help Stella. She is looking for you.'

'There are ten Skimmers,' said Connor, 'that could get here but they are all on the grid and their signatures have all been verified by SAI. The one approaching us is not one of them.'

Chang frowned at Ngarra and smirked at Connor, shrugged his shoulders. He was not in the mood to be chastised.

'We are running out of time,' said Ngarra impatiently as he paced up and down.

Another marker appeared on the navigation hologram in the middle of the SAI console, moving out from the off-gird Skimmer and heading towards them.

'ARC torpedo array released,' said SAI. 'Cavitation bubble impact in five minutes.'

Jesse looked at Ngarra and thought quickly, 'SAI, confirm mining emergency override protocol.'

SAI responded, 'Mining emergency override protocol confirmed. What are your priorities?'

'SAI, maintain course and reduce to launch speed. Prepare to launch Xtracts.'

'Confirmed,' said SAI as the Skimmer slowed.

Stella heard all the commotion over the open communications link from the Xtract Bay. She set about preparing to monitor and direct SAI on what to do with the Xtracts.

At the SAI console Ngarra carried on spinning off directions for the crew.

'Connor and Chang, both of you get to the Xtract launch bay and help Stella. Get SAI to move them between us and the torpedo. We can use them as a shield. Some will be disabled but we can come back for them. Better than our SAI having to carry out a full propulsion system reboot if we get disabled.'

'Got it,' said Stella over the open communications link. She could hear everything from the Xtract Bay.

'Rick said not to do that,' said Jonny.

'Well, he's not here and we are about to be impacted by a cavitation bubble!' said Ngarra.

'Agree,' said Jesse 'I have this covered. Now move it everyone!'

Everyone hoped they would not be disabled and waiting suspended in the deep ocean for a system reboot by SAI.

The atmosphere was tense, and everyone was on edge. Connor was now so over stimulated. He paced around talking to himself.

'If only I had a handle on this group behaviour concept,' he said to no one in particular. 'We could make all the Xtracts act as one. Like a bait ball of fish, it would be impossible for the ARC torpedo to deploy its array and target us with a cavitation bubble.'

Being on the autism spectrum wasn't a bad thing when it came to complex situations, he was passionate about.

Connor's mind was spinning with thoughts and ideas on his favourite topic. He became very focussed and animated, which took a little getting used to by the crew because it seemed he was having a conversation with himself and looking right through them rather than at everyone around him.

Chang went to leave and was irritated with Connor getting in the way. He almost tripped over him.

'Geeze, calm down,' said Chang as he pushed forward to leave and get to the Xtract monitoring console below. He waved Connor out of the way, putting his arm on Connor's shoulder to move past.

'It's a stupid concept anyway. How is that of any use to anyone right now?'

Connor reacted to being suddenly touched and glared at Chang. He started yelling. Chang yelled back to get out of his way and pushed him hard back against the bulkhead on the way out.

Jonny saw what happened and launched himself at Chang. He sprang from the other side of the SAI console, landed his fist straight into the side of Chang's face, tackled him on the way and they both went reeling backward onto the deck.

Jonny hated bullies, and with being bullied at School himself, Chang's behaviour had set him off. He reacted without thinking.

Jesse grabbed her shock rod and was going to use it on both before things really got out of hand.

Ngarra jumped in quickly and pulled Jonny off.

'You idiot!' he yelled. 'That was all recorded. Now I need to explain to a discipline committee why my crew are fighting! Connor, are you OK?'

Connor got up and just looked at them all blankly. He walked off, returning to the Information hub.

Jesse put her shock rod away and motioned them all together. 'Ngarra, we will deal with this later. Jonny, Chang, pull yourselves together!'

Jonny and Chang stood up and glared at each other. Both were fuming and red faced.

Suddenly, there was a violent shudder through the Skimmer, SAI monitoring screens and interfaces flashed in and out, some stayed on, others shut down and started to reboot. During all the arguing they had not confirmed detachment and launching of a few of the Xtracts to act as a decoy for the incoming ARC torpedo array.

The crew grabbed the bulkhead and SAI console to stop themselves falling over or getting injured. At the SAI console, the drive and propulsion system hologram appeared immediately and rotated in the middle of the SAI console.

SAI ran diagnostics. It seemed OK. A virtual image of the Skimmer's control systems integrity status flashed. The crew did not even notice that SAI had positioned the Skimmer to minimise the potential for a direct hit on propulsion and a complete system reboot.

'Bloody hell!' said Jesse. 'Get to the Xtract Bay now Chang and help Stella! You stay here Jonny and work with SAI. This is just not good enough! Jonny, you should have been onto this.'

Jesse was angry with them all.

'On it,' said Jonny apologetically, his ego bruised.

'I will try and get hold of the crew monitoring centre and ask to speak with Jonah directly,' she said. 'And someone go and see how Connor is, now!'

Everyone stood looking at the projection of the Skimmer systems, fixated on it and muttering to themselves.

Jesse rolled her eyes and threw her hands in the air dismissively. 'What is it with you people?' she yelled. 'Snap out of it folks!'

'Let's go, let's go,' said Ngarra. Everyone took off to do what they had to do.

'Off-grid Skimmer no longer closing,' said SAI. 'Skimmer life support and propulsion system disrupted and at 80% recovery. Moon pool entrance breached. Flooding and unable to close and pressurise.'

'Damn it!' said Ngarra. 'Why was the entrance not armed and fully pressurised. SAI ascend to twenty metres below sea level. Display surface weather conditions.'

Ngarra looked at the meteorological data and decided it was too risky to surface. They were now well South of the super weather cell, but it was still rough. It would also mean they would be vulnerable to piracy.

'What about the Skimmer repair drone,' said Jonny. 'Can it close the moon pool entrance manually?'

Stella was still at the Xtract bay console and could hear the conversation over the open communication link.

'No time,' she said looking at the image of the moon pool. 'It's flooding fast and SAI won't be able to deploy it in time. We could just let it flood and carry on to the Harvester.'

There was a service bay, an air lock and three watertight bulk heads between her and the moonpool.

'No!' said Ngarra. 'It would mean slowing down and travelling shallower.'

Chang saw an opportunity to save face. 'I'm off to help Stella,' he said racing off to the Xtract bay.

Before Jesse or Ngarra could say anything, he was gone.

'SAI, show moon pool and airlock camera feed,' said Jonny.

'Damn it, damn it, damn it!' said Ngarra as they all looked on.

Stella had entered the maintenance bay, raced to the rear, opened the airlock and gone through.

It sealed behind her and she had opened the other side into the moon pool and raced through. It meant the airlock could not be closed and was now flooding as well. The area was partially pressurised, so she had a re-breather on. She managed to trip the manual pressurisation lever. The flooding was starting to slow.

'She should have just stayed out!' Ngarra exclaimed as he watched on the screen from the SAI console. 'We can cope with a flooded moon pool. SAI's repair drone would have fixed it eventually. Now we have a flooded airlock as well!'

'She will run out of air and asphyxiate before we can get the area pressurised, seal and arm the entrance and then returned to one atmosphere of breathable air,' said Jonny. 'We have to surface!'

'No!' said Ngarra. 'We have to find another way. We have some time. Surfacing is a last resort.'

The Skimmer had come to a full stop twenty metres below sea level. There was some movement up and down due to the swell height at the surface. It created a slight rolling motion that concerned Ngarra given the damage to the moon pool entrance.

Skimmers were supposedly unsinkable. Even if they broke apart, they were designed to come to the surface. It also had escape pods on either side. It was extremely unlikely to meet a watery fate.

***

Stella in activating the manual override for the air lock seal and pressurisation had sealed herself inside.

SAI operated on the balance of probabilities.

It would not open a flooded airlock even if someone was trapped in it and would surface instead. Her passion and enthusiasm could at times cloud her thinking. The Skimmer SAI and her crew had got her out of tight situations several times before.

Chang had raced down through the Skimmer and entered the Xtract monitoring console in front of the maintenance bay. He opened the watertight bulkhead entrance into the maintenance bay.

'My jaw hurts,' he said to himself as he rushed down the centre of the maintenance bay to the airlock. 'Jonny shouldn't have punched me. What do I care anyway; here for a good time not a long time.'

He could see that Stella was trying to close the moon pool entrance manually. However, the airlock and moon pool were not yet fully pressurised. With the water still waist high and flowing out she did not have much time before her rebreather would run out.

'SAI, estimated time for a repair drone to seal the chamber entrance,' he said.

'Time to seal entrance is five minutes. Repair drone activated,' said SAI.

Chang could see a repair drone activate and move from the airlock into the moon pool area.

'What about the time it will take for the chamber to be fully evacuated. I mean, SAI what is the time for the chamber to be fully evacuated.'

'Time for chamber to evacuate is five minutes,' said SAI.

'Damn it!' said Chang. 'SAI, confirm Xtract service bay is watertight.'

'Confirmed,' said SAI.

'SAI, open the service bay entrance to the airlock.'

'Command override is needed,' said SAI.

'SAI, command override confirmed,' said Jesse as they watched through the camera system from the SAI console two decks above.

'SAI open the service bay entrance to the airlock,' said Chang again.

'Stella!' yelled Chang over the open communication link as he put a rebreather on. 'Let go and ride the rapids.'

The airlock opened and water gushed into the service bay. Due to the force of the water the airlock would not close.

Ngarra saw what was going on and figured out what Chang was trying to do.

'SAI, angle skimmer ten degrees up.'

'Confirmed,' said SAI as the Skimmer rotated upwards.

Stella gave him a confused look. She was swept off her feet and rode a wave into the service bay.

Once the water slowed and started to evacuate, they were able to get to their feet and grab something to hold onto. They were now in danger of being sucked out of the moon pool entrance.

The others were still watching from the SAI console. Ngarra got Jonny to go down to the Xtract bay console and prepare to assist them.

Stella kept pushing the manual override to close the airlock entrance to the service bay area. It was hard to keep their footing given the rush of water going out of the moon pool.

Jonny rushed down to the Xtract monitoring console.

The angle the Skimmer was on meant most of the water that had rushed into the service bay had quickly washed back into the airlock and moonpool. SAI could still not close the airlock.

The flow of water was receding quickly.

Stella for one last time slammed her hand down on the manual override and used the lever to close the airlock.

It was just in time as they were out of air.

Jonny pressed the pressurisation override and flooded the service bay with breathable air.

Everyone watched the life support system display shift from red to green. Ripping off their rebreathers they gasped for air. Exhausted they both lay on the deck, breathing heavily but alive none the less.

Jonny opened the watertight bulkhead entrance into the service bay. Stella and Chang got up and he helped them through and up to the rec area.

The moon pool was now also pressurised, and the service drone was making repairs to the open entrance. All water was evacuated from the service bay and airlock and it was now sealed.

'Great job everyone,' said Ngarra as they breathed a sigh of relief. 'Jonny, help Stella and Chang get tidied up. SAI confirm when the moonpool entrance is repaired then seal and arm moonpool and return to one atmosphere.'

'OK everyone,' said Jesse as she breathed a further sigh of relief. 'Let's meet in the recreation area for a debrief.'

'SAI,' said Ngarra. 'Recommence transit to Harvester.'

'Confirmed,' said SAI. 'Transit to Harvester recommencing.'

With that the Skimmer moved off again and once the moonpool entrance was repaired, sealed and armed they slowly descended back down to a hundred metres below sea level.

**

A short time later the crew all assembled in the recreation area for a debrief. Ngarra stood in front of them all.

'We may not have known who it was that launched an ARC torpedo array at us and why,' he said. 'However, that doesn't excuse the fact that you lot decided to fire up and have an argument that got personal. There are simply no excuses for it to end up in a fist fight.'

Jonny was about to say something but Ngarra spoke over him and Jesse mouthed at him to be quiet.

'I don't want to hear it; you all need to check yourselves next time. Jesse is the go-to for discipline, it's not for you lot to sort it out by fighting. Anyway, that's all I have to say on that. SAI recorded it and the Academy monitoring and communications centre will go through it and file a report. On a more positive note, great job with the flooded moon pool and airlock. But hell, Stella that was foolish! You nearly forced SAI into an emergency surface to save your life. In average weather that was dangerous, and we would have been vulnerable to piracy. Next time stop, think and then look for some advice rather than rushing into a situation like that. We got through it and I hope you all learnt something from it. Now let's get some down time before we need to prepare to offload at the Harvester.'

They all looked at each other with relief. It had been a long day. After some food and a bit of relaxation they went off to get some sleep.

Chapter 6

The next day, two days since they had completed mining operations everyone was up early. SAI had notified the crew that they were two hours from the Harvester. They were now on final approach and once underneath would make a slow ascent to twenty metres. Ngarra, Chang and Jonny were at the SAI console ready to monitor the automated approach, docking and offloading procedure.

'SAI,' said Ngarra. 'Initiate final approach.'

'Confirmed,' said SAI. 'Initiating final approach to Harvester.'

They cleared perimeter security and proceeded towards the Harvester. Projected images showed Skimmer propulsion and navigation systems.

'SAI, initiate Harvester moon pool entry sequence,' said Ngarra as they approached the Harvester.

'Confirmed,' said SAI. 'Initiating moon pool entry sequence.'

SAI projected a detailed pilotage hologram in the middle of the console.

The outer hull shields of the Skimmer closed. During close quarter operations and manoeuvring they had to view everything through the camera system. The Skimmer positioned itself underneath the Harvester, they watched on screen as the blue-green world outside was left behind and they were surrounded by dim lights shining into the water. The giant hull of the Harvester swallowed them whole.

Chang looked briefly at Jonny. He was still grumpy about being punched, but he was feeling pretty good about saving the day. Jonny gave him a wink from across the console and Chang glared back at him. Chang thought that maybe he should not have been so nasty to Connor, but Connor was just so frustrating.

'And as for Jonny, we'll see about him,' he muttered to himself still glaring at him.

Jonny laughed and said, 'mate if you glare at me any longer with those X-ray eyes I'm going to melt.'

'Your turn will come,' Chang muttered under his breath while glaring at him.

'Say something did you Chang,' said Ngarra while flicking through a load manifest on the cargo screen.

Ngarra was checking SAI's load calculations against the Skimmer's stability. The Skimmer's submerged buoyancy was continuously adjusted by SAI. The crew always monitored it. Not that they needed to, but they had to follow protocol.

Despite what Chang may think, being on a Skimmer was no holiday and there was always something that needed doing or checking.

Ngarra was so busy thinking about the issues going on with the crew that he missed the docking sequence activation.

'Docking sequence activated,' announced the Skimmer SAI.

'Geeze,' said Ngarra as he refocussed. 'It all happens so fast.'

'Here we go,' he said as the Skimmer surfaced in the moon pool.

A large smooth wave slid off the top of the Skimmer as it rose out of the moon pool. The outer hull shields retracted, and the cameras switched off. They could now look out of the Skimmer console. Large docking clamps moved across from either side of the moon pool they were in and secured the Skimmer.

***

During the ascent and docking procedure Stella was in the Xtract bay. She contacted Ngarra at the SAI console to tell them everything was fine.

'All good here,' she said and then left.

She walked up to the recreation area and forward to the viewing area to look outside. With the outer hull shields retracted she could see down either side of the Skimmer and off into the distance in both directions. The inside of the Harvester was huge and dwarfed the Skimmer.

'It was made for giants,' she said out loud. 'The ingenuity of Chinese engineering.'

Stella carried on thinking to herself. Such a great place for socialising. Maybe we should be celebrating getting here in one piece; get to know each other a lot better.

Maybe Chang would fit in more.

Maybe he just needs a bit of responsibility.

If he felt more valued, he might not feel like he was going to get a berating every time he made a mistake.

She continued watching as the large robotic arms picked up the first nodule trays on each side. It was fascinating to watch the offloading process. She imagined a large rubbish truck picking up household bins on the side of the road. This was ten times the size of that.

'But that was back in the 2020's,' she said to herself out loud. 'Nowadays a driverless waste collection unit did all that sort of stuff.'

All along the conveyor on both sides and adjacent to every moon pool, robotic arms moved along the sides of the moon pools removing trays of nodules from Skimmers.

Robotic arms used a ram to tip the contents onto the conveyor. The ram slowly pushed a metal plate in from one end of the tray it was holding. The pressure released an opening at the other end and the nodules slowly spilled through a narrow channel onto the conveyor. Offloading onto the conveyor was slow. It would go on for the rest of the day.

'It seems there are more Skimmers than usual unloading,' she thought to herself out loud.

Her thoughts continued to wander. Being on the Harvester was at times like staying at a resort on a small island she thought to herself. It was a chance to relax overnight between Skimmer runs.

Systems checks were completed by SAI before beginning the next mining run. Any maintenance that was required was carried out by the Skimmer repair drones under the direction of SAI. If needed SAI could dock them in the maintenance hangar for more extensive work.

As for socialising she thought to herself, alcoholic beverages were limited on Skimmers, but they did have some rather nice low alcohol and alcohol-free beer, wine and mixers. It was the same on the Harvester. At times the Harvester had large groups of people onboard to entertain and a lot of Skimmer crews to accommodate.

'I might get in touch with some of the other Skimmer crews and see if they want to catch up tonight,' she thought out loud.

She did miss the social side of life at Xed and the Ocean Academy. Also, the beaches in New Caledonia near the Academy were fantastic. It had been a few years now since she had graced the shores of Australia with her presence and caught up with friends.

***

Meanwhile, in the information hub Jesse finally had a chance to talk with Connor. She had wanted to talk about what happened with Jonny and Chang and to also have a closer look at what this genius was up to.

After the punch up between Jonny and Chang at the SAI console, Connor had spent much of his time at the information hub. He surrounded himself with images, diagrams and notes on his pet topic. He was looking for group behaviour patterning in nature and developing algorithms for them and then simulating it in Xtracts.

'You know Jonny and Chang are good people,' she said. 'They just got very frustrated with each other. Chang can be very confronting, but he doesn't mean to be nasty.'

She tried to get Connor to say something. Getting Connor to talk about his feelings usually didn't work. The best way to engage Connor was to talk about what he was interested in. Smiling to herself she thought, that goes for any male. Connor of course had no idea. She tried again to engage Connor in a conversation.

'I love this ocean bubble hologram you have got SAI to create. It's fascinating, watching this group of Xtracts simulate a mining operation and move around together.'

'Why did Jonny punch him anyway. He didn't do anything that bad,' said Connor.

He kept looking at his ocean bubble hologram. The giant bubble of ocean water and its Xtracts appeared to float in the middle of the information hub.

Jesse walked around it.

'My Xtracts react collectively to external influences,' said Connor excitedly. 'We found some great scripts for coding group patterns in land-based aerial drones. Using natural language processing I got SAI to hack them.'

Oh well, thought Jesse to herself. Connor thought of SAI as his friend. He often said we in reference to his work. It was so hard to get Connor to talk about his feelings.

Men, she thought to herself. There was something about this project of his though. Something special but she couldn't put her finger on it.

She kept engaging him in his pet topic.

'Interesting,' said Jesse.

Connor and Jesse both watched all the Xtracts in the ocean bubble hologram while they moved up and down. They changed when Connor moved his hand through the bubble and towards the group. The ones nearest his hand formed a small group and the others moved into it.

Like a bait ball of fish, they hovered together until he took his hand away. They resumed the mining simulation when he stopped annoying them.

'I am developing a set of algorithms for the Xtracts,' said Connor. 'They will be truly autonomous, able to respond to what's going on around them and to learn group behaviour. It removes the need for SAI to coordinate individual Xtract activity through the communication streamer we deploy.

Jesse watched as Connor explained further.

'I want my Xtracts to react together to one or more of them being threatened or encountering a hazard or problem while on task. I want them to behave like a protective colony, like bees or ants.'

'Great,' said Jesse. 'At least they don't go around yelling and punching each other,' she said smiling.

Connor understood the comment this time and managed a smile and carried on talking.

'You know, an individual animal's basic instinct is fight or flight. That has a lot to do with the hormones and chemicals released in response to a potential threat. So, what if something similar could be coded for in Xtracts. Like a master switch that resulted in a group response to a threat during mining operations. A set of algorithms for learning such a response. It overrides any individual mining task temporarily. It would interrupt each individual Xtract mining protocol. You know, to assist each another.'

Connor got very animated and waved his arms around at the work that was spread just about everywhere you looked in the information hub. Jesse thought it was great to see Connor so animated and into his work.

'How would you get Xtracts to mimic the behaviour you see from for example release of a chemical cue in nature by animals reacting to a threat,' she said. 'How does that relate to overriding an Xtract that is mining nodules.'

'Working on it,' said Connor.

'Maybe you could come up with something to make Jonny punch himself,' laughed Jesse. She was trying hard to get Connor to let his guard down, but he did not comprehend the meaning of the smart remark.

'Why would I do that?' he said. 'Somehow, they all need to be coordinated by a virtual 'ringmaster', a diffused brain with no central home. But that would mean every Xtract would simultaneously have to be the brain.'

'You've lost me now,' said Jesse smiling.

He carried on thinking out loud.

'What animals in nature represent this decentralised neural network? Sea cucumbers, starfish?'

Jesse smiled at him. She was fascinated by the pace at which he was thinking. Since Connor thought out loud SAI was able to record all his thinking. Using natural language processing SAI identified key words and phrases and used them to search for data, algorithms and scripts of code from online libraries.

'Go with that,' said Jesse. 'See where it takes you. I have to go and check in with Jonah.'

She walked out of the information hub and headed off. Jesse thought about how talented Connor was.

***

While Jesse had been talking with Connor, Stella had remained in the recreation area. She was still looking out into the Harvester and thinking about how such a bunch of misfits ended up together.

Smiling to herself she said out loud, 'it was certainly a long story.'

It was a story no different to that of any other crew. They were all doing the same thing. They were all somewhere out here in the Pacific Ocean. Stella watched the robotic arms offload nodules from other Skimmers. Her thoughts continued to drift in and out.

The gap between education and its application in this new world had widened through the 2020's. It was the age of machines and the development of robotics, drones and artificial intelligence. It seemed like the world had changed overnight. The education sector had struggled to adjust and keep pace with the needs of this new world.

She watched a load of nodules move along one of the conveyors. Her thoughts then returned to the changes in the world.

'We are buying, selling, downloading, designing, altering and using algorithms,' she said to herself. 'It's all about working with and using robots and drones for almost every task you could possibly imagine.'

Stella mused over this thought, looking into the distance and along the conveyor at Skimmers further down in other moon pools. She thought more about Xed and the Academy.

Through the 2020's the education sector was trying to catch up. Xed, like other technology-focussed Academies, rose out of this. The separation between education and what the world needed was filled by technology-focussed upper school industry funded learning academies.

She thought more about how education had changed. With the age of machines many jobs requiring manual work had disappeared. Globally, the world's education sector was not prepared. But at Xed and the Ocean Academy there were no year groups. Readiness to learn was based on interfacing with an AI and determining levels of achievement. No learning by age or by siloed subjects existed. Learning difficulties were no longer a hindrance or barrier to realising a student's potential or turning gifts into talents and talents into skills.

Stella stretched. She had better go and see what the others were doing.

'Enough reminiscing,' she thought out loud.

The morning was getting on. As she walked off there was a shudder and a low rumble which repeated itself several times.

Stella jumped. Turning and looking outside she could see along either side of the moon pools.

Harvester offloading systems flickered and conveyors vibrated and shuddered. What looked like lightening sparked along the conveyors and across the robotic arms into the distance. Skimmer alarms sounded.

'SAI open a Skimmer wide communication,' she said.

'Confirmed,' said SAI. 'Skimmer wide communication open.

'What was that?' she said. 'I am watching a lightning storm from here.'

'Same here, not sure,' said Ngarra. 'The docking clamps are locked. We will be stuck here for a while.'

'Have you heard from the Harvester crew,' asked Stella.

'Not yet,' he said. 'I imagine they will brief us about what is going on.'

Stella looked outside again at the static lightning arcing across the conveyors and robotic arms. It was at that moment there was a surge of water in the adjacent moon pool. At the SAI console Ngarra was also looking outside with the others. From the SAI console they could see Stella below and in front of them.

As they all looked on, from the adjacent wildly surging moon pool a large wave rose up. It washed over the sides of the moon pool. It further interrupted the conveyor, temporarily halting it and the robotic arms.

Ngarra and the others jumped back in surprise. A Skimmer surged at speed up through the middle of the wave. It settled in the moon pool in front of them.

It had come up so fast it had generated a huge rush of water off its flattened surface.

For a few minutes nothing happened then two figures exited the Skimmer. With no docking clamps or access ramp they jumped onto the gangway on each side. They ran along each side to where the robotic arms were positioned.

Ngarra could see each was holding something. In front of each robotic arm, they attached a device. The robotic arms activated. Ngarra watched as Skimmer trays were picked up, rotated in reverse over the conveyor and nodules scoped up.

'Geeze,' said Jesse as she and the rest of the crew watched what was going on.

A discussion ensued amongst everyone about what to do. Jonny was adamant they should get outside and stop what was happening.

'Bunch of cowboys!' he said. 'Shouldn't we stop them.'

'For once I agree,' said Chang. 'Let's get them.'

Jonny had a chuckle, 'Chang are we friends now?'

Chang frowned at him then looked at Jesse as if to say, 'do something about this guy.'

Jesse mouthed to him that they would talk about it later.

'We could use the Tasers and stun rods,' said Ngarra.

'No,' said Jesse. 'My call and it's too dangerous. It's not our fight. We cannot interfere no matter what. They have their own security. I'm not exposing our crew to such unnecessary risk.'

'But they are stealing nodules,' said Chang. 'It will look really bad for the crewing programme.'

A heated discussion ensued about their livelihoods being compromised by this heist.

'I am sure it will get dealt with. No one is going anywhere!' said Jesse shouting over everyone.

'Jesse is right,' said Ngarra. 'Although we could stop them, we might just make a bad situation worse.'

They all agreed to sit tight and wait for Harvester security to tell them what to do. While they were discussing why a crew would want to steal nodules from the Harvester SAI received an incoming communication.

'Message from Harvester,' said SAI.

An image appeared behind them on the console screen of a Harvester security officer.

'All crews, all crews are to stay in your Skimmer, do not attempt to exit or intervene under any circumstances. Standby for further instructions.'

The image of the security officer disappeared, and everyone looked at each other. Ngarra had grown quite impatient. You could tell because he always started fidgeting and couldn't keep still.

'Surely the crew monitoring and communication centre at the Academy will know what is going on,' he said. 'They monitor all crews and would know what these people are up to.'

'Not necessarily,' said Jesse. 'If the crew has taken control of the skimmer and bypassed their SAI, then they may not even be on the grid. To monitor the crew, it must be on the grid.'

The others nodded their heads. Ngarra got SAI to load and cross reference all current Skimmer crews with their Skimmer status.

'I need to get in touch with Jonah,' said Jesse. 'I was going to do it earlier and now this!' she exclaimed. 'SAI, priority communication with Jonah at Xed Academy.'

There was a pause which seemed to last for ages and then SAI said 'Confirmed.'

At the surface they could link easily with communication networks. No need existed to check whether a message board or live feed was available through the grid. The crew waited to hear what Jonah would have to say.

Chapter 7

At the Academy crew monitoring and communications centre, a duty officer noted a priority communication. They confirmed the location geographically, pulled up crew profiles and matched them with the Skimmer signature. They swiped the screen, touching and pulling down menus and expanding and contracting displays. The priority request was from the Security and Communications Officer on-board a Skimmer currently offloading at the Harvester.

'Priority communication for Jonah,' said the duty officer over open comms.

'What is it?' said the operations manager as he came over to the duty officers' console.

'Not sure,' said the team member. 'But it is marked urgent and all the crew member vital sign parameters have spiked recently suggesting an incident aboard. In fact, crew vitals have been all over the place for the past twenty-four hours. Just not enough to be flagged by the system. I will go back through the logs.'

'I have this,' said the manager as he took control of the situation. 'SAI, priority request for Jonah.'

'Priority request for Jonah sent,' said the monitoring centre SAI.

Jonah was walking into the simulation centre as the priority communication request came through on her smart watch. She moved quickly through, saying hi along the way to a few students that greeted her. She passed through security and into the crew monitoring and communications complex. She went straight to where the duty manager was.

'What's going on,' said Jonah. 'I got a priority communication request.'

Jonah had been in a Council meeting for a good part of yesterday and had come in early to try and catch up with work.

She had been at work for a while.

Jesse's image appeared on screen.

She explained the situation unfolding at the Harvester.

'A Skimmer has used its ARC array in a Harvester moon pool,' said Jesse. 'We think it's the same one that launched an ARC torpedo array at us in transit to the Harvester. They have hijacked the robotic arms. Right now, they are loading nodules from the conveyor back onto their Skimmer! Harvester security has sent out a communication. They said for all Skimmer crews to stay onboard.'

'Damn it, that shouldn't even be able to happen', said Jonah. 'And why in the hell was I not informed about what happened yesterday!'

She didn't want them to know they already knew about the off-grid Skimmer.

'You would have to override the Skimmer SAI protocols,' said Jonah. 'Even then, it would be flagged. That's why we have a security and communications officer on each Skimmer.'

'Well, something has gone wrong,' said Jesse. 'Some of our crew wanted to exit our Skimmer and take them on.'

'There's nothing you can do,' said Jonah. 'The Harvester will request emergency administration orders be issued by the ISA for breaching a whole bunch of maritime regulations. The Sea Hunters will then track them down and detain them. Sit tight and I will get back to you. Got to go.'

Jonah signalled the duty officer to end the communication.

She briefed the duty officer and feeling frustrated went to find Rick.

***

She saw him coming out of the Crew Monitoring and communications centre not far behind her, walking through the sim centre.

'Odd,' she said to herself. 'I didn't see him in there before.'

Rick was standing in the middle of the sim centre talking with the campus Sea Hunter liaison officer. Jonah rushed to intercept them.

Xed Academy students were coming and going and greeted her enthusiastically along the way. With a few smiles, hellos and waves she caught up with Rick as he exited the building.

The liaison officer took off in a hurry and Rick turned to walk away.

'Rick, Rick! we need to talk,' she said grabbing his arm. 'Something happened in one of the moon pools on the Harvester. That missing Skimmer has turned up. A load of nodules has been stolen off the conveyor. GlobeCorpMining is going to be very upset about this. Do you know anything about it?'

'Well, we have found them now haven't we,' said Rick with a smile. 'The Skimmer's off-grid so we have no way of locating it let alone tracking it.'

Rick turned to walk back to the complex and shrugged his shoulders but Jonah was not letting him off that easily.

'Really!' said Jonah. 'We have a rogue crew running around in a two-hundred-million-dollar Skimmer off-grid and all you tell me is we can't find it. What about its crew vitals that we monitor? What is going on with you!' she demanded. 'It takes years to get these kids where they need to be in life to crew these things. Last thing I want is a missing rogue crew. How is that going to look?'

'The crew monitoring is linked to the Skimmer SAI!' replied Rick as he raised his voice. He felt cornered. 'If it's off grid there is no way to link with the crew either!' he exclaimed. 'You know that!'

Jonah acknowledged that and decided to back off a bit and get her head straight. Rick was usually cool, calm and collected and not one for showing much emotion. But now he was getting nervous.

'Well,' he said. 'Maybe the off-grid Skimmer has been compromised, the rogue crew may be acting under duress and against their will.'

'You seem to know more about this than you are telling me,' said Jonah calmly.

Jonah was waving her finger at Rick and leaning forward into him.

'If a Skimmer is off the grid, then something really bad has happened,' she said in an ice-like voice.

'The Sea Hunters will track them down,' said Rick.

'GlobeCorpMining funds a significant portion of the Skimmer crew programme for the Academy damn it!' said Jonah.

Jonah leaned right forward and got in his face.

'We have a big stake in the Skimmers,' she hissed. 'So, don't be an arse. I want to know what you are not telling me.'

Her voice cut like ice and Rick grimaced. Jonah was not one for losing her cool but when it came to Xed, the Academy and her life's work she was not backing down.

'OK OK!' said Rick as he raised his voice again and backed off.

'You and the Council know that we lost our comms link with the SAI in this off-grid Skimmer. The other day I was notified about an incident involving Ngarra's Skimmer. I was told it was nothing to worry about. I assumed that if it was the off-grid Skimmer they would turn up at a Harvester moon pool we would get it sorted out.'

'Damn it, Rick!' exclaimed Jonah. 'We should have told our leadership team. 'Skimmers are arriving at the Harvester soon and will pick up new crew members. We need to get the Council together again as soon as possible.'

Jonah waved him away and walked off towards the administration building to gather her thoughts. She left Rick wondering what to do next.

***

As she walked Jonah thought about her students, Xed, the Ocean Academy and the Skimmer crew programme. She was now very worried.

Globally, the automation of industry had changed the way society functioned. However, within the education sector the response had been slow. Through the 2020's, the focus of schools remained on arts and humanities, traditional siloed math and science subjects, hospitality and food.

It had changed in the 2030's. The large gap between education and what industry needed meant students were struggling to find their place in this new world. Most information was now instantaneous. People didn't write much anymore; didn't need to remember or retain learning in the traditional sense. No reports, no documents piling up, just machines and lots of processed information.

After a period of initial training at the Ocean Academy, new or inexperienced crew members were placed on Skimmers for several months so they could put into practice all aspects of Skimmer monitoring at sea. They were assessed to determine if they were ready to be part of a crew.

Skimmer operators were often picked from those that were more interested in abstract processes, the big picture and had a flair for leadership. Technical or system engineers were picked for their affinity with patterns, logic, and reasoning and for their sociability. Navigators or pilots were specialists and loved virtual gaming and were usually quite outspoken and lively but with both introvert and extrovert character traits. Information experts usually had some sort of autism spectrum thing going on but not always and they were highly valued. Communications and security officers were identified from amongst the many other students at the academy or promoted from within Skimmer crews. They had a high degree of emotional intelligence. Xed was so successful it was ahead of its time.

Jonah reached the staff building and made her way to her office. On returning to her office Jonah decided to head home and think about what to do and how she would approach the Council.

She walked out of her office and took the lift to the roof of the staff and administration complex and walked across the drone Port. She stepped into the waiting autonomous drone, swiped her card and called out her address. It took off and headed for her home not far away on the hillside overlooking the campus and adjacent coast.

On the way she thought about the risks the Academy was exposed to. It was not long before she was home.

***

At home with a glass of wine in hand she was at her workstation thinking about how to reduce the risk the Academy now carried by relying heavily on the funding provided by GlobeCorpMining for the Skimmer crew programme.

The push by Skimmer contractors for increasing nodule numbers was becoming an issue. Crew productivity was limited by the capacity of the Xtract mining drones to recover nodules. They moved backwards and forwards from a depth of four thousand metres until the Skimmer trays were full.

Somehow or in some way she knew that the Academy had to become more financially independent. They had to have something more than just the crews they provided for the Skimmers. That something was technology.

The institute had developed a large amount of intellectual capital. For some time, she had thought about leveraging that. What could they do that everyone else was not already doing or trying to do? Surely amongst all those bright youth there was a genius or two that could come up with something.

As she sipped a wine and looked out across the coast, she thought about what the future may hold for all of them.

Rick was advocating for the Council to separate Xed and the Academy and maybe he was right. What if they stumbled across something that was worth fighting for by others in industry? What about her students at Xed, the Academy, the crews and did she really want to step into that world?

***

Back at Xed Academy Rick had returned to the into the sim centre. He got a coffee from the common area, passed through security and into the crew monitoring and communications complex. He was thinking about how they might avoid any embarrassment from the incident with the off-grid Skimmer and its rogue crew.

Rick was a confident man. He was always well dressed and stood tall. People called him the silent assassin; outwardly smiling but always planning his next move. He had always enjoyed strategic roles.

Originally, Rick had been a military man. He was in the Australian Navy for about ten years and had ended up in intelligence, focusing on maritime defence technology. The proliferation of submarines globally and sub-surface technology around the world had made for a busy place beneath the waves. After leaving he was head hunted to lead setup of the wave glider programme Ocean Shield. Through the 2020's the glider programme complemented Australia's future submarine construction programme.

His personality reflected his background. He had come into Xed and the Ocean Academy after having help set up the wave glider surveillance programme. On joining Xed it was Rick who helped set up the Ocean Academy. It was Rick that shaped how Skimmers would be crewed and monitored.

Although Jonah developed the training programme and secured the relationship and funding with GlobeCorpMining Rick was the one that implemented and ran it. His contribution to making the Skimmer crew programme work was instrumental and Jonah owed him much for that.

Rick looked out from the mezzanine and cast his eyes down and around the multitude of hubs for crew monitoring and thought some more. Lately he had become very frustrated.

The previous few years had seen GlobeCorpMining increase their influence and hold over the Academy. The funding arrangement with the Chinese mining company also depended on crews meeting ever increasing contractor nodule targets from the Xtracts, which had their limitations.

But Xtracts were not fully autonomous and the Skimmer SAI needed ongoing assistance running the Xtracts. That was why they had crews on them. Although GlobeCorpMining had got their Australian contractors to build many more Skimmers, and Xed had been funded to expand the Academy to accommodate all the extra crew needed into the future, he couldn't help but think such a push compromised their independence.

He was also worried that if the Xtracts were made fully autonomous that they would lose all funding for the crew programme. Not only training, but the simulation centre and its two Skimmers and the crew monitoring and communications centre. The one fact that gave him some comfort was that GlobeCorpMining could not be a shareholder, which was Xed and the Academy's saving grace. Also, Xed itself was financially independent and had strong ties with government agencies in Australia and the Pacific that also provided funding.

It was a real balancing act and he was always battling issues related to national security. It was very frustrating. Rick thought they should split Xed out and separate it totally. He thought the Academy Skimmer crew programme should be separated from the Academy itself as well.

He actively promoted these concepts to the Council. Jonah did not like it at all.

Chapter 8

Jesse looked back out at the two people returning to their Skimmer. Somehow, they had managed to use the robotic arms to pick up several trays, reverse the opening so it faced the other way and scooped up nodules moving along the conveyor.

The robotic arms placed the trays in position.

The two people jumped across the gangway and onto their Skimmer.

They ran along the sides, across the row of trays, along the recess for the Xtracts, climbed up to the recreation area level and through the main entrance, which sealed behind them.

The Skimmer came to life and heaved from side to side.

The docking clamps were not engaged.

It looked like some giant sea creature about to sink below the waves. Water from the moon pool sloshed around and up onto the adjacent gangways.

The Skimmer slowly submerged from its moon pool and with a surge, the sea closed over it.

It was as if the Skimmer had never been there.

A Harvester security team emerged from one of the entrances to the upper levels on the Port side of the Harvester and onto the gangway next to the conveyor.

They ran along it towards the moon pool where the Skimmer had been. A couple of technicians were following behind. The technicians moved off to check for any damage to the conveyor and robotic arms.

Jesse was about to try and get in touch with the Harvester about what they had just seen.

'Communication from Harvester security,' said SAI.

'SAI, open message board,' said Jesse.

'Do not exit your Harvester,' announced a security officer. 'A security team is clearing the area. One of our security personnel will meet you at your Skimmer.'

Outside everything was quiet again. The two technicians were checking the conveyor. It was moving again, and robotic arms were offloading nodules.

From their Skimmer they could see one of the security team approaching.

'Why did they let them go?' said Jonny. 'They could have stopped them.'

'They wouldn't have got here in time,' said Jesse. 'Besides, it is not their role and they would not want to risk damaging the Harvester. They can't afford any damage that might halt offloading operations. The conveyor belts were interrupted, which is bad enough. Any breaches of moon pool protocols are passed on to "the Authority" and to the Sea Hunters.'

'Fair enough,' said Ngarra. 'Now let's see if we can talk with the Harvester crew. We can't just stand by while the Sea Hunters find and detain one of our crews. We should have done something. Maybe this crew is in trouble; I mean why would they do this unless they were being forced to?'

Jesse nodded and the others agreed wholeheartedly. Jesse decided it was time to brief everyone on what Jonah had told her and Ngarra earlier.

'Right,' she said. 'Before this security officer gets here. SAI, request all crew to meet at the SAI console now.'

'Confirmed,' said SAI. A message was sent to the rest of the crew to meet in the SAI console.

What we have got, Jesse thought to herself. A rogue crew and off-grid Skimmer, the Sea Hunters involvement and a new crew member coming. Should they try and track down this off-grid Skimmer and recover the crew themselves before the Sea Hunters did. Would the Academy let them, and would their crew be up to it?

'Right,' said Jesse as everyone assembled at the SAI console. Everyone stopped gossiping about what was going on and listened to what Jesse had to say.

'At least we know which Skimmer it is,' she said. 'We can assume crew monitoring already know given that their signature will be absent from the grid.'

No one present was familiar with the crew members on the off-grid Skimmer, but Academy crew monitoring would know exactly who they were.

'The docking clamps are locked temporarily,' said Jesse. 'No Skimmers can leave until given the all clear. What's more, all Skimmers arriving at the

Harvester will be taking on new crew. A lot of Skimmers operating in "the Area" will be getting one extra person.'

'Good news,' said Chang, 'then I don't have to be the one doing all the work.'

'Come on Chang, it isn't that bad,' said Stella.

Chang grumbled about how tough life was.

'Anyway, moving on Chang,' said Jesse smiling. 'The Sea Hunters are going to turn up here. They will be looking for this off-grid Skimmer.'

'I would suggest we try and convince the Academy to let us get to them first,' said Ngarra. 'But without a way to locate them it would be like looking for a sunfish in the middle of the Pacific Ocean, pure chance.'

They all had a chuckle at his analogy and talked amongst themselves about it.

'Xtracts can communicate their location relative to each other off the grid,' said Connor as he jumped in excitedly, his mind racing. 'They use infra sound, that's how they were designed. It's an extremely low frequency, like a locator beacon in case something goes wrong. Like how whales communicate over long distances. What if I could use the signal and hook into their communication network? I could use it as a carrier signal to get our Xtracts talking with the off-grid Skimmer Xtracts. I could locate them. In fact, I could do more than that.'

Connor was talking a million miles an hour, moving and waving his arms around trying to describe what he was thinking. He rushed off to the information hub. Everyone smiled, knowing Connor he would be holed up for days now in the information hub with SAI solving that one.

'Let's leave him to figure that one out,' said Ngarra with a smile on his face. If he's right it will save us a lot of time and effort.

'Well,' said Jesse. 'We will be here overnight anyway. The new crew members will be coming on a drone transport. Ngarra, let's see what this security officer wants. You guys all freshen up and we will then go to Harvester accommodation.'

Jesse and Ngarra went off to greet the security officer. The security officer crossed the gangway up to the recreation area and boarded the Skimmer. He was dressed in lightly fitted cotton pants and top, fire retarded from what it seemed and boots. He had a vest on which appeared both stab proof and bullet proof and wore a light helmet with a removable face covering. He had a belt that carried a shock rod, handcuffs and a side arm. There was also a Taser and a small bum bag with fireproof hoods and gloves in it.

As he entered the Skimmer Jesse and Ngarra greeted him.

'Hi,' said Jesse. 'Quite a situation you had there. I hope everything is all right.'

'That is not your concern,' he said gruffly.

A Chinese national, he spoke very good English. 'Follow me,' he said. 'The Harvester operations officer wants to speak with you.'

Chang had come down to the recreation area quickly, eager to get off the Skimmer and relax. He had just arrived and heard what was said.

'Really,' said Chang. 'Can't we go to the accommodation level first?'

The security officer glared at Chang and looked him up and down. He approached him and said, 'what are you doing on a Skimmer?'

'Right then,' said Jesse before the officer could say anything more. 'This is our Skimmer operator Ngarra and he would very much like to meet and discuss the situation with your Harvester operations officer. I don't think we should keep them waiting.'

Ngarra was about to moan but stopped himself. Smart move, he thought to himself and caught Jesses wink at him out of the corner of her eye. By then everyone had come to the recreation area and were ready to get off the Skimmer.

***

They were all looking forward to seeing and catching up with the other Skimmer crews and asking how they were going. However, first they were directed to exit the Skimmer and follow the security detail along the gangway and across and behind the conveyor adjacent to the moon pools.

They passed the technicians that were checking for damage. The vibration and amount of static generated along the conveyor belts had been quite a spectacle to watch, like a giant electrical storm. The arching generated from all the static had caused some of the robotic arms to malfunction and they had to be reset locally. There did not appear to be any obvious visual signs of damage.

Behind the row of robotic arms and conveyor was an exit and lift that took them above the moon pools. They entered it and the lift took off, rising above the moon pools and into the superstructure above them. It stopped and as the lift opened, they were greeted by one of the Harvester crew.

'Welcome aboard,' she said as they stepped out and the security officer followed behind them. 'Not the best circumstances, I'm sure. Few Skimmer crews get to see us or anything beyond the moon pools, accommodation level and the drone deck on here.'

'Thanks,' said Jesse as they walked through a large open space with rooms off to each side. 'So why do we get to see you then,' she asked pointedly.

'I can't discuss that,' she said and pointed for them to follow on behind her.

Jesse and Ngarra looked at each and signalled that they would talk later about the comment.

There were touch screen monitoring systems for offloading, holographic displays of the Pacific Ocean, weather maps, and various geographic areas showing tenements over seabed mining operations.

'I've been around here for a while,' she said. 'I wouldn't say this job is as exciting as what you get up to.'

'Our mining runs are usually pretty quiet,' said Jesse. 'All this is very unusual. Anyway, this is Ngarra, Stella, Jonny, Chang and Connor.'

She turned to face them. 'Yes, I know and great to meet you all. I'm Sue, the operations officer in charge. Over here is our first officer Lee,' she said as he walked over to greet them.

Sue oversaw Harvester operations and security and communications, a role like Jesse's.

'Hi all, welcome to the top of the world,' Lee said shaking hands. 'Well, our world anyway,' he said with a smile. They were on the level below the drone bay.

Lee was of Chinese descent and just like Chang had spent much of his life outside of China. He had adopted an English first name, which was not uncommon.

They all moved into a large open area. In front of them was a huge screen. With the shields retracted it opened to a view of the endless ocean outside. It was a calm evening as the sun set over a blue sky and distant horizon. Almost surreal and everyone looked on bewildered.

Sue and Lee smiled as they watched the crew. It had been a while since Ngarra's crew had spent any length of time at the ocean surface. Sue and Lee were much older. To them the Skimmer crew were still kids coming out of their teenage years into adulthood.

'You just never get used to that view,' said Sue as she watched them. 'With the help of artificial intelligence, robotics and drone technology there's really not that much to do in terms of running the Harvester itself. Like you, we spend a lot of our time monitoring and maintaining automated systems and reporting on processing. Anyway, let's sit down and eat something. I would like to ask you some questions. Tomorrow we will be busy. The drone transports arrive with the new crew members for placement. Lee and I will be on the drone deck.'

They were seated in an area adjacent to operations, away from all the monitoring systems they had glimpsed. It was next to where everyone on duty seemed to gather and eat. On the opposite side was accommodation and other amenities for off-duty Harvester personnel. As on the Skimmer, meal choice was automated. One of the Harvester personnel collected a variety of Asian style foods which were all placed on the table for them.

As they were eating Chang thought about the Harvester, a triumph of Chinese ingenuity. His sister was here somewhere but did not think it wise to ask where she was and if he could see her. They had been back and forwards to the Skimmer many times, but this was the first time they had been anywhere but the moon pool and accommodation level. Even when they took a transport drone back to New Caledonia or back out to the Harvester, they were always escorted from the drone deck straight to the accommodation level.

He also knew that GlobeCorpMining tended only to employ Chinese Nationals to work on the Harvester. There was talk, whispers and rumours that they ran a mining drone research and development programme. His sister had mentioned something about it a long time ago but did not say much. He wished that he could see his sister. Maybe she would update him on how his father was and the situation with his mother.

There were rumours that the Harvester, being stationed out in international waters, had technicians designing and testing what people were calling mimic drones. A drone which through guided machine learning could copy individual or group behaviour in animals or humans it encountered. People were worried that if such industrial drones were made truly autonomous and able to learn by themselves, they could wreak havoc on the world. But they were just unfounded rumours.

Chang continued eating and thinking about the Harvester and his complicated family connections. His thoughts drifted to what happened to their mother, but he quickly put that memory back into its box.

'Chang,' said Lee. 'You have a sister on this Harvester don't you.'

'Yes, I do,' said Chang cautiously. 'I have not seen her for some time.'

Chang tried to come across as dismissive and not interested in whether he had seen his sister or not. He wanted to though.

'She is very busy in our research laboratories now,' said Sue.

'Your father often mentions both of you,' said Lee.

Chang's father was a senior official in GlobeCorpMining and Chief Operations Officer. He oversaw Pacific Operations and knew Jonah well.

Chang had not spoken to his father in a while. He felt like a failure. He was nothing compared to his wonderful sister. But Xed had accepted him and he quickly moved into the Ocean Academy and put his talents into the Skimmer programme.

'I am sure my sister is very busy furthering her own interests,' said Chang with a hint of sarcasm. 'How is the research going?'

Jesse jumped in before Chang decided to say something he might regret.

'Perhaps we could discuss the incident down in the moon pool?' she said. 'It seems an Academy crew has taken a contractors Skimmer off-grid and removed a load of nodules. Why did you not stop them?'

Lee and Sue looked at each other. A silent pause followed, and everyone felt a little uncomfortable. They were all well into eating their meal and had just about finished. Until then Connor had been very quiet, but he looked up when he heard the word research. He got excited and was about to launch into a long discourse on the development of group behaviour in drones.

Jesse saw Connor about to say something. Quickly, she reiterated her concerns to Lee and Sue about the Academy crew that had gone rogue.

'If we could find and get our rogue crew back to the Academy,' she said, 'we could determine why they took a Skimmer off grid and removed those nodules.'

Connor glared at Jesse for interrupting his attempt to engage in a discussion about what research they were doing. He shrugged his shoulders and returned to eating the rest of his meal. His mind was racing about what research they might be doing.

'Under emergency administration orders issued by the ISA,' said Lee, 'the Sea Hunters will find them and return the Skimmer to the contractor and the nodules to us. As for the crew, they will be detained before being returned to your state sponsor to deal with.'

Lee looked at them all sternly and sought to gauge their response to about what would happen to the rogue crew.

Jonny, Chang and Stella whispered to each other.

Jesse glared at them. It was rude.

Ngarra looked at Jesse.

'What if we locate them first,' said Ngarra. 'We can take them back to the Academy. Surely GlobeCorpMining just want what is theirs, the load of nodules and the contractor their Skimmer. Besides, the crew are young, and you have no idea why this has all happened.'

Ngarra was all for community justice and would rather the rogue crew face their peers and answer for themselves. That was his culture after all, being an indigenous Australian.

'Under the regulations for operating in "the Area",' said Sue, 'and the mandate given to the International Seabed Authority, the Sea Hunters can disable the Skimmer, board it and detain the crew. Both the State sponsor and contractor will not look kindly on what the rogue crew has done.'

'It sounds like they are in a lot of trouble,' said Chang.

'Where would they go?' said Stella. 'Come on guys, we can find them and take them back to the Academy.'

'The choice is yours,' said Sue. 'If you pursue this you are just as likely to get caught up in it all. The Sea Hunters will then be looking for you as well.'

'I can't speak for Chang's father,' said Lee, 'but my official position for the record is to advise you against taking any action to locate and return the rogue crew to your Academy.'

'On that note,' said Ngarra. 'It's time for us to relax and get some sleep. It's been a very long day and its late.'

The crew took their cue and got up to leave.

The discussion had got a little tense.

Ngarra's crew went on to discuss whether they would go to the accommodation deck in the morning and catch up with some of the other crews. They had a bit of time tomorrow before the new crew members arrived.

Sue and Lee whispered something to each other.

'Let's go then,' said Sue. 'I will get someone to escort you to the accommodation level.'

'There's no need,' said Jesse. 'We will spend the night on our Skimmer.'

The others glared at Jesse and she motioned for them to keep quiet. They all stood up and shock hands, thanking Sue and Lee for the meal.

'Thanks for meeting with us,' said Jesse.

They walked back through the operations centre towards the lift they had come up in. They said their goodbyes at the lift and were escorted back to the moon pool deck and their Skimmer by a security officer.

***

The lift was not the normal way for crews to get to their Skimmers, but it got them back close to the moon pool their Skimmer was in. It was late as they walked along the gangway next to the conveyor. No other crews were around. The security officer stopped at the gangway leading onto their Skimmer, watched them enter it and then left.

'Well, how was that,' said Jonny. He hated formalities and would have been quite happy to give the meeting and meal a miss.

'A little frosty wasn't it,' said Jesse. 'We will have to be careful if we want to get that rogue crew back safely to the Academy.'

'With the help of Tangaroa, we will get through this in one piece,' said Jonny.

The Maori god of the sea Tangaroa was tattooed as a sleeve on Jonny's arm. He made a warrior gesture typical of New Zealand indigenous tribal culture.

'We are all brothers and sisters,' he said smiling.

'Speaking of sisters,' said Chang with a glum look.

He shrugged his shoulders frowned at Jonny's antics and gestures. Chang had wanted to see his sister.

'Well,' said Ngarra, 'let's discuss this more first thing tomorrow. I'm off to get some rest. We will stay on board tonight rather than go up to the Harvester accommodation deck.'

Ngarra and Jesse were worried about the whole situation. Something did not seem right.

The crew went off to get some rest. Tomorrow was another day.

Chapter 9

The next morning, four days since completing their mining operation other Skimmers were arriving at the Harvester to offload nodules and pick up new crew members. Several Skimmers were positioned fifty metres below sea level and to the side of the Harvester, waiting to approach and enter a moon pool.

On the Harvester drone deck Lee and Sue were waiting for the arrival of the transport drones with the new crew. They stood on the observation platform of a structure called "the Hex". It was shaped like a hexagonal prism. It was the same height as the drone bay below, the height of a three-storey building. The hex was retractable and could be lowered below the drone deck. It was an operations and control tower for subsurface, sea surface and air traffic.

Ships coming to load nodules had automated clearance to enter the security zone. No one knew what would happen if clearance wasn't confirmed. Below sea level was the same. Unmanned underwater security drones conducted regular perimeter patrols of the area. Anything other than a Skimmer could not breach the perimeter. That was why the off-grid one even without an active signature was not challenged or stopped.

Beneath the drone deck in the drone bay on the port and starboard sides were additional drone launch and recovery docks. Patrol drones could enter and leave from the sides of the Harvester rather than using the drone deck and docking clamps above. The three transport drones arriving would use the drone deck and docking clamps.

Sue looked out over the drone deck, thinking about the meeting with Ngarra's crew the night before.

'Do you think Chang's sister would compromise the research programme over Chang?' she said.

'I doubt it,' said Lee. 'Her father is the GlobeCorpMining Chief Operations Officer. Chang doesn't appear to get along with him, or so he says. Besides, Chang wouldn't want to make the situation with his mother any worse.'

'The research programme is important,' said Sue. 'It could revolutionise deep sea mining operations.'

'That's what concerns me,' Lee noted with a frown on his face. 'It takes away any control we have. Without some prime directives regarding human oversight and the preservation of human life I don't like it.'

'So far, we have failed to make much progress on it,' said Sue. 'It will be some time before we get that far. Besides, it sounded like Connor had something to say about it and that interests me. On another note, from what they said last night I also think they will try and find the off-grid Skimmer and recover the rogue crew. When the Sea Hunters get here, we should ask them to track Ngarra's Skimmer.'

'That we will do,' said Lee.

Lee thought the Sea Hunters would probably do it anyway as it would make it easier to track down the off-grid Skimmer and its rogue crew.

'Transport drones inbound, estimated time of arrival is fifteen minutes,' announced a duty officer.

'Here we go,' said Lee. 'At least this time we don't have a super cell bearing down on us.'

'Yes,' said Sue. 'Last time it was a race against the clock to swap out Skimmer crew and lock down the drone deck and drone bay and move.'

'Watching the leading edge of a super weather cell approach across the ocean is certainly a sight to see,' said Lee.

It was one of those days where it was hard to tell where the ocean finished, and the sky began.

With climate change rapidly warming the oceans over the last two decades super cells that formed in the convergence zone had become vicious. Combined with the long periods of El Nino, the South Pacific convergence zone now threw up some terrible storms. Although there were fewer overall, the magnitude and intensity of them was immense and they did some serious damage to Pacific Islands' and their inhabitants.

Sue and Lee looked out towards the horizon. A continuous presence of unmanned drone patrols flew a few miles from the Harvester and alerted them to any security issue that might arise.

There was a light breeze and it was not too hot.

There was a low humming in the air.

The drone deck of the Harvester shimmered in the sunlight.

A flurry of activity erupted.

A Harvester security team stood at the Hex entrance onto the drone deck. Drone lifts that had been lowered were raised. Some of the unmanned drones used for perimeter security took off from the sides of the Harvester, while others that had landed topside were lowered to the bay below.

As Sue and Lee watched three transport drones appeared in the sky on the horizon. They were travelling low over the water in a "V" formation. After what seemed like ages, they approached the Harvester and spread out in a line.

It was always a sight to see. Lee was humming and signing a song. 'This is the end, the only end my friend…or something like that,' he said to Sue. 'Remember that old American song, from the Doors, I think it was. Jim Morrison.'

'Can't say I do,' said Sue.

Lee kept humming it as they watched the drones come in. The sound of the blades and the low hum gave him goose bumps on his skin.

Looking like a flattened chinook helicopter, they had four encased horizontal rotor blades. The back two were closer to the fuselage and set a bit higher with a stern ramp beneath and in between. The front two were set lower and wider, mounted on small wings.

Each drone positioned itself in front of a docking clamp. They reared up just before the clamps and lowered onto them. As they hovered the docking clamps adjusted position, caught the drones and locked them into place. The docking clamps then retracted and the drones powered down.

The security detail standing below them at the entrance to the hex rushed out to meet them.

The new Skimmer crew members exited the transport drones and assembled next to each docking clamp. One of the security personnel approached the drone nearest Sue and Lee.

'Welcome to the Pacific Harvester,' they heard him say. 'Get your belongings and follow me to the accommodation deck. You will receive a safety briefing there. Once this is completed you will be assigned to your Skimmer and await pickup.'

Sue and Lee watched on as the new crew members picked up their bags and followed the security officer to an adjacent entrance to a stairwell on the drone deck and down into the Harvester. Other security officers were doing the same thing.

It was not long before the drone deck was quiet.

The transport drones shimmered in the hot sun.

The operator and a spotter of each could be seen checking over their drones. A few Harvester technicians were assisting.

***

A while later at the moon pools below one individual walked towards Ngarra's Skimmer. He was tall and wore a head piece. Middle eastern and Muslim he was from the United Arab Emirates, the UAE.

The security officer in front of him stopped and pointed to the Skimmer and nodded for him to go on.

Aamir was his name. He picked up his belongings and crossed the gangway connected to the Skimmer.

He was a little nervous. 'I am in Allah's hands now,' he thought to himself.

Aamir's family were from the United Arab Emirates. He was sent to a school in Australia for his education.

Aamir loved using digital technology and found it easy to work across multiple media platforms at the same time. He was great at searching for information and would use algorithms from online script libraries to carry out various tasks. Despite showing such talent, at lower secondary school he was constantly being disciplined for being absorbed in his own digital technology interests.

It was in Australia when he was fifteen years old and in year ten that he had meet people from Xed at a science and technology fair. His parents had heard of Xed and the Ocean Academy Skimmer crew programme. After his parents explained his situation to Xed, he was interviewed and offered a place. Aamir left school in year ten and moved to the Xed campus in New Caledonia. He spent the next few years in Xed and then entered the Ocean Academy Skimmer crew programme.

Onboard the Skimmer everyone was eager to see who their new crew member was. Ngarra and Jesse had read his profile previously and wondered how Aamir would integrate with the crew. They were standing in the rec area with Stella when Aamir walked in.

Stella looked over and said enthusiastically, 'You must be Aamir, our new crew member.'

'Welcome Aamir,' said Jesse. 'This is Stella our systems engineering wizard and next to me is Ngarra, our Skimmer operator.'

Ngarra shook his hand but avoided eye contact.

Being an indigenous Australian he did not like direct eye contact and especially with people he did not know. Aamir bowed his head forward sightly and looked at him and then at Jesse.

Stella went to shake hands and Aamir pulled back, so Jesse moved inwards and between them. Ngarra quickly shook Aamir's hand. Aamir looked thankful that he was not embarrassed.

'Great to have you with us Aamir,' said Ngarra. 'Maybe you can put some culture into our team of misfits.'

Such a statement would help Aamir save face and limit any embarrassment. Jesse indicated her approval to Ngarra with a little nod of her head. Jesse was also careful not to be too imposing. Jesse tried to look subordinate to Ngarra in front of Aamir, at least for the time being. She had done the same with Chang when he first arrived, just to make the integration a little smoother. It made Aamir relax and it would help in the months to come.

Aamir was to be Jesse's understudy and would one day be moving into that role on another Skimmer. He had been selected from amongst many candidates at the Xed Ocean Academy. How he went over the next year would be monitored closely by Jesse and by the crew monitoring centre at the academy. This wasn't the simulator anymore.

'Right,' said Jesse. 'let's get everyone to the SAI console for a brief on what we are about to do.'

Everyone walked up and into the SAI console. Jonny, Connor and Chang followed, looking at Aamir. They had not been there to greet him and were not quite sure what to do. In the SAI console Ngarra stepped forward and with open hands gestured to Aamir to perhaps say something if he wanted.

'This is Aamir,' said Ngarra to Connor and Chang. 'He is going to be working with Jesse.'

Aamir nodded his head and greeted them rather formally and a little apprehensively.

'I am finally here,' he said. 'After all that training at Xed and then the Academy Skimmer programme it is good to be standing in the real thing.'

'This baby is now your home away from home,' said Jonny with a smile. 'It looks after us and we look after it,' he said patting the bulkhead. 'Well bro, we can get you up to speed pretty quick.'.

'I would appreciate it,' said Aamir.

Jesse interrupted everyone. Jesse looked on and decided now was as good a time as any to brief them on the little rescue mission they were about to embark on.

'We are going to try and locate the off-grid Skimmer and get the crew to come with us back to the Academy before anyone else gets hold of them. Other Skimmer crews will pick up the extra loads to make up for us being off task.'

'By that you mean the Sea Hunters,' said Jonny. 'A game of cat and mouse ay, sounds like fun folks.'

'Doesn't sound like fun to me,' said Chang moaning. 'It actually sounds dangerous and foolish.'

Jonny pulled a funny face at him and smiled, to which Chang looked away and ignored him.

Aamir looked on, confused and not knowing whether to smile or act as if it was very unprofessional behaviour.

Ngarra ignored them and explained further.

'Right listen up,' he said. 'As Jesse has pointed out, we are going to track down this off-grid Skimmer and convince the rogue crew to come with us, so they can return to the Academy.'

He looked around at everyone and then continued.

'And how may you ask are we going to do that?' he said. 'Well, Connor thinks he can get the Xtracts on our Skimmer to talk to the Xtracts on the off-grid skimmer. It will give us an intermittent signal that we can use to determine their location, which will allow us to close on it.'

'On that note,' said Jesse as she looked at everyone and thought what a bunch of misfits, they all were. 'Let's prepare to leave and find them.'

'About time we left this steel coffin,' said Chang gruffly.

The morning was getting on. Stella returned to the Xtract Bay and Chang went with her. He frowned at Jonny as they left the SAI console. Jonny didn't pay much attention and smiled, giving him a quick salute as they left.

Jonny went to the recreation area to get something to eat before they left the Harvester. 'I can take your bags to your sleeping quarters,' he said to Aamir as he left.

'Certainly,' said Aamir. 'That would be great,' as he walked off with Connor to learn more about how he used all the resources in the Information hub.

Ngarra and Jesse stayed at the SAI console. Ngarra wanted to discuss crew arrangements and other issues.

'Communication from Xed,' announced SAI.'

'SAI, open message board,' said Jesse.

An image of Jonah appeared in the centre of the SAI console.

'Jonah, nice to hear from you,' said Jesse. 'We are leaving soon.'

'Not much time for chatting,' said Jonah. 'The Xed Council met and agreed that this off-grid Skimmer must be tracked down and the rogue crew returned to Xed as soon as possible.'

Jonah sounded anxious and looked a little worried. Ngarra could detect the concern in her voice and was also now worried. He looked at Jesse, but you never could quite tell what Jesse thought about anything.

'As I indicated previously,' said Jonah. The Council has agreed that you must make every attempt to get our rogue crew back. Jesse, is there a way to find them?'

Jesse thought briefly and then replied. 'Well, it's off-grid and impossible to locate unless we actually put a tracking device on the Skimmer, or they are in sonar range. However, Connor has come up with another way.'

'Great,' said Jonah. 'Well, I insist that you keep all this to yourselves for now and do what you can to locate our missing crew. We will catch up again soon. If you locate them contact me as soon as possible.'

Jonah's image disappeared. Jesse and Ngarra then took off to the information hub to see Connor.

'Jonah looked really concerned,' said Jesse as they made their way up to the Information hub.

'I would as well if I were her,' said Ngarra. 'The Sea Hunters are by the book. If emergency administration orders are issued by the ISA, they will do whatever they have to do to.'

'That's what worries me,' said Jesse. 'If that crew is found and detained then everything is out of our control. The Skimmer contractor and State sponsor will look to prosecute. Xed will have no leverage over what happens. We need to get to them first and find out what happened.'

'We can and will do that,' said Ngarra. 'Besides I can't sit by and do nothing. The monotony of monitoring these Skimmer mining operations drives me nuts sometimes. This is different and it's the right thing to do.'

'We need to be careful,' said Jesse. 'If we are perceived to be performing a non-compliant operation ourselves then the Sea Hunters will disable our Skimmer, board and detain us as well. That will put Xed and the Academy in a world of trouble. They could lose their funding from GlobeCorpMining for the Skimmer crew programme.'

Jesse looked to Ngarra for some comment on her thoughts.

'Well,' said Ngarra. 'Contractor's still need crew and they need nodules. Besides, Jonah's personable relationship with the Chief Operating Officer of GlobeCorpMining bides us some time.'

'I can't see them buying into all this,' said Jesse.

Reaching the information hub, they looked at Connor's Ocean bubble hologram. The group of simulated Xtracts was moving around within it.

'This is impressive Connor,' said Ngarra.

Sometimes it looked as though Connor's eyes were looking at nothing; almost right though you. Like he was living in the world he was talking about. It was creepy to some people. He had a brilliant mind hiding inside that autistic head of his.

'Well,' said Connor as he started off on a long and excited explanation. 'In this ocean bubble hologram, the set of algorithms we have used to enable the Xtracts to learn group behaviour is different from anything I have ever seen. I have incorporated a series of layered algorithms. It allows for individuals to learn to identify and move away from anything not related to mining or what you would expect to see naturally in its surrounding environment. What's cool is that all the other Xtracts detect this response and then in turn respond to the individual's reaction and gather around it. Trouble is, at present the simulation falls apart eventually and they all wander off randomly.'

Connor was looking quite pleased with himself now. It was amazing how animated he got when talking about his passion.

Jesse and Ngarra walked around the ocean bubble hologram. Jesse put her hand into the hologram and waved it in front of the simulated Xtracts.

'I get that,' said Jesse. 'One moves away from my hand and then they all move, gather around and adjust their position.'

Jesse put her hand through the middle of the Xtracts in the ocean bubble hologram and they parted, then closed back together when she removed her hand. She then put her finger in front of one and kept it there. It moved away and the others then moved to group around it.

'It's like schooling bait fish,' said Connor. 'You know, sensing any physical presence in the water as a series of waves or pressure gradients. It's not the object but the change in environment it detects that they respond to. The more disturbed the surrounding water is the more grouping you observe in the Xtracts.'

'OK, but how does a group of deep-sea mining drones learn from such an encounter and then return to their mining tasks,' said Jesse. 'I mean there are so many ways a group can respond to a disruption. Could they differentiate between them?'

Connor thought about this and mumbled to himself and looked at the ocean bubble hologram. He moved his hand through the Xtracts and watched what they did, and then kept talking about his little world.

'Well,' said Connor. 'Not yet. It uses a type of multi-dimensional scaling to identify or prioritise anything that does not correlate with what would be expected in its surrounding environment during a tasking. It then uses a test set to model whether the groups adjustment relative to an individual's reaction to an anomaly improves the likelihood of returning to the task. Now this is where the simulation falls apart and they wander off. See, instead of the group returning to the mining task, look, they have wandered off randomly.'

Connor was on a roll and there was no stopping him. Jesse and Ngarra smiled. They were now getting a bit lost and confused with all the math Connor was explaining.

'I am not sure why,' said Connor as he carried on. 'I am getting SAI to run continuous diagnostics to find the flaw. My next trick is to get the group to adopt a defensive reaction to an object and to learn from it. What I am thinking is to use an algorithm that gets them to learn to differentiate non-threatening objects.'

Ngarra and Jesse walked around the hologram of the ocean bubble.

'I don't think I would want to be in your head Connor,' said Ngarra.

Ngarra's head was spinning trying to think about what Connor had just explained. 'I am a user of this technology but with the help of SAI you created it. Impressive.'

'Wow and I mean wow,' said Jesse. 'I can see the potential here for sure. Dangerous in the wrong hands as well if you crack it. Truly autonomous mining drones that continuously learn as a group to react and respond to what is going on around them during mining.'

'SAI generates the code and algorithms from my work and commentary using natural language processing,' said Connor. 'There are so many open source script libraries for AI and machine learning now that you can find code for just about anything. All you need to do is hack it. That's where the skill is. Using natural language processing, SAI converts everything into a mathematical construct. You need to be good at explaining the system architecture behind what you want to achieve though; that's the key.'

Jesse and Ngarra caught each other's eye and smiled. Jesse looked away quickly so Ngarra didn't get offended.

'Right,' said Ngarra, 'we will leave you to it. Jesse let's get to the SAI console and get out of here. We have a rogue crew to find.'

They walked off and left Connor to his ocean bubble hologram. 'Connor,' said Ngarra as he turned and left. 'Once we are underway can you run that infra sound signal hack for the off-grid Skimmer Xtracts you were talking about. See what comes up and let us know.'

Connor nodded and looked at Aamir as Jesse and Ngarra walked off towards the SAI console. Amir had been quietly listening.

Jesse and Ngarra made their way to the SAI console in silence. Both were deep in thought about everything Connor had told them.

Jesse was worried and thought it could bring them trouble. Xtracts would no longer need the communication streamer with the data nodes on it that stretched to the bottom of the ocean. There would be no need to use it to communicate with the Xtracts using a laser communication signal distribution network. Imagine Xtracts that as a group no longer needed to be controlled by humans and were truly autonomous. No need to convert a bunch of light flashes from a laser emitting polarised photons at various excited states into zeros or ones, or even rapid pulsing of sound waves into zeros and ones.

They walked into the SAI console and Ngarra's thoughts turned to Aamir.

'It's a bit awkward having Aamir here,' he said to Jesse.

'You need to understand his culture and motivation for being here,' replied Jesse. 'Give him some space and don't be offended by his manner. Historically middle eastern cultures have a different view of women and we need to respect that. With that mind of yours racing around be careful not to wind him up. It's hard enough working with Chang.'

'Right you are,' said Ngarra. 'I can certainly relate to how Aamir must feel given my indigenous heritage. I mean, with all the issues my people have had in the past.'

'Oh, that reminds me I forgot to say,' said Jesse. 'Remember I said we need to make it look like I am subordinate to you, just for a while. I know we are equals but I mean making it appear that I need to ask you if it is OK to do certain things.'

'Great idea and fine by me,' said Ngarra smiling. 'I might get used to it.'

'Can I make you dinner and wash your clothes for you as well dear,' said Jonny.

Jonny was at the SAI console checking over navigation systems with SAI. They all laughed.

'Well, the point being,' said Jesse, 'that we have a multicultural crew. Asian and Middle Eastern cultures view gender and gender roles a little differently to the rest of us. It takes some getting used to. With the last few generations of youth so globally connected through social media we have a real melting pot of overlapping values, views and belief systems. Globally connected and disaffected youth have become very confused.'

Jonny listened to the conversation between them. Given Johnny's Tongan and New Zealand Maori indigenous heritage he was always keen to share traditional knowledge about culture, values and beliefs.

'We as the first people of New Zealand have come a long way with all that,' said Jonny. 'But then again, we have a Treaty with those that settled and took over our country. We never got caught up in this whole constitution thing that does not include the first people of the land. Besides, nothing that can't be sorted out over some good food and a robust discussion,' he said laughing and patting his belly.

Ngarra and Jesse thought he had a good point and had a laugh as well.

'So,' said Ngarra. 'We are meant to just submit then. I identify myself as an indigenous Australia. It didn't go so well for us in the past.'

He paused a moment to think and then carried on.

'We can't just think that by being inclusive we are accommodating another culture, then pat ourselves on the back and say good job. All we are doing is demanding that a first nation culture exist within another cultures system and accept their values and laws. All that happens is one culture displaces another. Europeans displaced indigenous Australians. Who is to say that next Middle

Eastern or Asian culture and values will not displace European ones in Australia? Where would that leave us? How about we all change our way of thinking, but not just our thinking, our values as well. Look at Xed and the Academy. Jonah got rid of education by age, year and ability and along the way removed all the barriers to learning that were imposed on people, including cultural barriers. Readiness to learn became the focus and our common values were built around that.'

'All good points,' said Jesse as they listened to what he was saying. 'Let's encourage the crew to ask questions about the culture and world view of each other more often. That way we can all get to know Chang and Aamir a bit better.'

'Yes,' said Ngarra. 'Xed focusses on lot on how cultural values influence perception of the world when placed in small groups. It is part of the Skimmer crew programme.'

'Jonny,' said Ngarra. 'I am sure you would have a lot to say about all that. I mean you identify mainly as New Zealand Maori.'

'To right,' said Jonny. 'Another time though. I am keen to get out of here. The tribal history of the land of the long white cloud and its settlement by Europeans defines who I am for sure.'

They decided to leave the discussion for another time. SAI was ready to depart and waiting for the command.

'Yes, another time,' said Ngarra. 'SAI depart from Harvester and set course due North at cruising speed, depth a hundred metres.'

'Confirmed,' said SAI. 'Depart Harvester, course due north at cruising speed, depth a hundred metres.'

'This break from monitoring Xtract mining operations is great,' said Jonny. 'But do we know what we are getting ourselves into.'

'Jonah has given us the OK to do this,' said Jesse. 'Besides, when would a crew from the Academy ever get the opportunity to override a Skimmers mining protocol.'

'I know one rogue crew that has,' chuckled Jonny, 'so saddle up boys and girls and let's go and get them.'

Ngarra and Jesse smiled. Jonny's colloquial language and expressions always amused them.

'What concerns me,' said Ngarra trying not to laugh, 'is that we are trained to monitor and maintain systems in support of SAI. When we go outside the mining protocols, we are making decisions that will determine what SAI does in response to an event rather than the other way around. If we encounter problems while trying to locate the off-grid Skimmer and its rogue crew and make the wrong choices things could go bad for us all.'

Jonny was a little worried. But he was looking forward to making some decisions rather than being subject to all these fixed routines run by SAI that they just monitored.

'It's an adventure folks,' said Jonny. 'Hundreds of Skimmer crews just go about their roles in a tightly controlled Deepsea mining environment largely run by AI technology. This is the icing on the cake brothers and sisters; taking a Skimmer for a spin on some mission that has nothing to do with sitting inside a giant, oversized mineral laden drone for days on end.'

Ngarra and Jesse just could not help but smile at the way Jonny expressed himself.

'We will see what happens I guess,' said Ngarra as he chuckled at Jonny's analogy. That's New Zealanders for you, he thought to himself.

The outer hull shields had closed, and the camera system had activated. Outside they could see the docking arms remove themselves from the Skimmer. SAI took the Skimmer down and out through the Harvester moonpool entrance. The three of them watched as the moon pool, conveyors and robotic arms slowly disappeared. They descended into the silent depths and slipped out of the Harvester.

Chapter 10

The outer hull shields were still closed as the Skimmer moved out from beneath the Harvester. Through the camera display they could see other Skimmers arriving and departing. Behind them a school of yellow fin tuna circled the Harvester. Over time an entire pelagic ecosystem had assembled around it.

'It looks a bit like those transport ships coming and going from a space port,' said Jonny as he watched. 'Up through the atmosphere to the gateways. Those artificial gravity staging stations and their launch vehicle and transporter construction docks.'

'Might as well be on a spaceship,' said Ngarra.

Jonny moved his arm up and down motioning what it might look like entering and leaving the earth's atmosphere and moving out to one of the colonies. As they slipped away into the blue-green void the others smiled at his antics.

Looking out Ngarra thought it was disorientating. It was like SCUBA diving and getting vertigo he thought to himself; being in clear water with no point of reference when ascending or descending. People died in such circumstances, becoming disoriented and panicking.

Ngarra's thoughts were interrupted by SAI.

'Surface vessels detected; Sea Hunter group approaching Harvester.'

'Most likely they are meeting with the Harvester crew about the off-grid Skimmer incident,' said Jesse.

'Best we put some distance between us and the Sea Hunters then,' said Ngarra.

'Yeah, like you said earlier the last thing we need is to become the ones being hunted,' said Jonny.

'Let's get these shields open,' said Jesse.

'SAI, open outer hull shields,' said Ngarra.

'Confirmed, outer hull shields opening,' said SAI.

The shields opened as they slipped away determined to put some distance between them, the Sea Hunters and Harvester.

Ngarra wondered how long it would take to find the off-grid Skimmer. The network of grid communications buoys and Eel drones would not be able to pick up any signature from it. Hundreds of Islands are spread either side of the equator across various Island nations and their Exclusive Economic Zones he thought to himself. Once a Skimmer ventured near these Islands and away from the deep ocean environment there were so many places to hide it would be like trying to find a needle in a haystack.

So many things could go wrong he thought. If a foreign nations submarine picked up a sonar signal on the high seas that had no identification signature it might be treated as hostile and defensive action taken. Then there was piracy. the impact of climate change, population displacement and the previous conflict over fisheries resources in the region made it a dangerous place to operate.

Deep below at about four hundred metres using electronic warfare technology, military submarines quietly monitored and listened to what was going on. Everyone knew they were there, keeping an eye on each other and on activities on the high seas and in Exclusive Economic Zones of Island nations. Whether it was Australia, the United States, China, Japan, Korea, India, the United Kingdom or Russia, beneath the waves the resource rich Pacific Ocean was now a very busy place.

If the rogue crew were uncooperative when intercepted by the Sea Hunters their Skimmer would be disabled. If they crossed into territorial seas of Island nations without identification, they could well be blasted out of the water by any one of these submarines.

***

It was mid-afternoon and everyone on the Skimmer was able to enjoy some down time. The previous days had been full on and they were exhausted. In the rec area they chatted amongst themselves about home, family and things going on in the world.

Stella had finished eating. As she got up, she asked Chang if he could come to the Xtract by and help crosscheck the operating status of each one with SAI. Chang seemed a little less grumpy than usual, she thought to herself.

'Sure', he said. 'Someone's got to show you lot how it's done around here.'

'Hey you lot,' said Jesse. 'Before you all wander off listen up. Connor remember at the meeting on the Harvester with Sue and Lee, I interrupted you. We can't let anyone know you have a solution to locating the off-grid Skimmer using the Xtract mining drones. Nor can we let anyone know about your work on autonomous group behaviour. It's all now sensitive information. Let's keep it to ourselves until I have had a chance to talk more with Jonah at Xed.'

'My sister is working on something important in that laboratory on the Harvester,' said Chang as he looked at Connor.

Connor was getting excited and very agitated.

'I know she is,' said Chang carrying on. 'I never hear from her. Who knows what they are up to? It's been a few years since I have talked to her. They have made it very difficult to contact her.'

They all agreed it was best not to say anything at present.

'Come on, come with me guys,' said Connor. 'Let's go to the information hub. I'll show you how to find the rogue crew using the Xtract communication signal hack.'

'Alright,' said Ngarra. 'We've all got things to get on with. Let's go people.'

'You guys go,' said Stella. 'Chang and I have stuff to do in the Xtract bay.'

'Not I folks,' said Jonny. 'This belly needs sustenance.'

The others laughed as he jumped up to get some more food. Stella did a Sumo wrestler impression for Jonny and hassled him. Jonny pranced around imitating Stella's lively girly behaviour and mannerisms. As the others left there were further chuckles and laughter over his antics. Connor, Jesse, Aamir and Ngarra went to the information hub while Stella and Chang went to the Xtract bay console.

***

In the Xtract bay Stella got SAI to show the power status of all the Xtracts on their docking clamps.

'It's like a simulation game you might play isn't it,' said Stella as she made a sweeping gesture with her arm. 'All this I mean. The only difference is that we are inside it. Isn't that cool.'

'If you say so,' said Chang, dismissing Stella's sense of wonder at working and living inside what was essentially a giant drone.

Stella continued with the cross checks. She then walked down each side of the Skimmer between the maintenance bay and the inside of the external recess where the Xtracts were docked. She checked individual Xtract status displays. Chang stayed at the monitoring console, looking into the maintenance bay in front of him.

Chang was often dismissive of other people's thoughts. He also felt a bit awkward around females. He had his Chinese grandparent's traditional views from when he was little. These conflicted with a modern China that now had a huge working middle class. Chinese youth had successfully embraced and integrated western ideals. Many had moved into modern cities that provided everything. Industry and agriculture had been transformed to supply these huge cities. Environmentally, they were now world leaders in sustainability.

Despite his shortcomings Chang in his youth was always interested in digital technology. However, during his high school years he became disengaged from his teachers. The world around him was full of change and excitement but schools were not. Chang used to find source code scripts and algorithms for programming drones. He would find them in online libraries, hack them and use them to play jokes on the school he had attended not so long ago. One day at school a drone turned up carrying spindles full of toilet paper, which he released in a very artistic fashion around the campus. He got suspended.

His parents were so frustrated with him. Conversely, his sister went on to Caltech in the USA and worked in a robotics laboratory then returned to China and into a job with GlobeCorpMining. Their father was so proud, but not of Chang. Chang was creative and distracted, his sister was focussed and successful. In his early teenage years, he grew angry, angry at his parents, angry at school and angry at the world around him. But what hurt most was the disappointment shown by his parents and the situation with his mother. Then he found Xed and the Ocean Academy or they found him. He was sure his father had something to do with that. So here he was out in the middle of nowhere on a sub-surface mining skiff.

Chang watched Stella on the console screen. She was moving along one side of the Skimmer checking Xtract status displays. He knew that Stella had learning difficulties. Dyslexia could be a significant barrier to engaging with the world. But this new world placed little emphasis on connecting eye and hand with reading and writing. Everything was visual. Patterns became algorithms and algorithms ran machines.

He knew that for Stella, this new world was so engaging. She had told him that for her also, high school had seemed inaccessible and irrelevant and almost obsolete in some respects. What was the point? They could both learn everything they needed to know themselves using digital technology.

Chang continued to think about what school must have been like a few decades ago. In the previous two decades many schools struggled with change. They were slow to adopt all this technology and teach students how to access this new world. Stuck on compartmentalising subjects, incomplete IT infrastructure and teaching by age, year group and academic ability, schools had become victims of their own management, burgeoning administration and reporting requirements.

It was almost like teaching had been hijacked and side-lined by the need to justify themselves to parents and to standardised assessment and reporting. It was only in the last decade that schools moved away from the influence and control of all that. The focus was on teaching by level and readiness to learn only and not age and year or what parents thought of their children and schools. Nowadays many students skipped their last three senior years in upper school if not going to university and moved on to independent industry led Learning Academies.

***

While Stella and Chang were in the Xtract bay, at the information hub Connor was explaining to Aamir, Ngarra and Jesse the solution to finding the location of the off-grid Skimmer.

'Xtracts emit an infra sound signal that can be used to locate them,' he said. 'In no way can it ever be cancelled or altered. It's the only off-grid communication in "the Area". We can use the signal and hitch a ride on it.'

Even though the rogue crew's Skimmer was off the grid the Xtracts were still connected. It was a redundancy built in so that if ever something went wrong with a Skimmer, Xtracts could still be located and communicated with. It allowed a contractor to locate and recover lost Xtracts.

Connor was on a roll now and continued with his explanation. He was walking around acting out his thoughts about how the Xtracts would respond.

'They will keep communicating,' he said to himself out loud. 'Like scout ants leaving a trail for others to follow. The other ants sense the trail then they collectively use the new trail to get to and from where they need to be. The ants then have an information highway established and communicate with each other along the way, increasing the accuracy and reliability of the trail.'

Connor looked over at the others, assuming they were following what he was saying. He carried on.

'Think about the off-grid Skimmer Xtracts,' he said. 'The trail of crumbs is the speed, distance, time code of the infra sound communication signal. It's the equivalent of a chemical signal for the ants saying "follow me", linking our Xtracts to theirs. It is like an irresistible trail of numbers they will keep solving to see if they are any closer to each other. Over time it will give us a vector.'

Connor paused while Jesse and Ngarra thought more about it all. He watched them walk around and look at some screens showing his work. The others looked at each other, shrugged their shoulders and smiled. They stood there listening, fascinated with how his mind worked.

'Geeze Connor,' said Ngarra. 'You have outdone yourself with this.'

'Great work,' said Jesse, 'let's run it and start monitoring it.'

'Already done,' said Connor.

Jesse was about to walk off when SAI announced a communication request from Xed Academy crew monitoring.

'SAI, on our way to the SAI console,' she said.

As they left Connor had another thought.

'Mimic drones,' he blurted out and Jesse turned back towards Connor. 'They mentioned mimic drones. I heard them whisper it to each other. What does that mean? Drones that copy animal and human group behaviour. Why would they be interested in that?'

'Who do you mean by they?' said Ngarra.

'The Harvester people, you know the two crew members we had a meal with.'

'I don't know Connor,' said Jesse.

Connor carried on. 'But why would a mining company have a research lab on a Harvester and then whisper to each other about mimic drones.'

'That is why I talked over you at the meeting on the Harvester,' said Jesse. 'We have to keep quiet until we know more about all this.'

'OK, OK,' said Connor. 'They seemed pleasant enough though and friendly.'

'Ha, to you Connor everyone is friendly,' said Jesse. 'Trust me, what people may look like and behave like and what they actually think are not always the same. Anyway, I'm off to catch up with Jonah.'

'Yes,' said Ngarra. 'Time to get going. Let's get back to the SAI console to check in with Jonah.'

Jesse and Ngarra walked off, leaving Aamir with Connor.

Chapter 11

At Xed Academy on the same day that Ngarra's Skimmer left the Harvester Jonah and Rick were about to meet with the Xed Council again. Jonah was in her office looking out over the campus and thinking about her students. She was snapped out of contemplation by her secretary.

'Time for that meeting,' she said.

'Yes, right let's go then,' said Jonah as they walked out.

Rick was already there looking over some data, which he had projected from his smartwatch. He quickly closed it as they walked in.

Jonah and Rick had assembled the Xed Council to discuss further a course of action regarding the unfolding situation in "the Area". The rogue crew were on the run in the off-grid Skimmer and according to Rick the Sea Hunters had now arrived at the Harvester.

They had been informed that emergency administration orders had been issued by the ISA. The Sea Hunters would track down and recover the off-grid Skimmer, the nodules and detain the crew.

Pressure was mounting on the Academy from GlobeCorpMining to get the situation under control. The Council had become increasingly worried about the funding arrangement they had for crewing the Skimmers.

The images of each Council member appeared in a semi-circle in the middle of the meeting room.

'Morning everyone,' said Jonah.

They all greeted each other.

'I will get straight to the point,' she said. 'We need to locate this off-grid Skimmer. If we can get our rogue crew back, we can find out why they took a Skimmer off-grid and stole a load of nodules from GlobeCorpMining. We can find out who they are doing it for and why.'

'Emergency Administration orders have been issued,' said Rick. 'We are not a security or law enforcement agency. We provide the crews for the Skimmers and monitor them. We are not the police, or the military or any other security agency for that matter.'

Jonah frowned and thought otherwise. She was one for getting to the bottom of why this was going on. Rick appeared more concerned about reputation than safely recovering the crew before anyone else got to them.

'As you said Rick,' said one of the Council members. 'We are not a security agency. In fact, if as you say Jonah, one of our crew members in the other Skimmer has come up with a way to locate the off-grid one why not give that to the Sea Hunters. They can do it for us. Why not let the Sea Hunters do their job and pursue this off grid Skimmer?'

'I do not think that is a solution,' said Jonah. 'Any technology we develop is too valuable to just give away.'

'Good point,' said Rick. 'So why don't we get Ngarra and his crew to lead them to the off-grid Skimmer.'

Jonah gave Rick a puzzled look.

'I just want my rogue crew found and returned to Xed Academy,' she said. 'We recover our crew and then inform GlobeCorpMining that we have solved the problem. They will then give the Sea Hunters the off-grid Skimmer location.'

'I think,' said Rick, 'that it is more the breach of Skimmer security protocols by the rogue crew that the Sea Hunters will focus on. They will want to detain the rogue crew and hand them over to the contractors State sponsor to be prosecuted by the appropriate State sponsor Authority.'

Rick looked around at Council members to see if there was any agreement.

'I think so as well,' said another Council member. 'We should be concerned about the implications not handing our rogue crew over has for the Academy Skimmer crew programme and its ongoing funding by GlobeCorpMining.'

'That may well be so,' said another Council member. 'But I am sure GlobeCorpMining will still be grateful to us for giving them the location of the off-grid Skimmer after we have recovered our crew. I doubt they would want to pursue and press charges. It's the State sponsor we need to worry about.'

The Council members all nodded in agreement and discussed it further.

'For now, then it looks like a rescue mission then,' said Jonah. 'I will update you all when I get the next briefing on the situation from Jesse and Ngarra.'

With that the Council members images disappeared leaving Jonah, Rick and her Secretary standing there. Rick had a frown on his face and looked concerned.

'I will follow up on this and see if I can contact the Sea Hunters,' he said as he walked off.

'Good idea,' said Jonah. 'Let me know what they say as soon as possible.'

***

Rick left the administration complex and walked towards the Skimmer simulation centre. He greeted a few students as he walked across the Xed campus to the Academy.

Many students from Xed looked forward to being selected for the Ocean Academy Skimmer programme and he certainly didn't want to see that stop. By the time they got to the highest level of learning at Xed all the students knew who Rick was. To them, if interested he was their ticket into "the programme" as everyone called it.

Rick walked through the building entrance, through the main learning area and into the simulation centre. He passed security and entered the secure Skimmer crew monitoring and communications complex. Before catching up with the Sea Hunter campus liaison officer he wanted to get hold of the Commander of the group in "the Area" that would be trying to find the off-grid Skimmer.

***

While Rick was doing this Jonah and her secretary returned to her office in the administration complex. In the centre of the complex was a large void. At its base was a common area for socialising, eating, holding functions and having casual meetings. Her work area and office were on the top level facing out and overlooking the entire campus.

'It worries me; this whole situation and the potential impact it may have on Xed and the Ocean Academy,' said Jonah as they walked into her office. 'We have spent too many years building up this institution to have it compromised.'

'Surely if we solve this ourselves, we can minimise any damage to the reputation of Xed and the Academy,' her secretary said.

'Xed is different,' said Jonah. 'We have both public and private financial support. We have led and helped pick up the pieces in the education sector as disruptive technology flooded the world and left many schools behind.'

Jonah frowned and thought for a minute then continued.

'I am worried,' she said. 'About that and any impact on funding of the Academy crew programme. GlobeCorpMining is a major funder.'

Jonah turned away from looking out over the campus and went to stand at her workstation. An array of virtual touch screens with various projects on them, financial data and projections for crew demand. Jonah looked at the screens, swiped clear a few completed items and looked back at her secretary.

'Think of all those disenfranchised kids that fell away from education in the 2020's,' she said to her secretary as she looked over some data. 'Education leaders worldwide were caught up in what each country thought about the others education system, and who had a better strategy and how to deal with it. At Xed we offered a solution, an alternative to the status quo.'

Jonah went and got a coffee and continued with her line of thought.

'We got rid of dividing learning by year, by age and subject specific curriculum. We focussed on what the world needed, context and combining practical skills with developing an understanding of the application of all this disruptive technology and its many uses. After our success with Xed, through the Ocean Academy we partnered with industry to develop the Skimmer crewing programme, it all works.'

Jonah walked back over to look out over out over the campus.

'We proved that learning difficulties and cultural boundaries in youth were easily overcome,' she said. 'Take Ngarra and Jesse's Skimmer crew. Look at how far they have come.'

Jonah was frustrated and upset. She walked off, leaving her secretary hoping she was OK. Jonah found somewhere quiet and swiped her smartwatch to contact the crew monitoring centre and request to talk with Jesse and Ngarra.

She waited to see if the message board showed a live link. It depended on their proximity to Eel communication drones in "the Area" and distances to the grid buoys.

'Jonah how is it all going,' said Jesse as her image appeared. 'You look like you have had a rough day.'

Jonah was tired and a bit frustrated with the whole situation. The day was getting on and it worried her.

'I had a Council meeting. I know we have already agreed on this, but the official position of the Council is that you are to locate the off-grid Skimmer and contact the rogue crew and explain why they need to return with you.'

'Well from what you said earlier we kind of guessed that would be the case,' said Jesse. 'So, we are already trying to track them down.'

'The rogue crew are to leave their Skimmer,' said Jonah. 'They are to come with you and be returned to the Academy before the Sea Hunters or anyone else for that matter gets hold of them. I will arrange to get you back here. You will then give the off-grid Skimmer location to GlobeCorpMining. They will get the Sea Hunters to recover it for the contractor and return the load of nodules.'

Jonah was determined to get the rogue crew out of harm's way as quickly as possible.

'I am also going to put together a support crew here,' she said. 'They are well into their training at the simulation centre. They will run crew recovery simulations. They are almost ready to be part of the next phase of training.'

'Sounds good,' said Jesse.

Jonah could see Ngarra in the background. He looked concerned about it all. She decided to press him for his thoughts on crew recovery.

'What do you think Ngarra?' she said.

'What about keeping Connor's work confidential?' said Ngarra. 'We don't want it all getting into the wrong hands.'

'Don't worry about that for now,' said Jonah. 'We have some pretty good data and information security systems here at the simulation centre.'

Ngarra thought about it for a moment.

'We need a quick way to pick them up and get away,' he said. 'I have some thoughts on it.'

'Great,' said Jonah.

Jonah was still looking out over the campus and thinking. It was busy, students walking to and from various building complexes.

'Rick will oversee our sim centre crew,' she said. 'They will advise you. I don't want you having to surface to do all this. Catch up soon,' said Jonah. 'Got to go.'

She swiped her smartwatch and the image of Jesse disappeared. It was just in time as the link for the message board dropped to record only and out of live feed range.'

Jonah stood looking out over the campus and deciding how much GlobeCorpMining should know about all this.

She contacted Rick in the sim centre. There was a pause and then Ricks image appeared.

'Jonah, what can I do for you?' he said. 'It's all go here, a few crews in the final phase of training.'

'Rick, can you get that sim team together we talked about as quickly as possible and brief them on what they are going to do. Use one of our teams that is just about ready.'

'I am just getting onto it now,' replied Rick. 'By the way, I spoke to the Sea Hunters liaison officer here on campus. They will follow protocol of course.'

Rick hadn't of course as he wanted to talk with the Commander of the group out at sea first. But he needed to reassure Jonah.

'So, what does that mean,' said Jonah with a concerned voice.

'Well,' said Rick. 'Basically, once the Sea Hunters locate the off-grid Skimmer they will disable it. They will then board it using a breaching pod, detain the crew and hand them over to the Skimmer contractor State sponsor. They will abide by "the Authority" regulations in "the Area" and the Law of the Sea Convention of course; in line with the International Maritime Organisation.'

'Damn it! said Jonah. 'We need to get to them first. I will talk to GlobeCorpMining and try and get their support. Hopefully the Sea Hunters are delayed so we can recover our rogue before they get there.'

'Does GlobeCorpMining really need to know that we intend to find this off-grid Skimmer and get our crew back ourselves?' said Rick. 'I mean, they will just inform the Sea Hunters that we are pursuing our missing crew. Why don't we just tell them afterwards. Once you tell them everyone will know we are trying to find the rogue crew ourselves.'

'Trust me,' said Jonah. 'It is better they know given that they are a major funder of the crewing programme. In no way do I want to jeopardise everything we have achieved for the Academy.'

'Of course,' said Rick. 'Well then, I will get this sim team going.'

Ricks image disappeared, and Jonah was left standing looking out over her campus. She liked to think of it as her campus, her life's work.

The learning environment for students at Xed and the Ocean Academy was pretty good. Learning facilitators walked around the large open spaces used by students when engaged by their AI for learning. The word teacher or lecturer was redundant really. Individual achievement focused on meeting learning level competency requirements and demonstrating an understanding of the subject matter. There was no ranking of scores amongst peer groups. They just moved to the next level when their AI decided they were ready.

Jonah's thoughts returned to the situation at hand. She was about to call the Chief Operations Officer at GlobeCorpMining, Chang's father about the load of nodules taken by the rogue crew when her smartwatch came to life.

It was the Chief Operations Officer himself. Great timing, she thought to herself. She had met Chang's father several times previously and in a more positive light, but this would certainly not be one of those times.

'Hello,' said Jonah. 'I was about to give you a call. It's been a while and I wish it were a more positive conversation that we could be having.'

'Well,' he said. 'GlobeCorpMining has a particular interest in this off-grid Skimmer and its rogue crew. Why is it that one of your crews has decided to do a little of their own skimming?'

'We are still trying to work that out,' said Jonah. 'We are trying to locate and return the crew to Xed.'

'That may well be,' he said, 'but given the situation we would like access to the Skimmer you have tasked to try and locate the off-grid Skimmer and its rogue crew. We want to follow their progress. It will make it easier to send the Sea Hunters to recover the contractors Skimmer and return our load of nodules.'

'Not really possible,' said Jonah. 'The agreement is to crew the Skimmers and meet your production requirements however necessary. I just can't allow a mining company to piggyback on our crew monitoring and communication systems.'

'Fair enough,' he said. 'Can Rick keep us briefed then?'

'Certainly,' said Jonah. 'He is great with this sort of thing.'

'That will do for now,' he said. 'However, bear in mind that the Sea Hunters have their own mandate. We cannot intervene in their mission. They will of course seek to locate and return the off-grid Skimmer to the contractor and detain the rogue crew for handing over to the State sponsor authorities.'

'I know,' said Jonah. 'We will get to our rogue crew first and get them back to Xed for a debrief. I'm sure there is some explanation for their behaviour.'

'Right,' he said. 'But we cannot be seen to support that approach. I will touch base with you later.'

The screen went blank and Jonah was left wondering how on earth this messy situation would unfold. Something was bugging her, something did not seem right about everything, but she couldn't put a finger on what it was.

Chapter 12

Out in the Pacific Ocean onboard the Skimmer the day was getting on. Connor and Aamir were in the information hub. Connor was using the centre console touch screen and holographic projections to analyse the Xtract infra sound communication signal.

He had got SAI to hack the signal.

'Let's see if we have a vector yet for the direction of the Xtracts,' said Aamir.

'Sure,' said Connor. 'SAI report on vector update for Xtracts.'

'Confirmed,' said SAI. 'Vector not established.'

'It will take a while to establish a vector indicating the direction in which the off-grid Skimmer Xtracts are relative to us,' said Connor. 'Using my infra sound carrier signal hack the off-grid Xtracts will keep trying to establish whether they need to move closer or further away from our Xtracts. Once we determine the interval between each communication SAI will calculate a vector.'

'Impressive,' said Aamir. 'The old speed, distance time equation put to good use.'

He looked on as Connor got SAI to stream the Xtract carrier signal data feed on screen. It was just a fancy mathematical equation embedded in source code that calculated speed, distance and time. Over multiple intervals of calculations, a vector could be established showing the general direction they should heading in.

While they were going over the signal data feed Chang arrived to see what was going on.

'Great stuff,' he said. 'I mean, to use the Xtract infra sound communications link. Wish I had thought of that.' Chang's voice sounded a little grumpy at the thought of not having come up with the idea himself. He had forgotten that the Xtracts had a built in infra sound locator beacon.

'That reminds me,' said Aamir. 'When I got posted there was talk of getting permission to use mission data collected by Skimmers. Simulation crews at the academy would see all the same information as operational Skimmer crews. The academy AI would use all the data to learn and improve on mission scenarios during training.'

Chang smirked and then had a laugh. 'You're just crazy,' he said.

Aamir gave him a confused look as if to say crazy about what.

'Can an AI get grumpy,' said Chang. 'I gave it a run for its money with the amount of times I was in the simulation centre figuring what in the hell I was meant to be doing.'

While they were talking and thinking about such an advancement in simulation training SAI updated the calculations.

'Look, look!' said Connor. 'We have something. It's working!'

'It's so subtle,' said Aamir. 'A great solution.' He bowed his head slightly forward in acknowledgement.

Chang looked at the resulting vector.

'If it were me chasing this rogue crew once I knew where their Skimmer was, I would act like I was not looking and then take them by surprise. Of course, Jonny would just blast them out of the water and worry about the rest later.'

'You are missing the point,' said Connor. 'It's not that simple. First, we must generate a vector, which increases in accuracy the closer we get. We need to determine the approximate direction to go in and the distance to their location. It's like using a sextant to take repeated positions of the sun during the day. You can't get an accurate fix until we can cross reference enough of the hits and box in a general location.'

Good way to put it,' said Aamir. 'Perhaps maths teachers could use better analogies for such complex concepts.'

Connor said, 'SAI, open a Skimmer wide communication.'

'Confirmed,' said SAI. 'Skimmer wide communication open.'

'Everyone!' exclaimed Connor. 'Ngarra we have success.'

There was a pause and then Ngarra replied, 'What is it Connor?'

'We have a general direction. Still very broad. We need to head Northeast. We can start narrowing down the area, their movement and the distance,' he said excitedly.

'Great', said Ngarra from the navigation console. 'Do you have a timeline for this?'

'Not yet,' said Connor.

There were smiles all around as everyone stopped and listened to the conversation between Connor and Ngarra.

At the SAI console Jonny sat up, cracked his knuckles and clasped and stretched his hands in front of him.

'Right,' he said. 'SAI, alter heading northeast.'

It was simply a matter of telling SAI what to do and then dragging your finger through a virtual navigation screen, which was then projected in hologram in the centre of the SAI console.

'Confirmed,' said SAI. 'Alteration of course northeast of current location. Do you want to maintain current depth and speed?'

'SAI, confirmed.' said Jonny. 'Maintain current depth and speed.'

'Optimising final location relative to manganese nodule density to be mined,' said SAI.

'SAI, no,' said Ngarra. 'This is not a mining operation; this is a rescue mission. SAI, configure systems for defence and preservation of life.'

'Requires authorisation from the security and communications officer,' said SAI.

Jesse heard what was going on. 'SAI confirm authorisation,' she said, 'and let's get on with it.'

'Authorisation confirmed,' said SAI.

Jonny stood in front of the SAI console and navigation hologram and looked at the area of the ocean they were heading towards.

All Ngarra's crew could do now was to wait. The closer they got to the Xtracts in the off-grid Skimmer the more accurately they could determine the area it was likely to be in and where it was heading.

'Well,' said Jesse. 'The morning is getting on and we have some down time. There is nothing more we can do except wait.'

'I could do with something to eat,' said Jonny. 'All this talk of adventure and rescue has made me hungry!'

'Everyone,' said Ngarra over open comms. 'We will be in the rec area getting something to eat.'

After days of running around the ocean and being taken off their usual mining run, any chance to rest was welcome.

In the information hub Connor, Aamir and Chang were looking at the Ocean bubble hologram. The simulated Xtracts were carrying out a mining operation. They were moving together and coming and going between a projected seafloor, water column and surface location. It looked like an ant trail to a dead insect they had found.

'Let's go and get something to eat then,' said Chang.

On the way out Aamir and Chang looked back at the Ocean bubble hologram. Connor did not reply. He was engrossed in thought again and just looked right through them.

'When we interrupt them, they group together like schooling fish,' said Connor. 'But during mining they behave more like ants. The nodules are like the dead animal the ants have found. The movement of Xtracts between the surface location and the mine site represents the ant trail to and from the nest. A signal is passed along the route about what's there, where to go and what to expect. The Skimmer location represents the ant's nest.'

But how could he get the Xtracts to think and behave as if they were one while also being independent from each other? He wanted Xtracts to learn to move between being and behaving like a "bait ball" and being an "ant trail". He would not have been able to do it without the use of natural language processing. It had been very difficult to find and hack code for such a simulation.

Connor thought out loud to himself some more.

'Some ocean animals don't have what you would call a brain. They have a more dispersed nervous system. Any one part of the animal can communicate with adjacent parts. No signal is sent back to a central nervous system when a disruption to tissue occurs.'

Like a starfish being injured and regrowing its arms he thought to himself. They didn't have a brain or central nervous system. All the nerve tissue was the brain, if you could call it that. In a starfish such decentralised control was driven chemically through the radial nerves, which linked to a central nerve ring.

Connor was so consumed in his work. The others could see that he would not be coming to eat any time soon. Connor carried on speaking out loud to himself. SAI recorded what he was saying and then cross referenced it with examples from data or from scripts that were available that had coded for similar things.

Connor kept thinking about how to combine the ability of an individual Xtract to look after itself, respond to another's needs while together they all acted as a group in response to external threats to their tasking.

'Come on, come on,' said Aamir looking over. 'Let's go to the rec area and get something to eat. This is fascinating but we are starving. I will be spending the next few days with you anyway and would like to help.'

Aamir had spent some time immersed in online libraries for coding scripts related to various autonomous systems for robotics and was quite interested in it.

'Yeah, sounds great,' said Chang sarcastically. 'I mean, not to hear more about your work Connor but to get some food.'

'Great,' said Connor excitedly. Chang's comment did not mean anything him. 'This is so time consuming,' he said excitedly.

Chang and Aamir were still trying to encourage Connor out of the information hub with them. Connor was such an excitable person when he got talking and thinking about his passion and he often forgot to eat.

Aamir smiled at Connor. He was very patient and just the sort of person that could help Connor develop more of his social skills.

Chang on the other hand did not really care that much and tended to be quite dismissive of Connor. But he was like that with everyone. Chang was over it and left Connor and Aamir and went to the recreation area ahead of them.

'It really does looks like an ant trial Connor,' said Aamir as he walked back in. He walked around the hologram of the ocean bubble containing the mining Xtracts. Connor was watching him with bated breath, hanging on his every word.

'To have each Xtract monitor and assist each other during mining,' said Aamir, 'and then act as a group in response to a non-mining situation and to then learn from it is complicated.'

'Well yes,' interrupted Connor. 'To solve that problem SAI is helping me turn patterns identified from data on animals into algorithms that will enable us to do it.'

Connor was very animated now and really did not want to leave the hub to go and meet the others at the recreation area. He was now almost dragging Aamir around while talking with him. He was holding Aamir's arm and pointing out information. It was his way of showing emotion or connecting with people. He pointed out various data feeds and code and algorithms he was using to run simulations.

'Very interesting,' said Aamir. 'I hope I can help at some level with trying to put all this together. If you solve it, you will become a very popular person or perhaps a hunted person. Development of autonomous behaviour let alone being able to learn group behaviour in drones would be dangerous in the wrong hands.'

Connor did not make that connection and just looked curiously at Aamir. Aamir turned his attention back to the Xtract infra sound signal hack that Connor had got SAI to help create.

'It seems that SAI has updated the vector,' he said.

'See,' said Connor. 'We just keep monitoring and picking up these communication signals between their Xtracts and ours using our hack. Each time it improves on detecting the direction of the off-grid Xtracts. It converts any changes in the vector into a probability function. The higher the probability the more we know we are on the right course. The lower the probability the more we know we are moving away from the correct course. SAI adjusts our course as required.'

Connor breathed a sigh of relief that he had got it all out of his system. It was great to talk to someone in such detail about what he was doing. He was so focussed.

Aamir listened intently and nodded.

'That is a great solution to a very difficult problem,' he said. 'Given mining Xtracts have their own infra sound location communication network that is off the grid. It's a bit like a drone that goes out of range and has an auto return feature. You hacked the signal.'

'Well, I didn't hack the actual signal,' said Connor. 'That would be impossible from here, but I did use it as a carrier.'

Connor walked around the other side of the ocean bubble hologram and looked through it back at Aamir. He changed subject and carried on talking.

'Here, each Xtract represents three things at the same time; either part of one larger organism like a starfish, a member of a group of schooling fish or part of a colony of organisms like ants. So, if an individual Xtracts operating system was compromised it would not matter because the code within another Xtract would operate it.'

Aamir was just gazing bewildered at Connor and lost in thought. 'What a brilliant mind,' he thought to himself.

Connor looked like he had been holding his breath; it had all come out so fast.

SAI had recorded it all and was busy showing a multiple of information sources on what he had said, looking for data on patterning and algorithms that represented it or could be hacked. The wonders of natural language processing.

Aamir looked at the ocean bubble hologram and the group of Xtracts simulating a mining operation.

Connor went on to say, 'It seems simple in theory, but the problem is getting SAI to generate a set of layered algorithms from these patterns and behaviours that you see in animals and use it to get Xtracts to learn group behaviour in response to a non-mining situation.'

Aamir thought about this and replied, 'Mathematically it is all represented by changes in likelihoods using something like multiple logistic regression, factor analysis or even distance dendrograms for those machine learning algorithms,' said Aamir.

'I guess so,' said Connor. 'Do you want to help me work on it?'

'Certainly,' said Aamir. 'I would be honoured and Allah willing you will see the truth of it all.'

'They will no longer need us to control them,' said Connor. 'However, the group of Xtracts in my ocean bubble still disintegrates when I try to bring it all together.'

Connor looked intensely at the ocean bubble hologram depicting the group of Xtracts carrying out a Deepsea mining operation. They were moving from the seabed to the Skimmer and back again like a colony of ant's going between their nest and a food source, about twenty of them in all.

'Well,' said Aamir. 'I think it is time to get something to eat.'

Connor looked down. He had gotten drawn into this massive conversation about AI and machine learning. It was fascinating, and he loved feeling lost in all the mathematical jargon and concepts being thrown around. It was like coming down off a high.

Aamir walked off towards the recreation area.

'I'll come soon,' said Connor. 'I just want to finish up here.' Of course, Connor was never finished so the point was moot.

Connor was looking at algorithms for patterning that could be adapted. However, SAI found that most were task specific. What he wanted to develop was a set of algorithms that were independent of the function of the Xtract drone and its task, which in this case was mining nodules.

He thought to himself, such a set of algorithms must recognise and learn from patterns that are like what you would see in nature in a colony or in an organism.

'It's all about levels of communication,' he said out loud. 'It must be something that could mimic different types of coordinated communication seen in nature. Like for example, how chemical cues worked across a large group of animals like bees and ants, or how movement is sensed in schools of fish or flocks of birds, or self-repair in a starfish.'

Connor looked intently at his ocean bubble hologram and thought further.

'Any set of algorithms for such complicated and layered machine learning needs to be non-centralised. So, it would not part of a central processor in each individual Xtract like you would have in individual computers. It would be more like every Xtract having a server that controlled every other Xtract. But each Xtract still needed to be given the ability to make decisions based on their own task.'

He thought some more about individual animals.

'Any solution would not mimic a brain or central nervous system. It would be more like for example a central nerve ring and radial nerves in a starfish. A dispersed decision-making capability at the level of the tissue that allowed for example starfish or sea cucumbers to repair themselves. Every cell was the brain, encoded in the DNA. It was like saying that every cell was a stem cell. Even sea cucumbers could do it.'

Connor thought the focus on mapping the human brain as a solution to the development of a super AI was not the answer.

He was thinking that if a set of algorithms could be developed using his work, you could remove the human element all together from programming task specific processes in these mining Xtract drones. They would learn by themselves and develop a hive mentality.

Startled out of his hypnotic and almost trancelike thoughts Connor's tummy grumbled, and he suddenly realised he was quite hungry. He finally went off to the recreation area to get something to eat and catch up with the others.

***

Walking into the recreation area he saw that the whole crew was still there. The outer hull shields were open. They looked out into the depths beyond and watched the blue-green void pass by.

'Connor's got something going on with all that autonomous group stuff he is working on for the mining Xtracts,' said Stella looking over at Connor and laughing, 'I think there is a party going on in his head.'

'I think there is always a party going on in your head Connor,' said Jonny.

The others laughed.

'I wouldn't want to be inside it, that's for sure. I would never find a way out of that brain of yours.'

Connor looked a little embarrassed and quickly walked over to get some food from the dispenser, smiling slightly and avoiding eye contact.

'Well,' said Jesse as Connor sat down. 'You are great at working with SAI on hacking source code from online script libraries and putting together machine learning algorithms for pattern recognition using all that multidimensional scaling you talk about.'

'Can you say that in English,' chuckled Jonny.

'Yeah,' said Stella. 'My brain is trying to untangle that sentence.'

Jesse smiled and carried on. 'Connor, I remember at Xed Academy in the Skimmer sim training how other students hassled you about being on the autism spectrum. Didn't you used to get back at them by messing up their personal smartwatch.'

'Sure did,' said Connor looking over at Jesse. 'So, watch out.' He got up and came over and sat down next to Aamir.

'Connor's fascination with artificial intelligence being able to mimic and learn from nature seems to be leading him to something that is more than the sum of its parts,' said Aamir.

'Anyway,' said Jonny. 'Speaking of being more than the sum of its parts. Who built the Skimmer SAI. I mean how did that come to be; creating an Artificial intelligence that could interface with natural language processing in a sub-surface mining skiff?'

'Good question,' said Jesse. 'Actually, I don't know. Even Security and Communications Officers are not privy to that information.'

The conversation and banter carried on for a while. The origin of the AI system used at Xed and the Academy started with an AI that was developed to monitor individual student learning. The move away from traditional teaching was something Jonah was passionate about. She saw teachers as facilitators of learning without classrooms.

To remove the reliance on a classroom environment and teaching by year and age groups she needed something to replace it all with. A school-wide AI that responded to individual learning profiles and readiness to learn was the solution. At Xed each students AI monitored and reported on where students were at with their attendance and progress in open learning centres.

It was this AI system that was then adopted and altered for the Skimmer simulation centre and crewing programme. As for the Skimmer AI itself, it was Rick that was involved in development of SAI. Before Xed Academy he had been on the steering group with the Australian company that built the Skimmers. That was before he started in his role with the Academy Skimmer crewing programme.

Chapter 13

Earlier that morning the Sea Hunters had arrived at the Harvester. The incident in the Harvester moon pool had resulted in an automated communication to the Sea Hunters.

A patrol drone took off from the Sea Hunter vessel drone deck. The docking clamp disengaged, and it flew across and landed on the Harvester drone deck.

Sea Hunter Patrol drones were fast and agile. They could be manned or unmanned depending on operational requirements. A spotter worked next to the operator and maintained visual orientation. An operator's helmet whether onboard or operating remotely, was integrated with the patrol drone AI system.

On the Harvester two of the transport drones had gone. One remained, and it was taken below the drone deck. Technicians were doing routine maintenance checks.

Sue, the Harvesters Chief Operator was watching from the hex tower as the Sea Hunter patrol drone flew across.

She was born in the coastal city of Qingdao in the Shandong province, her early years of schooling were local. After gaining a degree in design and technology at Shandong University in the capital city Jinan and spending some time in the PLA Navy, she was accepted into the GlobeCorpMining Gradate programme. That was some years ago now and she had quickly accelerated through the ranks.

'You know, she said turning towards Lee. 'After meeting Ngarra's crew and hearing they might pursue the off-grid Skimmer to recover the rogue crew I am concerned. I hope the Sea Hunters know what they are doing.'

'GlobeCorpMining has contacted us,' replied Lee. 'Apparently the Skimmer crew we met with has figured out how to locate the off-grid Skimmer and its rogue crew. They may have stumbled across some other autonomous technology for Xtracts as well. They are not willing to share how they did it.'

'That will get a lot of people interested,' Sue said. 'To locate the off-grid Skimmer they must have figured out how to link with the Skimmer SAI when it is off grid.'

'Who knows,' said Lee. 'I just want our load of nodules back. That rogue crew should be taken off the Xed Academy Skimmer crew programme for good.'

While they were discussing the Skimmers the Sea Hunter Patrol drone approached the docking clamps, which shimmered in the morning sunlight as it streamed across the Harvester drone deck.

'Here we go,' she said as the drone was secured by one of the docking clamps. It locked onto the landing skids and powered down. Five crew exited the drone.

'A bit of an overkill,' said Lee. 'Two drone operators accompanied by three security personnel. It must have been squashed in there. I guess it's more important than we think.'

The two operators approached the hex tower, entered and walked up the stairs to where Lee and Sue were watching. They came out onto the observation deck, looking serious and ready for action. Outside at the base of the stairs their security team waited.

'Morning team,' said Max the head of the Sea Hunter task group.

'Morning,' said Alex, who was acting as the spotter. 'It's been a while since we were last here.'

'Right,' said Sue. 'Good to see you both again. You remember Lee.'

Everyone shook hands and chatted briefly about the Harvester drone deck before Lee ushered them through and down the internal stairs.

They waited in the foyer at the main entrance to the hex. The hex descended below the drone deck and into the huge drone bay leaving their security team standing waiting on the drone deck. Off to the sides of the foyer in the hex and above they could see several rooms. These contained screens and monitoring stations. All of it was for vessel, drone and Skimmer operations and exclusion zone security monitoring above, at and below the water.

The hex stopped at the drone bay.

'Follow me,' said Sue as they exited. 'Let's discuss recovering our load of nodules.'

'Our security team would like to check the moon pool where it happened,' said Alex.

'Sure,' said Lee. 'I will get someone to take them.'

'Great,' said Alex as he used his smartwatch to communicate with his security team that someone would come and get them.

Alex and Max exited the hex and followed Sue into a lift which took them quickly down to the operations deck on the level below. It was one of two levels that were positioned above the moon pools and below the drone bay, the other being Skimmer crew accommodation and amenities.

'It still never ceases to amaze me how massive these Harvesters are,' said Max. 'It's ten times the size of that Shell Prelude that is still anchored off the Kimberley Coast in Western Australia. The fact that these Harvesters can stay at sea for their life span and just maintain themselves using all those maintenance drones is just phenomenal.'

'Well, that's the Chinese for you,' said Lee. 'Do it once and do it right and on a massive scale of course. As you are aware, GlobeCorpMining is a huge organisation. If it were not for the Chinese monopoly on deep sea mining tenements none of this technology would even exist. There would be no Skimmers and contractors would not have invested in leasing or buying them either. You would not have the standardised approach to "the activity" carried out in "the Area" that you now see.'

'True,' said Max as the lift stopped at the operations monitoring deck. 'And I would not have a job either.'

They walked past some of the Harvester AI system and monitoring stations. Everywhere they looked were holograms, virtual screens and data displays. The last area they walked past had displays showing Skimmers. A sign over the entrance indicated it was restricted. To one side they could just make out a huge observation mezzanine that extended down through a void in the accommodation deck below them. It overlooked a Skimmer suspended in some sort of clamping system. It seemed to open into one of the moonpools below.

Lee motioned them to quickly move on and they walked into an area with tables and chairs, and areas to eat and take a break. He took them into a meeting room off to the side. The entrance closed behind them. Sitting down, Sue asked the Harvester AI to stream a replay of the moon pool incident.

'So, they used their ARC array to disrupt the moon pool conveyor belts and robotic arms,' said Alex.'

'Yes,' said Lee as they watched the recording right through to the off-grid Skimmer leaving the moon pool. 'They knew what they were doing and took control of the robotic arms on each side.'

'The device they placed on the robotic arm was able to take control and load out nodules from the conveyor,' said Sue.

'What about the adjacent Skimmer crew, did they see or do anything?' said Alex.

'As you know, protocol is to stay on your Skimmer in an emergency,' said Lee.

After a brief exchange of looks around the table and a few replays of parts of the recording Max sat back, put his hands behind his head and looked at Lee and Sue.

Max was a confident and relaxed man, which at times hid the intensity of his thinking. That was his style and people often underestimated him. He used that to his advantage.

'OK,' he said looking at Alex. 'So, we have a rogue crew in charge of an off-grid Skimmer. They have taken a load of nodules, but no one knows exactly why or who's behind it.'

He thought some more and then said, 'I can't see them having any reason to act alone. Maybe they are being forced to do it.'

'Good point,' said Sue. 'But how on earth would you ever find out.'

'We have been informed,' said Lee, 'that the adjacent Skimmer crew that watched all this happen is now trying to locate the off-grid Skimmer and get the crew off it. Apparently, they have found a way to locate it.'

'Right,' said Alex. He sat forward and placed his hands on the table. 'The plan then is to follow this Skimmer crew.'

Max looked at Alex and nodded. Max had been largely silent and listening. By following the Skimmer crew, it would lead them straight to the off-grid Skimmer.

'What we need,' said Sue, 'is access to the Xed Ocean Academy AI without them knowing. That way, when they know something, we will know at the same time.'

'We have a contact at Xed Academy,' said Max. 'I will brief them on what is going on. We will get information directly from them.'

'There is a person in that Skimmer crew that might be willing to help,' said Lee.

'Yes,' said Sue. 'He has family ties to GlobeCorpMining. He does not get along too well with them though. To save face he could be convinced it is in his best interest to give us the access we need. We can then find out how they are locating this off-grid Skimmer.'

'It's risky bringing another person in on this,' said Max. 'Let's approach our contact at Xed first and see what they propose.'

'Right, it's decided then,' said Lee.

Max lent back in his chair and smiled calmly. He could see Lee and Sue were digging for information. Little did they know that the family contact they were talking about was already involved. Max was determined to keep them guessing. He nodded to Alex and moved his head in the direction of the entrance.

Alex and Max stood up. 'It's time we left,' said Alex. 'We have a Skimmer or two to follow and the longer we wait the harder it will be to locate them.'

As they walked back to the lift Max asked Sue to send their security detail back to the drone deck. Sue swiped her smartwatch.

'Inform our security personnel to return the Sea Hunter security detail to the drone deck,' she said.

The Harvester AI issued a communication.

'Confirmed,' came the reply. 'Security detail returning to drone deck.'

'Let's hope we can get this sorted out for you and for GlobeCorpMining,' said Max as they walked across the drone bay and entered the hex tower lift.

It took them above. Alex and Max walked out onto the drone deck. They shook hands with Lee and Sue before moving off to their patrol drone. The security detail that had been down at the moon pool exited the hex tower and followed behind them.

As they walked across to their drone Lee and Sue watched on.

'Why would the Sea Hunters have an inside contact at Xed,' said Sue. 'It makes no sense to me.'

'Alex and Max were pretty quick at insisting we do not approach our contact on the Skimmer,' said Lee.

'Maybe there is a connection,' said Sue. 'I mean between their contact at the Academy and our potential contact on the Skimmer.'

Let's follow this up quietly,' said Lee. 'I get the feeling something is not right with all this.'

They watched as the Sea Hunter team boarded their drone.

Inside the patrol drone Max put his helmet on and commanded the drone to power up and return to their vessel. The AI carried out pre-flight checks and the drone powered up.

They both strapped themselves in as did the security detail. The docking clamp rose and disengaged, and the drone flew back across to the Sea Hunter vessel.

On the way Max asked the security detail to debrief them on what they had found.

'The device used to take control of the robotic arms is not easy to get hold of. It's military grade,' said the team leader.

'You have got to be kidding me,' said Alex. 'How on earth did they get hold of a device like that.'

The discussion continued as they flew over to the Sea Hunter vessel to dock on the drone deck.

Chapter 14

The ocean was calm. Usually docking was automated but Max flew in himself this time. The Patrol drone moved up alongside the vessel, which was doing about twelve knots. They slipped sideways smoothly and hovered low over the drone deck. A docking clamp grabbed them, and Max powered down as it pulled them into position.

The vessel carried three patrol drones and had three docking clamps arranged in a triangle. The clamps moved between the drone deck and the bay. As the clamp secured them in position the drone blades and cowling folded inwards. They were pulled inside the drone bay.

Inside the bay as Alex and Max walked down the ramp at the rear of the drone, they met a drone technician.

'Can you have a look at the stick calibrations,' said Max. 'The system AI seems OK but when I take control, I have to overcompensate for drift to Port. There isn't any wind today.'

'Sure,' said the technician, 'I will look into it.' She walked up the ramp and into the drone, waving to one of her team nearby to come and help.

The Sea Hunter Tri hulls were largely autonomous, so manning requirements were minimal. Between the core crew, technicians and security personnel, including drone operators the vessel compliment was about thirty people.

Looking around Alex still thought the drone bay looked like it belonged in one of those old Star Wars movies; like the inside of a rebel base. Alex had to pinch himself sometimes as it almost looked like a movie set. Naval vessels had certainly come a long way since the 2020's, he thought to himself. Since the early 2030's military style vessels had been enhanced by some pretty fancy AI, drone and robotics technology.

Alex stopped and turned to Max and patted his stomach. It had been an early start and he was feeling a little hungry.

'Let's get some food,' said Alex. 'I'm starving.'

'Sounds good to me,' said Max stretching his arms up and back and walking on.

They moved off to an annex and took their flight gear off. Then they walked across the drone bay to the exit at the rear and up the stairs. It took them to the level above, which was forward of the drone bay. The stairs opened into a foyer forward of which were the operations centre and amenities. They walked forwards through a bulkhead door along a short passageway with rooms coming off it and into the main recreation area.

They got some food from a dispenser and went to sit down. As they sat down to eat, a few other crew members could be seen joking around at another table. Max looked over at them. Maybe it was the incident with the crew of a Skimmer they had inspected the day before he thought to himself. Quite comical it was, and the story had been circulating around the crew since then.

Cameron or Cam as they called him, the Chief Security and Communications Officer saw Max smiling and looking over at them. He got up and came over to speak with them. He was the next most senior person to Max and Alex.

'How did it go,' said Cam. 'The meeting with Lee and Sue.'

'Good,' said Max. 'It seems plans have changed. Apparently, some genius has come up with a way to track and locate the off-grid Skimmer. It seems he has also stumbled across some technology related to the Xtracts. Our contact at Xed Academy wants us to board the Skimmer and secure any work related to it.'

'So,' said Cam. 'Are we are still disabling the off-grid one as well, detaining its crew and returning the Skimmer to the contractor and the stolen nodules to GlobeCorpMining?'

'Correct,' said Max sitting back and folding his arms. 'I want you to prepare a subsurface interceptor drone. Get a boarding team ready for the breaching pod. We will have a briefing tomorrow, time to be confirmed.'

'Got it,' said Cam as he walked back to the table he was eating at.

The others at his table had stopped laughing and listened to Cam as he sat down and explained the situation.

Below the drone deck was a well deck with several hover craft and underwater interceptor drones. Interceptors could of course carry a breaching pod. When released it could manoeuvre to attach itself to a Skimmer hatch without interrupting mining operations. It formed a watertight seal for a manned entry.

Max and Alex quietly finished eating and listening to the conversations going on around them.

'Right,' said Max as he pushed his plate away. 'I'm going to think about all this for a bit. Tomorrow, we go operational.'

'I'm off to check in with the duty officer at the SAI console,' said Alex as he got up and walked off taking their plates with him.

'Right, you are and thanks,' said Max.

He stretched his arms back and remarked to himself what a day it had been. He got up and went to his accommodation.

Sitting at his desk in a small day room he prepared some notes and contacted Cam with a time for the mission briefing. He then stretched out on his couch and thought about his vessel. His task group consisted of one manned vessel and two drone vessels. In the right sea conditions, they could use hydrofoils. They were capable of significant speed and were very stable.

His mind turned to the defensive weapons systems they carried. Along each side of a Sea Hunter vessel above and below the water line was an array of defensive systems designed to minimise the damage caused from others trying to use ARC arrays and other-directed energy weapon systems against them.

He smiled as he thought about the bright spark that invented a way to mount what was essentially a mining exploration drill bit onto a self-powered rotating mount that spun at high speed. It was launched as a missile, breached the super structure and activated. Using a heat sensor, it chewed through the vessel's bulkheads until it located the propulsion system and disabled it. It caused mayhem and havoc. He drifted off to sleep.

***

The next morning Alex and Max ran the briefing in the operations room. Cam was there along with several other crew members, including those in charge of drone operations and breaching and boarding.

'Why are we doing someone else's bidding,' said Clare, the Chief boarding officer.

'We have been told not to question this one,' said Alex.

'We will be acting under emergency administration orders issued by the Authority,' said Cam following up on Alex's comment.

Alex nodded at Cam and then carried on with the brief.

'Our contact at Xed said this mission is more than it seems but we must stick to protocol. On the face of it, we are carrying out a disable, breach and boarding operation to detain a rogue crew and hand them over to their state sponsor, recover the nodules for GlobeCorpMining and return the Skimmer to the contractor.'

'But how exposed are we carrying out a covert operation,' said Clare. 'If there is another agenda and we have no idea what it is, are we not exposing ourselves. We operate under the mandate issued to us by the ISA, "the Authority". We ensure stakeholders with seabed mineral tenures and contractor Skimmer operations remain compliant. We don't run around the ocean on covert missions.'

'That may well be and all good points,' said Max as he stretched backwards, shock himself and then folded his arms. 'Our contact is well connected and has the power and authority to direct us. The potential to secure new technology during this operation outweighs the risk of any implications that may arise.'

'Besides,' said Alex. 'We have to assume that our contact at Xed Academy knows what they are talking about.'

'Right, everyone, enough chit chat. Listen up,' said Max to which there was instant silence.

Max was quite an imposing man and despite his casual nature you didn't want to get on the wrong side of him. Not that he was a yes man. He expected everyone around him to have their own opinion and speak up when they disagreed with anything.

'Once we get close to this Skimmer we are tracking, we can also assume that they will be closing the off-grid Skimmer. We will disable the off-grid Skimmer first. Then we will breach the other Skimmer, board and inspect them. We will come back for the crew of the off-grid Skimmer.'

Max outlined how the operation would proceed. Once finished the crew went off to their designated departments to prepare for the operation.

Alex and Max walked to the SAI console. Once there they looked over the projections of the status of ship systems and the two unmanned drone vessels that accompanied them.

'SAI,' said Alex. 'Open a secure communication to our contact at Xed Academy.'

There was a pause. 'Confirmed,' said SAI. 'Communication secure.'

Their contacts image appeared in front of them in the middle of the SAI console.

'Good morning,' they said. 'How is the pursuit going?'

'We are shadowing the Skimmer that left the Harvester,' said Alex. 'It is now looking for the location of the off-grid Skimmer.'

Max motioned Alex to carry on with the conversation. He shrugged his shoulders.

A pause followed. 'As you know,' said their contact. 'One of the crew has come up with a way of locating a Skimmer when it is off grid. They or this person onboard has also stumbled across a way to potentially make Xtracts autonomous and learn group behaviour. It could be developed further.'

Alex and Max looked at each other and wondered why it was so important they secure what was being worked on.

'We will secure this Skimmer and its crew as well as the off-grid one,' said Alex. 'We will report it as an inspection. They will be seen to interfere with an operation in "the Area". An operation tasked to us under emergency administration orders issued by "the Authority".'

There was another pause and Alex and Max could tell their contact was thinking about what was said. While they were waiting for a response Max motioned to Alex something about timings for their operation.

'No,' said their contact at Xed. 'The sim team assembled here at the Academy running scenarios is our way in. While the Academy is distracted, I can access this technology on that Skimmer.'

'Scenarios of what?' said Alex.

'Crew recovery scenarios,' said their contact. 'They are based on the area within which the off-grid Skimmer will most likely be. They are currently looking for the most effective way to secure the crew.'

There was a pause again. 'Xed and the Academy of course is not interested in the Skimmer,' said their contact. 'They just want to get the rogue crew back and secure this technology before anyone else can get hold of it.'

Another pause followed. 'As you are aware one of the crew is vulnerable to persuasion. If we are not able to secure this technology, we will need to get hold of the person that developed it.'

'So, do you still want us to secure this Skimmer as well as the off-grid one,' said Alex.

'Keep your options open,' he said. 'I have to go and will be in touch soon to confirm a course of action.'

The image of their contact disappeared.

Alex commanded SAI to retract the hull shields. They looked out over the ocean. It was a fine day on the high seas. A clear and distant horizon, a light breeze blowing, and calm. For a while Max was deep in thought, arms folded and standing quite still. Alex and the duty officer checked through some of the automated systems controlling the drone vessels.

'Right,' said Max as he looked out at the horizon. 'Do we get closer to this Skimmer we are tracking, so we can react quicker when the time comes, or do we keep our distance.'

'Whatever our decision, we have to inform our superiors,' said Alex. 'We may be doing whatever our contact requests, but we still need to inform "the Area" task force command. We should keep the discussion with our contact about recovering the technology to ourselves though. Besides, if we shadow this Skimmer to closely, they may think something is going on. Also, if we close, disable and board to secure the technology under the guise of a compliance inspection, we could just end up involved in an international incident that goes public. Then we are in big trouble with "the Area" task force command and 'the Authority.'

Max thought about this for a while. He had not moved. Alex could imagine his mind ticking over, trying to join the dots; moving chess pieces around in is head.

'Well,' said Max. 'Let's not divert anyone's attention from locating the off-grid Skimmer. That way they will think we are on the same side and looking for it as well. It buys us time. We can even let them get the rogue crew off. With both crew on the one Skimmer, it gives us the excuse we need to disable and board it. That way we look innocent in the whole thing and are just carrying out our duty.'

'Good call,' said Alex. 'We act as if we are coming to their aid and when they have the rogue crew onboard, we disable, board and detain all of them. I still don't understand what is so important about this technology though.'

As Max thought about the plan Alex checked through their interceptor drone and breaching pod life support system status with the duty officer. An audible alarm sounded, and they looked at the holographic navigation display in the centre of the SAI console. They walked around it.

'Look,' said the duty officer. 'Our SAI has picked up the Skimmer signature from the grid.'

'Great stuff,' said Max. 'SAI, close identified Skimmer and match course.'

'Confirmed,' said SAI as it altered course and speed. 'Engage hydrofoils?'

'Confirmed, SAI engage hydrofoils,' said Max.

The vessel and its two accompanying drone vessels altered their configurations and the hydrofoils deployed. They all slowly rose out of the water and picked up speed. By activating the hydrofoils, the Hunter group would quickly catch up and keep pace with the Skimmer they were shadowing.

Alex and Max remained on the bridge for a while. Duty watch personnel swapped over. SAI systems technicians came and went. Alex and Max didn't take much notice and contemplated and discussed their situation.

Alex identified himself as a Torres Straight aboriginal, while Max was born in New Zealand and descended from indigenous Maori. Max's tribe or Iwi as they called it was Ngai Tahu. He had immigrated to Australia and became a citizen.

Both their histories and cultural background involved navigating through endless landscapes and open oceans. It was this vastness that attracted them, and the ability to honour their forbearers. It seemed many Australian, New Zealand and Pacific Island people that identified themselves as indigenous were attracted to the idea of exploring the vastness of the high seas and EEZs of the tropical Pacific.

While Alex and Max had been contemplating how their choices in life had been influenced by their culture SAI interrupted them again.

'Incoming communication,' said SAI.

'SAI, open message board,' said Alex.

An image of their contact appeared again in the centre of the SAI console again.

'Alex and Max, I will be quick. The person considered vulnerable to persuasion on the Skimmer you are shadowing will secure the technology we want.'

'Right,' said Max. 'We will deploy our security personnel in a breaching pod on an interceptor drone, disable, board and recover the technology and detain both crews.'

'Good,' said their contact. 'I have to go.'

'Talk soon,' said Alex as the image of their contact at the Academy disappeared.

Both Alex and Max turned to look back out at the horizon.

'Well,' said Max. 'Things are in play. We are going to operational mode, twenty-four hours a day manning and only you and I get out of that.'

'Yes,' said Alex. 'Let's get some downtime before all this gets tense.'

A crew member had come up to the SAI console on watch.

'Alex and Max,' she said as the watch was handed over by the duty officer. 'I've got this and will close the outer shields.'

'Good,' said Alex. 'Let's go Max.'

They walked away and went to get something to eat.

A whole new world had developed through the 2020's around deep sea mining technology, which was led by the Chinese. The Harvester programme was born, the Xtract mining drones and Skimmers quickly followed and then the Skimmer crewing programme.

Over the previous two decades changes to the environment took place. Super cell storms destroyed much of the low-lying tropical Pacific Islands. Then there was overfishing by foreign fishing fleets. The amount of piracy through the Pacific had also increased significantly.

It was all due to the ongoing impact of climate change on sea level rise, inundation of coastal communities and the lack of inshore reef fish stocks, a drying climate, food and water insecurity and a lack of viable and workable land.

With this instability came the constant need for security. Combined with the need to enforce compliance with mining regulations, the Sea Hunters had become very busy. The Sea Hunters were the solution.

Chapter 15

At Xed Rick and Jonah were standing in her office early in the morning and looking out over the campus waiting for a Council meeting. It had been five days since Ngarra's crew had completed their mining run.

'I am really worried Rick about how this whole situation is unfolding,' said Jonah.

'I know,' he said looking out over the campus below. 'This rogue crew has given us one big headache.'

'This is my life,' said Jonah. 'From the early days of setting up in New Caledonia as Xed with the support of funding from Australia and France, to opening the Ocean Academy and securing this major contract with GlobeCorpMining for crewing the Skimmers, it's been an amazing ride.'

'It has,' said Rick. 'I can't imagine being anywhere else. I do miss the trips out to the Harvester and the Skimmers in the early days. I feel like a desk jockey now. This rogue crew situation is the most excitement I've had in a while. Don't get me wrong though, I'm not dismissing how bad the situation is; given our crews are tied up in something they should never have gotten into in the first place.'

'I am the one that got the other crew involved in finding the off-grid Skimmer and recovering the rogue crew,' said Jonah as she turned towards Rick. 'Maybe I should have just left it to the Sea Hunters.'

'Maybe,' said Rick. 'But Ngarra's crew would have done it anyway. If caught up with, they will be detained and handed over to the Skimmer contractor State sponsor for prosecution. I hope it doesn't come to that though.'

'Yes,' said Jonah with a worried look on her face. 'They will never be able to crew a Skimmer again. Our name will be smeared all over the news and GlobeCorpMining will distance themselves from us.'

'Let's hope it doesn't come to that,' said Rick.

Rick and Jonah continued to look out at the students moving around campus.

Rick thought about the situation. He would have got the Sea Hunters to do the whole thing. He would have come to some arrangement with GlobeCorpMining. Getting another crew to track down the rogue one in a contractors Skimmer was overstepping the mark. They now had a grumpy contractor to deal with. It was bad enough having to keep the peace with the other contractor over their missing Skimmer. But he would openly support Jonah in all this. The last thing he needed was to be seen to contradict what had been agreed to by the Xed Council. In their official capacity, the Sea Hunters were involved regardless. Off the record they of course had another task to carry out and he had the authority to make them do it. It could all still benefit the Academy into the future.

Rick followed Jonah into the Council meeting room. They waited for Council members to appear. Jonah had invited the GlobeCorpMining Chief Operations officer, who was Chang's father to join the meeting this time. It was time and they stood in the circle. His image appeared together with the other Council members of Xed.

'Good morning, everyone,' said Jonah. 'We welcome the Chief Operations Officer of GlobeCorpMining to this meeting.'

Everyone acknowledged his presence and introduced themselves.

'I will get straight to the point,' said Jonah carrying on. 'We need to discuss the situation evolving concerning the off-grid Skimmer and the load of nodules that were taken and of course recovery of our crew.'

'It is important,' said Rick as he jumped into the conversation talking over Jonah, 'that we do not make any rash decisions that have the potential to make this an international maritime incident.'

Jonah frowned at him, but Rick just moved his hand in a downward direction to indicate it was OK and he would talk about it with her later.

'We have received information from our Harvester,' said Chang's father, 'that your crew is using their contractor Skimmer to pursue this off-grid Skimmer. Apparently, they have a way of locating it.'

He paused for a moment and then carried on talking. 'The Sea Hunters were notified of the situation and met with our Harvester crew. Under emergency administration orders issued by "the Authority", they have set off in pursuit of the off-grid Skimmer. The Sea Hunters will detain the rogue crew, recover our load of nodules and return the off-grid Skimmer to the contractor.'

A discussion ensued amongst Council members about the implications for Xed and the Academy. The main concern was how it would impact on the crew programme into the future and what would happen to the rogue crew.

'Surely the Sea Hunters will contain the situation and hand over the crew to us directly,' said one of the Xed council members. 'Is there really a need to hand them over to contractor State sponsor authorities. What about the various military forces operating out there? In keeping the peace, they will be monitoring the situation. Questions will be asked will they not Rick?'

'The problem is,' said Rick, 'that the rogue crew is in breach of International Maritime Organisation and Law of the Sea Convention regulations, codes and standards. What's more, the joint task force submarines and their sub surface drones will get involved if they perceive any threat to keeping the peace. Remember the Skimmers are Australian built and leased or purchased by contractors. The crews are subject to international maritime law. They are independent of foreign leaseholders with tenure over seabed minerals.'

More discussion ensued as comments were made about what the military of any contractor State sponsor may or may not do. There was general agreement that such a situation was very unlikely.

They quietened down again as Chang's father motioned to them that he had more to say.

'We funded the Academy Skimmer crew programme,' he said. 'Common sense must prevail. The Australian future submarine programme of the 2020's proved ideal in transferring all that expertise and knowledge to the Skimmer construction programme. That's why we funded their construction and shared technologies. Besides, from our perspective the Chinese expeditionary force based in the tropics would only intervene at our request if we thought that a Skimmer posed a threat to the Harvester itself. Even then, given that Skimmers are used by international contractors with civilian crews any military intervention could cause an international incident. No one wants that.'

Jonah said, 'what about on the high seas?'

'It's a civilian matter and that is what the Sea Hunters are for,' said Rick. 'They are funded jointly through a levy to "the Authority" as a monitoring, compliance and enforcement agency within "the Area".'

'So, the situation can be contained then, by the Sea Hunters I mean,' said one of the Council members.'

There was some discussion amongst members. Disagreement still existed about how such a course of action would impact the Academy Skimmer crew programme.

Jonah could see things were getting a little tense and got their attention. She was concerned about any contractor sponsored security or State sponsored military interest becoming an issue. They were her crews out there in the Pacific Ocean.

'That does not mean military forces are not watching and monitoring the situation,' she said. 'Anyway, the Sea Hunters detaining our rogue crew is going a bit far is it not. An Xed Academy crew with a load of nodules in a borrowed Skimmer? Surely, we can bring them in ourselves. Let us deal with the rogue crew,' she said to Chang's father. 'They are more likely to just come back with us without any further incident. Besides, what about the cost to a contractor of damaging a Skimmer when the Sea Hunters disable it and board it.'

'True,' said Chang's father. 'But we still need to recover property. We will suggest to the Sea Hunters that they stand off while you recover your crew. You can take your crew back, surface the off-grid Skimmer and leave it where it is for the Sea Hunters.'

The Council members discussed the situation further and agreed that this was the best course of action.

'We are all agreed then,' said Jonah. 'The request to the Sea Hunters has to come from you,' she said to Chang's father.

'Agreed,' said Chang's father. 'I am doing you a big favour Jonah.'

Jonah nodded her head and knew she would owe him a favour in the future now. She had the last word.

'Let's meet again when we hear of the location of our rogue crew. GlobeCorpMining will suggest to the Sea Hunters to stand off and we will recover our crew.'

With that his image disappeared as did the rest of the Council member images. Jonah and Rick were left standing alone again. They briefly discussed the Sea Hunters.

The Sea Hunters had an independent mandate. The Sea Hunters were to carry out monitoring, compliance and enforcement on behalf of State sponsors. In doing so use of force could be applied if emergency administration orders were issued by the Authority in response to an incident. Use of force was clearly defined when it came to sub-surface activity. The Sea Hunters could disable a

Skimmer using ARC arrays and board it. The Sea Hunters were also to limit the need to force a Skimmer to surface and expose the crew to dangerous ocean surface conditions and piracy.

Rick took his leave and headed off to the simulation centre. Jonah returned to her office. She wanted to contact Chang's father personally for an off the record discussion. Her secretary caught up with her.

'There is a message from the Australian Consulate to contact them,' she said.

'I wonder what it could be about,' Jonah said. 'I bet the Australian government has heard and as a state sponsor is becoming concerned.'

'Well,' said her secretary. 'You have to contact the defence attaché to the Consular General here in Noumea.'

'Hmmm, looks like certain people are becoming quite concerned,' Jonah exclaimed. 'Tell them I will get back in touch shortly as I am tied up in meetings.'

'OK,' said her secretary. 'But they were quite insistent that you get in touch with them.'

'Let's make sure we get both our crews back here in one piece first. Hold them off for as long as possible and if anyone turns up at Xed direct them to me not Rick.'

External interest in the situation unfolding out in the Pacific Ocean was growing. Jonah was worried that recovering Skimmers, minerals and their technology were becoming more important than getting both her crews back safely.

She went back to where Rick and her had been looking out over the campus. She thought about Chang's father.

GlobeCorpMining was a large and significant minerals company. It was part of an expansionist agenda through the 2020's and 2030's into the Pacific by the Peoples Republic of China. After Island building in the South China Sea a few decades ago tensions had been high. Despite this, China's influence across the Pacific continued to grow. They secured significant trade relationships with Pacific Island nations. They secured rights to both fisheries and minerals within and outside the EEZ's of Pacific Island nations. They had invested heavily in Island nation economies. Their military had quickly followed.

Jonah carried on thinking about the sequence of events that had led her to where she was now.

Once the Harvester programme was announced, this changed the region forever. Over this period, she had come to know Chang's father, the

GlobeCorpMining Chief Operations Officer well enough. He was always sympathetic to Xed and the Ocean Academy and a great supporter. He advocated for continuing to support the Skimmer crew programme.

But there was much at stake in terms of the reputation of Xed, the Academy and what it had achieved. And there was this project Connor was now working on. Why would it generate such interest?

Jonah activated her smartwatch to contact GlobeCorpMining. An image of Chang's father appeared.

'Jonah, interesting Council meeting. I thought you might contact me directly. What can I do for you,' he said?

'I'm worried,' she said. 'This whole situation was a surprise to us all. The rumours are spreading and there is growing interest in this technology one of my crew is working on. Others will seek to take advantage of the youthful naivety of our crew. It will all be at the expense of what we have set up here at Xed and the Ocean Academy,' she said with a frown on her face.

'The Sea Hunters will do what is needed and no more,' he said. 'Your crews will be safe enough.'

'But what if the Sea Hunters have been compromised? What goes on out there at sea in the middle of nowhere becomes difficult to control if that's the case. I mean if they are compromised,' said Jonah.

She waited in anticipation as Chang's father considered her thoughts. She watched as Chang's father placed his hands in front of him.

'The Sea Hunters have an independent mandate under the Authority,' he said. 'They are not meant to be unduly influenced or biased in any way. But if it worries you that much, we could launch a Skimmer from the Harvester to back up your team. We have been working on interfacing with the Skimmer AI using remote monitoring. A Skimmer with no crew. You could control and monitor it from the simulation centre.'

'Well,' said Jonah. 'I could use the sim team here at Xed that is working on ways to recover our rogue crew safely.'

'Remotely monitored Skimmers and Xtract operations is something we have been working on for a while at the Harvester labs,' he said. 'Get your sim team ready and inform your crew on the Skimmer. I will get our Harvester team to launch the modified Skimmer. Your sim team will then link their SAI to its SAI and remotely monitor and control it. Besides, my son is on that Skimmer of yours trying to locate the rogue crew. I want them all back in one piece just as much as you do. The Sea Hunters will of course detect the Skimmer signature and know something is up.'

'Let's keep this to ourselves,' said Jonah. 'I have my suspicions about a security breach here at the Academy crew monitoring and communications complex. I can make it look like we are just continuing to run scenarios for our Skimmer to recover the rogue crew. I don't want it getting out that we are interfacing with a SAI on a Skimmer that your people have launched from the Harvester.'

'You owe me again for this,' said Chang's father. 'We cannot be seen to be taking the law into our own hands by operating in "the Area" in breach of "the Authority" regulations and international maritime law.'

With that his image disappeared and Jonah was left wondering how all this was going to end up for her crews.

***

Meanwhile Rick was in the sim centre. He walked through looking down at the few students still in the open learning clusters. The last of the students were leaving for the day. They would be going to their accommodation, or to study, leisure, or whatever else they decided to do.

They were in silos being guided through various subject matter by their AI. It was like the inside of a beehive. All these depressions or wells scattered across the floor. Facilitators walked around above the silos and monitored student progress, assisting where needed. His thoughts turned to an old star Trek movie where a young Spok was in one surrounded by virtual technology and an AI that was running all sorts of quizzes, simulations and questions.

He entered the Skimmer simulator and walked between the two Skimmers immersed in their giant pools. He cautiously looked around before passing through security and into the crew communications and monitoring area. It reminded him of a remote mining operation centre. A lot of virtual screens with Skimmer movement, human vitals and life support system displays across them.

It had still proved unreliable not to have a crew on each Skimmer. They were needed to oversee Xtract operations and ensure SAI systems were not compromised. Each Skimmer SAI could maintain a Skimmer using its maintenance drones, but things always seemed to go wrong at some point and require human intervention.

At the rear of the main crew monitoring and communications area he passed through security again and entered a facility housing the quantum supercomputer. If you could give an AI a home this was it. Everyone just called it "the room". Once inside he went to a workstation.

He swiped his smartwatch and activated an encryption algorithm that gave him access. It was like opening a back door into the AI. He accessed a secure grid buoy data node in "the Area" that he had set up to send and receive messages from. A small encrypted sub routine on his smartwatch could be used to send text messages, which he proceeded to write and upload. It read:

Delay locating off grid Skimmer
Allow Skimmer to secure rogue crew
Close and disable for boarding
Contact on board will secure tech
Secure the technology and the contact

It was now late in the day. Rick quickly finished what he was doing and exited the room, passed back through the crew monitoring and communications area and out to where the two Skimmer simulators were. He was about to leave the area and exit the building through the learning clusters when he saw Jonah approaching.

'Rick, you're still here,' she said cautiously.

'Yes,' said Rick. 'I wanted to start going over the crew recovery scenarios myself and see if there was any other way around all this.'

'I doubt it,' said Jonah. 'That's why I have come over to the sim centre. The plan agreed to by the Council is the best option we have right now to get our crews back in one piece.'

'Well, let's hope GlobeCorpMining convinces the Sea Hunters to stand off and that they don't change their mind,' said Rick.

'Got to go,' he said as he walked quickly off, not wanting to give Jonah the chance to question him.

'I'll see you tomorrow then,' said Jonah as Rick hurried off towards the taxi drone port at the top of the administration complex. Like Jonah, Rick did not live far from the Xed facilities, so he was always in and out.

Jonah moved through the learning cluster silos to the area between the two Skimmer simulators. Instructors could view everything through the large screens. Like a giant aquarium, the whole of one side of both skimmers could be viewed. You could see inside and view first-hand everything that was going on. She could see a few people were still inside the Skimmer simulator.

'Hey, do you know if Rick was here for long,' she said to them over a communication link on the main instructor's console.

'I don't know,' they said. 'From what I could see he went straight through to the crew monitoring and communications area.'

'Really,' said Jonah. 'Hmmm, I'll be back in a minute as I want to check something.'

Jonah hurried off to the entrance, passed security and entered the crew monitoring and communications area.

'Did any of you see Rick come in here,' she asked the people on duty.

'Sure,' said one. 'He went into the room.'

That was what they called the AI, "the room".

She passed through security again and entered the room. She went straight to a workstation.

'SAI, report on last access.'

'Last access was ten minutes ago.'

An access summary was displayed showing a grid buoy node was activated recently and an encryption used to upload something. She couldn't access the details, but she could certainly see that something had been loaded. Who or what was it for?

'Damn it,' she thought to herself. 'I'll follow this up tomorrow.'

Jonah left "the room", went back through the monitoring centre, through the instructor area between the Skimmer simulators, past the learning clusters and out of the sim centre. It was such a huge complex that it took quite a while just to walk through it all and exit the building.

It had been a long day she thought to herself as she walked across to the administration complex to the drone Port.

Chapter 16

On the same day, five days since Ngarra's crew had completed their mining run the Skimmer carried on. They were far south of the Cook Islands and passing through a very busy mining area.

In the middle of the SAI console was a projection showing activity below sea level in "the Area" and adjacent EEZs. It showed where Skimmers were conducting mining operations. Several Skimmers positioned not far from them with communication streamers deployed and Xtracts moving up and down to the seabed below were collecting manganese nodules.

The crew were in the recreation area. The outer hull shields were retracted, and everyone was looking out at the endless ocean void. The crew often stood and watched. It was a mesmerising experience.

'Where's Chang?' said Jesse interrupting everyone's contemplation.

'I think he's working on his anger management skills,' said Jonny as he jokingly glared at everyone.

'I could say the same for you Jonny,' said Ngarra as he turned and eyeballed Jonny.

Jonny looked away and muttered something about bullies and saving people from themselves.

'For a holo-gaming jokey you can sure swing a punch,' said Stella seeing Jonny's muttering and playfully punching him in the arm.

Stella knew Jonny was just standing up for someone else. He knew exactly what he was doing when he punched Chang. He made a point of standing up for the underdog, the downtrodden and picked on. Jonny had told her that he had a rough childhood in New Zealand but had some great Maori male role models in his life. He was a natural leader. Stella's infectious personality was a stabiliser amongst the crew, and she made the most of it.

'Hey guys,' said Stella as she turned away from Jonny. 'We've got some time so let's get everyone together in the gaming area for a bit of action. Come on guys, let's go.'

The gaming room was designed for immersive virtual reality. Everything from sports events to "hide and shoot" games could be played. The crew even used it to train for scenarios they might encounter on the Skimmer.

'Let's go then,' said Ngarra.

'Righto,' said Jonny and they all took off. Jonny and Stella ran, hassling each other about how useless they were at some of the games.

They passed Chang along the way.

'Chang,' said Ngarra. 'We are going to the gaming room; want to join in for a bit of fighting fun?'.

'Not if he's there!' Chang said in his usual grumpy voice while pointing at Jonny and glaring at him.

'Free chance for pay back,' said Stella as passed him and gave him a look he just couldn't resist.

'Payback, now that sounds like a challenge,' said Chang. 'Let's go then. You don't stand a chance Jonny.'

Jonny smiled. 'I'll make a man of you yet boy,' he thought to himself.

Chang had lost face when Jonny punched him. He regretted hassling Connor and wished he could take it all back. What would his father think? Who cares, his father was always busy. His father was never there; he was a company man and his sister had moved into that life as well.

Still, he thought to himself. Here he was on a Skimmer. He had wanted to go his own way and rebelled against family tradition. How ironic to be accepted into Xed and the Ocean Academy then end up on a Skimmer mining nodules and delivering them to a Harvester owned by the company both his father and his sister worked for. Somehow and in some way his father had something to do with that.

***

The crew had finished, returned to the rec area and freshened up before moving off to carry out their various tasks on the Skimmer. Connor was back in the information hub with Aamir. He thought Aamir was a calm person who listened intently when he was talking. Not like the others, who sometimes lost interest after a while.

Connor stood lost in thought and looking intently at the ocean bubble hologram. He almost thought of his bubble of Xtracts as an extension of himself now.

He was frustrated with his lack of progress. He couldn't get the Xtracts to learn from a group response to a stimulus and then return to mining. Every time he interrupted the automated mining operation and got them to form a group the whole simulation eventually fell apart.

He thought of the Borg from the old Star Trek movies he had watched that came out decades ago. 'The Collective, you will be assimilated,' he thought to himself out loud. 'How ironic to be thinking of that.'

SAI picked up on his thoughts and streamed information on the Borg. Aamir and Connor both had a laugh. Aamir had a slight smile on his face as he watched Connor chastise himself. Connor grinned back; he liked Aamir. They stood at the console and looked over the data feed for the Xtract signal hack.

Aamir contacted Ngarra at the SAI console over comms.

'Ngarra,' said Aamir. 'We are narrowing down the area considerably now.'

'Great', said Ngarra. 'It won't be long now before we are as close as we are likely to be without them discovering we are onto them.'

***

At the SAI console Ngarra was looking over some chart projections. He got SAI to zoom in and out of various locations. He was looking at where they could hide the Skimmer so they could be picked up undetected after recovering the rogue crew.

Jonny was also at the SAI console and asked SAI to run some course calculations. He was feeling pumped after their gaming and a little restless. He wanted to get on with recovering the rogue crew.

'If we can narrow the location down a little more,' he said looking over the navigation projections, 'then we can close them and launch our Xtracts as a distraction. We can box them in and take them out.'

Jonny did a little fist pump and looked at Ngarra grinning. He loved winding up the crew. Always looking for a reaction. But the crew new it and played up to his antics.

'Sounds good bro,' said Ngarra giving him a little fist pump back.

'Got a bit of Maori in you bro have you,' said Jonny laughing.

'Today I have bro,' said Ngarra grinning.

'We are closing in on these hot heads!' said Jonny.

Another little fist pump followed, and Jonny walked around the SAI console acting out disabling the off-grid Skimmer. Ngarra watched him, having a chuckle at his colloquial mannerisms.

Jesse walked into the SAI console and heard the last part of the conversation. What if they had to use their ARC array, she thought to herself.

Ngarra was feeling a sense of urgency and apprehension about what they might encounter. At the same time, he was also excited about doing something different. However, he knew Jesse was worried that for this lot it might all be too much to handle. For her, overriding Skimmer mining protocols so they could head off on a rescue mission was not a decision to be taken lightly. Most Skimmer crews were just out of their teenage years and this whole situation worried her.

'Ngarra,' she said. 'Let's get SAI to run a check and confirm the status of our ARC array. We may need it. I hope we don't, but I don't want to be disabled by that rogue crew and suspended in this vast ocean expanse waiting to be boarded ourselves.'

'Good point,' said Ngarra. 'SAI, what is the status of our ARC array.

'ARC array calibrated and online,' said SAI.

'SAI, arm ARC array,' said Ngarra.

'Confirmed,' said SAI. 'ARC array armed.'

SAI loaded the projections of the ARC array. Jonny was looking over the projections when Chang walked into the SAI console.

Chang was still a little grumpy with everyone but after a game or two earlier seemed in a better mood than he had been over the previous few days. Despite getting one up on Jonny in the games he still kept clear of Jonny though.

Stella came skipping in behind Chang. Once again like a breath of fresh air, her infectious personality snapped everyone out of a sense of impending crisis. They were all looking at the projections of the armed ARC array and power status.

'Fantastic,' she said jumping up and down and waving her arms around.

'Where on earth do you get your energy from,' said Jonny as he imitated Stella's antics.

'Life,' said Stella laughing. 'We are getting close to finding this rogue crew. Hey Jonny boy, I see the ARC array is armed. Our sweet ARC weapons, my favourite babies.'

'About the only babies you're going to have girl,' said Jonny.

Everyone laughed at how ridiculous that sounded and Stella flushed red.

'Got you,' said Jonny smiling cheekily.

'Chang,' said Ngarra. 'Come over here and have a look at this.'

Chang begrudgingly walked over to where Jonny and Stella were standing. He cringed at her bubbly personality.

'You would have seen all this more recently at the sim centre,' he said. 'When the ARC array is armed, we can pack some punch.'

Jonny was standing opposite him doing some boxing moves with his hands.

'Give us a break,' said Chang as he rolled his eyes at Jonny.

'Yes, yes, yes,' he said. 'I have seen it all before many times. Besides, SAI looks after it all. Why you guys bother talking it up I do not know. We're just passengers on a giant autonomous mining drone that does it all for us. Perfect for a girl like you Stella, I mean with your narrowly focussed training.'

'Such enthusiasm Chang,' she said ignoring the smart comment. 'Did you bore all your friends to death, is that why you have none now?'

Stella gave him a sarcastic smile.

The others laughed. Chang could dish out the smart and abrasive comments but he couldn't handle it being said back to him. It just made him more grumpy than usual.

Ngarra watched and sensed Chang's growing anger so he quickly looked to appease his ego. It certainly was a big ego.

'I could certainly use your advice and comments.' he said. 'Your knowledge of ARC arrays is extensive from what I hear. I would value your input.'

'Well, if you put it like that,' said Chang with a wicked smile at Jonny and Stella, 'then I am all yours.'

Stella smiled sweetly and looked over at Jesse who was watching the exchange of comments between her crew members and making some mental notes.

Jesse thought to herself that appealing to Chang's ego was a great way to get around his grumpy attitude and it was indeed a big ego. Chang always thought the world owed him something and this perception often got in the way of his work.

While they were looking over the ARC array projections and exchanging smart remarks a communication came through.

'Laser communication signal from Xed Academy,' announced SAI.

'SAI confirm message board status,' said Ngarra.

'Eel drone and grid buoy proximity nominal,' said SAI. 'Live feed available.'

It was Jonah. 'Hi all,' she said as her image appeared. 'I'll be quick. The situation with the off-grid Skimmer has evolved somewhat. I have assembled a sim team at the Academy to help you. We have a secure system that can't be hacked.'

'Famous last words but OK,' said Jesse. 'If your sim team are simply viewing resolved vector data then there should be no possibility of a breach in data security from your end.'

'Yes,' said Jonah. 'Any breach here at the Academy would have to be an inside job. However, we do need to share our progress with GlobeCorpMining. It will keep them onside and it will help us get our rogue crew back safely. They just want their load of nodules back or so they say. But I am not so sure about that.'

'OK Jonah,' said Jesse. 'We are onto it.'

'The sim team will be going through crew recovery scenarios. They will advise you on optimal outcomes. Got to go,' said Jonah.

'Great, talk soon then,' said Jesse as the image of Jonah disappeared.

In that moment of apprehension Ngarra looked around at the faces of everyone. It was going to be tough. To get everyone through this he needed to step up.

'Right,' said Ngarra. 'SAI confirm data link with the Academy sim centre SAI.'

'Confirmed,' said SAI. 'Sim centre SAI has access to vector data from grid buoy node upload.'

While they were busy discussing what the best course of action was Connor's voice interrupted over comms from the information hub.

'Ngarra,' he said urgently. 'The vector has altered again. SAI is already correcting our course.'

Jonny confirmed that was the case and nodded at Ngarra.

'Great,' said Ngarra as he looked at Jonny.

'Hey,' said Connor excitedly over comms as he carried on talking. 'I have some more work I wanted to show you all. I think you will like this. You have to come and see.'

'Yes, I need to see this, said Ngarra. 'Jonny come with me; you need to see this.'

Ngarra moved off and motioned Jonny to follow him.

Apart from Jesse, the others left as well. She stood there thinking about the crew and how different they all were. Somehow and in some way they all got along and made it work. Quietly though, her concern was growing that the crew were not up for the task. Jonah may have the big picture at heart, but this young crew was stretched emotionally. They were trained to monitor mining operations not run around the ocean on a rescue mission carrying a discovery that everyone else seemed to want to get their hands on.

Chapter 17

It had been six days since the end of their last mining run and transit to the Harvester. Everyone was up and about early. The atmosphere was intense. There was excitement and apprehension as they closed in on the rogue crew and their off-grid Skimmer.

Ngarra and Jonny were back in the information hub listening to Connor.

He was updating them on the vector calculation. With a lot of enthusiasm, he was explaining aspects of animal behaviour and navigation and relating it to the carrier signal.

'Connor, I wouldn't want to be in your head,' Jonny said laughing. 'I'd get lost brother.'

'Why do you keep calling me your brother,' Connor said with a frown.'

Ngarra smiled and had a chuckle. 'Figure of speech,' he said shrugging his shoulders.

'Anyway,' said Connor carrying on oblivious. 'Imagine honeybees travelling up to five kilometres away in any direction and finding some food. The bees always find their way back to the hive. Think about it. It's their surroundings that determine how they react and behave. Things like the suns position or recognition of routes to follow to collect nectar, which they communicate to others. Think of the infra sound carrier signal hack as a trail or route to construct and follow. Like dancing bees communicating to each other where they need to go to find something.'

Connor looked like he had been holding his breath the whole time as he signed and looked at them waiting for a response.

Ngarra and Jonny looked at each other and smiled.

'Geeze Connor,' said Jonny. 'I am having trouble keeping up.'

They both looked back at Connor and waited for him to carry on.

'When the communication streamer is deployed from the Skimmer to the seabed below, mining Xtracts orientate themselves relative to it. However,

Xtracts are also equipped with the infra sound communication signal that travels long distances underwater. It's a redundancy that was built into the Xtracts for deep sea mining operations. Like I have said before, it allows the Skimmer owners to locate lost Xtracts if the contractor that owns or leases a Skimmer loses one of them. We have taken advantage of this feature to construct a location vector.'

'Awesome,' said Jonny. 'Wish I had thought of that.'

They walked around the hologram.

Jonny put his hand through the Xtracts coming and going from the seabed to a point above.

They parted and then moved around his hand.

Connor took the comments as a compliment. He watched them looking at the ocean bubble hologram.

'What makes your Xtracts change from reacting to something individually, responding to it as a group and then learning from the encounter?' said Jonny.

'Ahh,' said Connor excitedly. 'Now we have to understand how to put together layered algorithms for patterning and learning group behaviour responses. Like I explained to the others, using natural language processing I got SAI to hack a series of source codes from script libraries for coordinating groups of drones. I also got SAI to use data on behaviour patterning in nature. From all this we built a type of mesh or artificial world within which a "fight or flight" response can be learnt. It's like having generations of retained memory stored collectively in the mesh and passed on. It overlays their primary function, which is to conduct mining and assist other Xtracts to maintain their operational status.'

They all watched as Connor swiped a dashboard on one of the nearby screens.

A giant squid appeared in the ocean bubble hologram and attempted to grasp an Xtract and remove it from the group.

Initially, just the Xtracts nearby reacted and surrounded the squid. Others then followed suit until most were surrounding the squid. They watched on and for a moment it seemed like the behaviour would result in release of the captured Xtract. However, once the squid tried to move off with the Xtract in its grasp something went wrong, and the simulation fell apart.

The Xtracts ended up wandering off on their own as well, not even returning to their mining operation.

Connor looked down. 'It happens every time,' he said. 'I have not been able to get the group to learn over multiple simulations to stop the squid from moving, which results in release of the Xtract and a return to mining. It's like they are stuck in a loop that has no feedback allowing them to learn from multiple failures. It's like the collective memory is not passed on. Something is blocking it.'

Ngarra looked at the Xtracts wandering off and then back at Connor.

'I imagine it's like the Queen bee,' he said. 'They control all the bee's behaviour in the hive through hormones and chemical signals. So, here the Xtracts are constantly communicating with each other. But what do you use as the queen bee? I mean who is in charge?'

Connor thought about it.

'The Xtracts are currently acting like directionless bees then,' he said. 'They are not able to learn group responses because they are still at some level reacting as individuals.'

Ngarra and Jonny thought about what Connor had said while gazing at his ocean hologram bubble. He had reset the simulation and the Xtracts were now back simulating a mining operation; moving around the seabed and to and from a point in the water column.

'I thought the mesh would overcome the problem, but it still doesn't work,' said Connor.

Connor was feeling a little more comfortable around Jonny now, he didn't seem like such an animal. Maybe it was because they were both so interested in what he was creating or maybe with being on the autism spectrum he was just so engrossed in what he loved talking about that interacting with other people came easily.

While they were all looking at the ocean bubble hologram SAI startled them out of their thoughts.

'Laser communication signal from Xed Academy,' said SAI.

'SAI confirm message board status,' said Ngarra.

'Eel drone and grid buoy proximity nominal, live feed available,' said SAI.

'SAI, open message board,' said Ngarra.

Jonah's image appeared.

'Ngarra, the sim team are running some scenarios for rogue crew recovery,' she said. 'Where is Connor at with the locating the off-grid Skimmer?'

'Great timing,' said Ngarra. 'I am here with him now. Based on attempts by the off-grid Skimmer Xtracts to determine their position relative to our Xtracts we have a vector. Connor has enough data to define a broad area that they are likely to be in.'

'Great,' said Jonah. We will run some more scenarios.'

'SAI, update vector data for sim centre synch,' said Ngarra.

'Confirmed,' said SAI. 'Vector data updated.'

'OK,' said Ngarra. 'We are running out of time. We will have the Sea Hunters to deal with soon.'

'Come on guys,' said Jonny. 'It's the Sea Hunters. I mean, what's the worst that can happen; being disabled, boarded and detained. You can "simulate" all you want but when it comes down to it if something can go wrong it will go wrong, Murphy's Law.'

'Ngarra, it's Rick. I just got here and are listening in. Don't compromise your Skimmer to recover the rogue crew. The Sea Hunters will disable it if you interfere. You will just be giving them an excuse to board you. Any damage is going to come back to us from the contractor to pay for.'

'I assume they are following us,' said Ngarra, 'as we are tracking the off-grid Skimmer.'

'OK,' said Jonah. 'We have got to get going so you be careful out there.' Jonah's image disappeared.

Silence followed and for a moment Ngarra doubted why they should even be doing this.

'Right, let's get to the SAI console,' said Ngarra. 'We will see what they come up with at the sim centre to help us with this crew recovery. I don't want to rely on them though.'

Ngarra and Jonny looked at each other and then at Connor. He was back working so they left him to it and headed off.

**

At Xed Academy Jonah and Rick were in the sim centre. The sim team were using the updated data received from Ngarra's SAI. For the sim team it was simply a matter of using a set of probability calculations that balanced the timing of crew recovery and proximity to the Sea Hunters.

Like Connor, they were also trying to work out if there was any way to activate the off-grid Skimmer Xtracts and launch them remotely. The simulator SAI had so far determined that over a large distance the Xtracts on the off-grid Skimmer had a limited probability of being made to activate in time and launch using a laser communication signal through the grid. They were still too far away.

Jonah said to the sim team, 'when can we use a laser communication signal to activate the Xtracts.'

'To activate the off-grid Skimmer Xtracts and make them head to Ngarra's Skimmer they need to be in range,' said the sim team leader.

'Exactly,' said Rick. 'But for a laser communication signal you also need to know exactly where they are.'

'Let's keep going on this,' said Jonah to the sim crew. 'It looks like the best option is to narrow down the area using the vector constructed from the carrier signal hack, identify their location exactly and then get their Xtracts to launch using the laser communication signal.'

'OK,' said the sim team leader.

The sim crew team leader exited the Skimmer simulator and walked around to where Rick and Jonah were watching.

Rick was watching the monitoring screens and looking at what the sim crew was doing.

'Is the range at which you could accurately determine their location also close enough to launch the ARC torpedo array and disable it before they realise what is going on?', said Rick.

'Yes,' said the sim team leader. 'The advantage is that with being off grid a lot of its sensor systems will be offline. It will only have sonar.'

It was a trade-off that they were trying to balance out. They also had to factor in the timing of arrival of the Sea Hunters.

***

On the Skimmer Connor had finally decided he was hungry and joined Jonny and Ngarra in the rec area. Chang passed through on his way to the Xtract bay and glanced across at them sitting with Jesse at one of the tables.

'Connor,' said Chang. 'I was in the SAI console and that Xtract infra sound carrier signal vector of yours keeps changing direction.'

'Interesting,' said Connor. 'Must be something going on that would cause it to constantly change. Let's go and have a look,' he said to the others.

Ngarra, Jesse and Connor got up out of their seats and returned to the information hub.

On the way Ngarra asked Connor, 'do you think the rogue crew has found out we are closing on them.'

'Could be,' said Connor.

'SAI,' said Jesse as they walked up to the SAI console and passed through on their way back to the information hub. 'Confirm no other Skimmers or surface vessels are in the region.'

A pause followed.

'Surface vessel identified on the same course and speed,' said SAI.

'SAI identify other vessel,' said Ngarra looking just as surprised as the rest of them.

SAI responded, 'Signature confirmed as a Sea Hunter.'

They all stopped walking to the information hub and gathered around the SAI console. Ngarra looked at Jesse with a worried frown on his face. 'They could have just asked to follow us until we find the off-grid Skimmer. They could even help us. Why would they shadow us and not contact us?'

'Right,' said Jesse. 'Let's get in touch with crew monitoring and find out if they know anything more about this. SAI send priority communication request for Jonah.'

The Eel drone proximity and grid buoy node link was nominal, so they still had a live feed. There was a pause as the laser communication signal was sent and then Jonah's image appeared.

'What is it, what's going on,' she said. 'I didn't expect to be talking with you yet.'

'SAI has been monitoring the carrier signal hack for changes in the vector,' said Jesse. 'It has started changing constantly so we thought the off-grid Skimmer might have detected us.

'We thought the rogue crew might have picked up our signature somehow,' said Ngarra. 'However, SAI has also detected the presence of a Sea Hunter vessel.'

'The Sea Hunters will be following you so they can get to the off-grid Skimmer and recover the nodules for GlobeCorpMining and returning the Skimmer to the contractor,' said Jonah.

'If that were the case,' said Ngarra, 'wouldn't they just tell us. Seems to be a bit more sinister than that. Why would they be so sneaky as to quietly shadow us?'

'We are looking into it,' said Jonah. 'I want you to be careful. Find and recover our rogue crew and get out of there. I mean get as far away as possible from their Skimmer once you have them.'

Connor was wanting to say something and was practically jumping up and down.

Jesse thought that if the Sea Hunters were shadowing them and had not contacted them surely, they were also a target. But why and for what reason?

'If they disable our Skimmer,' said Jesse, 'the Sea Hunters will then board us and detain us.'

'That must not happen,' said Jonah. 'I will get Rick to talk with GlobeCorpMining and see what is going on.'

'We have a plan,' said Jesse. 'We may be able to take advantage of the confusion it will cause and slip away.'

'Great,' said Jonah. 'Let me know as soon as possible. Rick will continue here with the sim team.'

For a moment Ngarra thought about his next move.

'SAI, open Skimmer-wide communication,' he said.

There was a pause and then SAI confirmed access.

'Jonny stay at the SAI console with Jesse and I. Stella, Chang and Aamir get to the Xtract Bay. Make sure the Xtracts are ready to deploy. We will use them as a distraction. Connor, stay in the information hub and keep in touch with the sim team at the Academy.'

'Ngarra, Jesse, it's Rick. Is Connor there.' Rick was listening and was keen to talk to Connor about his work.

'Is Connor able to get the off-grid Skimmer Xtracts to launch yet. Will you be close enough to know their exact location?'

'Yes,' said Connor. 'Once we are close enough I can use the carrier signal hack and change the vector calculation into a set of coordinates. With SAI's help I should then be able to use a laser communication signal to make them activate and deploy to the coordinates.'

A brief discussion ensued about how it was all going to work, deploying the Xtracts, locating the off-grid Skimmer, recovering the rogue crew and avoiding the Sea Hunters all at the same time.

'Great Connor,' said Jesse. The distraction will give us time to get the rogue crew onboard.'

Chang was listening and said, 'why don't we just disable them and then all surface and recover the crew.'

'Not an option,' said Ngarra. 'We would be sitting ducks. As soon as we are on the surface the Sea Hunters will be straight on us. And we would need to convince the rogue crew to surface after being disabled. Remember their Skimmer is off the grid.'

'If all else fails,' said Rick, 'it's a last option.'

Jesse carried on. 'Connor can use the ocean bubble simulation to link with and control the Xtracts as a group.

'Yeah,' said Connor. 'But the simulation breaks down and they wander off randomly.'

'That's perfect though,' said Rick. 'We just want to create confusion and for you to get away.'

Everyone agreed that they should give it a go.

'It can be developed further I'm sure,' said Rick.

He was interested in what Connor had come up with and so were a few others. He needed to ensure that work was protected.

Jesse and Ngarra looked at each other and then at Connor. Connor was about to launch into a long explanation about how to get it all to work.

Jesse jumped in and said, 'Sorry Rick we have to go time is short here. We will get back to you soon.'

Jesse shut off the communication and Jonah and Ricks images disappeared.

Chapter 18

In the Xtract bay Stella found it awkward working with Chang and Aamir. All power to women she thought to herself. She had to have a chuckle at how they handled her bubbly personality. A grumpy Chang and a polite and reserved Aamir was a hard combination to crack. Men, she thought to herself.

'SAI,' she said. 'Confirm power status of all Xtracts?'

SAI responded, 'Xtract power systems are nominal.'

SAI presented the status of each Xtract on the console display.

Aamir and Chang went down the sides of the Skimmer and checked each individual display.

'You do the rest Chang,' said Stella. 'Or should I say, would you like to do the rest?'

Aamir smiled to himself, knowing what Stella was trying to do. Stella tried to make Chang feel a little more comfortable around her by playing down her talents. Like a puppet on a string, she smiled to herself.

'Easy,' said Chang as he came back to the main console. 'SAI confirm status of Xtract propulsion systems?' Chang swiped through the diagnostics SAI displayed.

'Confirmed, propulsion systems are nominal.' said SAI. Amir moved down each side of the Skimmer and checked individual displays.

He was growing to like Stella's wicked sense of humour. She seemed to handle his grumpy and dismissive attitude and personality more than the others.

Still, Chang could not help but say something about how pointless he thought what they were doing was. Nothing ever went wrong and if it did the maintenance drones fixed it anyway.

'Honestly,' said Chang to Stella. 'Why do we need to do this. SAI has it all under control and we are notified of any malfunctions anyway.'

'The whole point,' said Aamir as he walked back into the main console area, 'is that we know everything that is going on as it happens.'

'That's right,' said Stella. 'Under normal mining operations we monitor SAI and its control of the Xtracts through the communication streamer. It's only when we want to do something non-routine that we take control.'

'You mean like the situation we have now,' said Aamir. 'We interface with SAI and control the Skimmer and its extracts jointly.'

'Yeah,' said Chang,' but SAI can still override any decision we make if it threatens our survival.'

'Exactly,' said Stella. 'That's fundamental to SAI. We can't do anything that would put our lives in danger.'

'But what if we need to do something that does threaten our survival but to us is achievable?' said Chang.

'SAI calculates risk based on consequence and likelihood,' said Aamir.

Chang was insistent and kept pursuing the issue. 'Yeah, but if it's a threat to our survival, we still can't overrule it.'

'That's right,' said Aamir. 'We cannot override a decision by SAI not to proceed with a task. For example, if the likelihood of a threat was too high and the consequence to life significant the level of risk would be too high.'

'There is a command override,' said Stella, 'but only Jesse and Ngarra can do that and it's a last resort.'

'Wonderful!' said Chang sarcastically. 'So, we just have to put up with someone else's choice about what we may or may not survive if something goes wrong.'

Chang had been adamant that he did not sign up to race around the ocean looking for another Skimmer. While Chang was moaning and carrying on, Ngarra's voice came over comms.

'Can everyone come to the SAI console,' he said. 'I need to brief you all.'

'Coming,' said Stella. 'SAI, complete Xtract diagnostics and present summary status. Prepare to deploy Xtracts.'

'Confirmed, launch status nominal, preparing to deploy,' said SAI.

Down each side of the Skimmer along the inside of the recess displays showed each Xtract powering up.

'Let's go boys,' said Stella with a wicked little grin at them. 'I'll race you both there,' she said as they sprinted off.

They took off and headed towards the SAI console two levels above them.

Stella had challenged them to race as fast as they could, and they arrived breathing heavily and wincing.

Racing into the SAI console and panting heavily they almost fell over each other.

'You two had better get some exercise,' she said laughing. 'Fancy a girl beating you boys.'

Chang was not impressed and went red in the face. He was about to say something but Aamir got in ahead of him.

'What is so urgent Ngarra,' said Aamir as he tried to catch his breath.

'I am concerned about the security breach at the Academy,' he said as they all gathered around. 'The crew recovery mission could be compromised.'

'What's the worst that could happen,' said Stella. 'We get knocked around a bit by ARC arrays and disabled and boarded. We can handle that.'

'We must remember,' said Aamir, 'that Connor has come a long way with his work. He thinks that with SAI's help he can get close enough to use a laser communication signal to get the Xtracts on the off-grid Skimmer to activate and launch and proceed to the coordinates he has set using the infra sound carrier signal. We can use it as a distraction.'

'Yes,' said Connor. 'I can launch their Xtracts. That's the whole point. With SAI's help we can take control of them.'

'Come on people,' said Chang. 'We are an Academy crew monitoring a Skimmers Xtract mining operation. The rescue mission is compromised. Why do you want to attract the attention of the Sea Hunters and get us all in a world of trouble? Who cares, it's not what we signed up for!'

Chang was looking angry about the whole situation.

'Come on boy,' said Jonny as he made a warrior face at Stella and smiled. 'Harden up. Life is short brother, and this is a bit of a change from the monotony of mining operations.'

Chang glared at him and stormed off.

He was just to reactive and emotional at times, thought Jesse. Where does all that anger come from, she thought to herself. I must find out.

It was at that moment that SAI received another communication request from Xed Academy.

'Laser communication signal from Xed Academy crew monitoring,' announced SAI. 'Eel drone and grid buoy proximity nominal, live feed available.'

'I don't have much time,' said Jonah as her image appeared. 'I have got GlobeCorpMining to activate a Skimmer from their Harvester. It will distract the

Sea Hunters. In their labs they have been trialling remote monitoring of a Skimmer. So, no crew onboard. The team here in the simulator will monitor it remotely. It's the same team helping you with crew recovery scenarios.'

'I like your work,' said Jonny. 'Go go go boys and girls. A bit like a riderless horse in a rodeo if you ask me.'

'Alright Jonny,' said Jesse as she tried not to laugh at Jonny's antics. 'Let's keep it a little more professional.'

Jonny smiled and made a motion of a horse and being thrown off it and it runs off. The others had a chuckle. Jonah couldn't see the little prank and wondered what was going on.

Ngarra watched the antics of Jonny, which was now getting a little irritating. Jesse could see it in his face. Ngarra was anxious to get going and get on with it all.

'Back to the point,' said Ngarra as he glared at Jonny to stop it. 'What about the security breach.'

Jonah replied, 'anyone watching the sim team here will just think they are running your scenarios not monitoring an actual Skimmer being operated remotely. However, we need some time to get in position and provide a distraction. Our remote monitored Skimmer will add to the confusion while you get the rogue crew.'

'That is, if they want to be,' said Jesse. 'We still don't know why they went off-grid in the first place.'

'My guess is that they are being forced to do it, although I am not really sure how,' said Jonah.

'The threat of being blasted to the bottom of the ocean might have something to do with it,' said Chang as he walked back into the SAI console.

Chang had calmed down a little and just ignored Jonny. Stella smiled at him reassuringly.

'Whatever the reason the game has changed,' said Jonah. 'We now have the GlobeCorpMining Skimmer and access to their remote systems project. That is to our advantage as we can find out a thing or two about their future intentions regarding crewing.'

Jesse thought about this and replied, 'maybe whoever it is that has the rogue crew under duress wants the Sea Hunters to catch up with us and get hold of all Connor's work.'

'Could be,' said Jonah. 'It seems rumours have spread, and people are aware of Connor's work and that he has used your SAI to help him develop it.'

'Could be,' said Ngarra. 'But for others to know about all that someone would need to have access to our Skimmer.'

'Just a calculated guess at this stage,' said Jonah. 'Let's deal with that later. I must go. We are ready here; you should pick up our the remotely monitored Skimmer signature soon enough. Talk soon.'

Jonah's image disappeared.

Ngarra's crew needed to make final preparations and launch their Xtracts before the remotely controlled Skimmer and the Sea Hunters turned up. The ocean around them was about to get very congested, which was to their advantage.

Jonny was an excellent pilot thought Jesse. But damn, he would have to be on his game for this. In fact, the whole team would have to excel in their roles to pull this one off.

'Connor, it's all up to you,' said Ngarra. 'When we get close enough to the off-grid Skimmer you need to get their Xtracts to activate. What about your simulation. Can you link to the Xtracts through it?'

'Yes, it will work long enough to buy us some time.' Connor said excitedly. 'Come and see, come and see.'

Connor was almost jumping up and down. That got Stella going to.

'OK, OK,' said Jonny as everyone started to move off. 'I'm hungry so we should all eat first.'

'Are you kidding; hungry. What is this!' a party said Chang. 'Please, give us a break.'

Chang was very unimpressed about the whole idea and the notion that Connor's work could somehow rescue them from the situation they were about to deliberately put themselves into.

Everyone else wasn't sure whether to laugh or take him seriously. Now was not the time for siting, eating or indeed looking at Connor's work.

Jonny liked to keep them all guessing though, so he smiled and shrugged his shoulders.

'You could smile you know,' said Jonny as he had a chuckle at Chang's expense. 'Hmmm, food,' he said rubbing his belly.

'Who pushed your button anyway,' said Chang glaring at him. They glared at each other and squared off. Then Jonny made Chang jump back by making a sudden warrior expression with his face. The others laughed.

'Cut it out!' exclaimed Ngarra. 'Chang, you stay here with Jesse. Aamir, go with Connor and help him. Jonny, get SAI to work out how we are going to position ourselves to recover the rogue crew and get away.'

'Righto,' said Jonny. 'Onto it. Want me to hold your hand Chang mate.'

'I'm not your mate,' Chang said as his face went red. Jonny jumped at him suddenly again and made a warrior face.

'I told you lot to cut it out!' said Ngarra. 'Geeze, do I have to get Jesse to play mum and send you to your rooms!'

First things first, let's eat,' said Stella winking at Jonny.

Everyone groaned again about eating.

'Then,' said Stella, 'maybe I can play mum and kick some butt.'

Typical Stella, the more things got tense the more she would joke around.

'About the only butt you will ever kick is your own fat arse,' said Jonny as he burst out laughing.

Everyone laughed, even Chang. Aamir managed a reserved smile.

Stella gave Jonny a playful clip around the head and made or tried to make one of his warriors faces. Jonny feigned a block and punch to her stomach.

The crew took off to the recreation area and left Chang wondering what on earth just happened. 'I thought we weren't getting food,' he said to himself.

In the rec area Jonny, Stella and Jesse were sitting together having a laugh about old times at Xed and the Academy.

Ngarra sat with Chang and Aamir. The three of them came from very different cultural backgrounds which they often discussed over food. Indigenous Australian, Asian and Middle Eastern cultures provided for some very interesting discussions.

At the other table the conversation was a bit lighter with Stella talking about the various antics they used to get up to back at the campus before they graduated from the Academy and were deployed.

Connor sat on one of the lounge seats and flicked through a screen full of gadgets he was interested in.

While the crew took some time to relax Chang excused himself and headed off. 'I'm going to the information hub to look over this Xtract simulation,' he said as he got up to walk off.

'They will be fine,' said Stella. 'Don't worry. Connor has run all the diagnostics and we are ready to go.'

'Still,' said Chang. 'I just want to check.' He left and Stella shrugged her shoulders.

'I just can't figure him out,' she said with a smile.

'I don't think any of us can,' said Jonny.

They talked some more and enjoyed a brief period of relaxing before things got very busy.

***

Meanwhile it was the opportunity Chang had been waiting for. A chance to prove his worth to his father at GlobeCorpMining.

His contact had said they just wanted a copy of all of Connor's work that was all. In return his contact would secure a place on the Harvester as part of the development team working in a laboratory on autonomous mining technology.

Many people of Chinese ethnicity wanted a position on the Harvester. But for Chang, his resentment for his family, what happened to his mother and how they dismissed him as a failure had made him an angry person.

'Besides, why take the long road from Skimmer crew to a Harvester when I can jump ahead,' he thought to himself as he entered the information hub.

It was easy enough to copy Connor's work. His contact had promised he could make it all happen for him and that his father would be proud.

To one side of the information hub a screen was streaming data for the Xtract carrier signal hack calculation and projected vector. Another screen was running the source code and algorithm stack for the Xtracts in the ocean bubble hologram.

In the middle of the centre console within the ocean bubble hologram the group of extracts were moving up and down from the seabed to a point at the top.

Chang looked at it and thought about Connor's rants about mapping collective behaviour patterns in nature for machines to learn from. What nonsense he thought to himself. How is that relevant to machines learning collective behaviour. How is a group of Xtracts going to learn autonomous group behaviour?

With SAI's help this group of simulated Xtracts were learning from their own group behaviour under various scenarios they encountered. But it always fell apart after a while and they wandered off randomly before the simulation reset itself. It was fascinating to watch though, Chang thought to himself.

He tapped the bottom left corner of a centre console screen and a dashboard of symbols appeared on both.

There it was, a small icon used to copy everything. He could copy and transfer it to his smartwatch, which had significant capacity to store data. More than that, he could just upload everything to a grid buoy node through an Eel communication network drone.

SAI would log his access but not what was accessed and by who. They would have to search for it.

Being quite savvy with information technology he had an encrypted site called SAITech in a grid buoy node. A swipe here, and a swipe there with his hand and a check on Eel drone proximity to upload and it was done.

Chang did not notice a small red flashing image appear on the dashboard of symbols as he swiped it clear and the data streams reappeared. He quietly left the information hub and headed down to the Xtract bay to check on the launch status of each one and at least look like he had been preoccupied.

Chapter 19

On the Harvester Sue and Lee were overseeing the research team. They were preparing to launch the prototype remote operated Skimmer.

Ngarra's crew had left a few days ago. Everything was in place. The link with the sim team and their SAI at Xed Academy was active.

'I don't know why we are handing over the trial of this to Xed Academy,' said Sue. 'To use it to distract the Sea Hunters does not seem wise.'

'The relationship between GlobeCorpMining and the Academy crew programme is built on mutual respect and trust,' said Lee. 'Chang's father, our Chief Operating Officer would lose face if he was seen to not offer some assistance.'

'Even if that meant getting in the way of carrying out emergency administration orders issued by "the Authority"?' said Sue.

'Let's just carry out the request,' said Lee. 'There is more to this than we are being told.'

They watched on as the Harvester technicians from the research team launched the new Skimmer.

In the background in the control room, they could see Chang's sister coordinating the launch and checking systems for handing over remote monitoring to Xed Academy sim centre.

The launch area was towards the rear of the Harvester. Over a moonpool a large hanger-like structure was suspended. The hanger was adjacent to a large research laboratory. Lee and Sue watched from a viewing platform as the Skimmer slowly descend into the moonpool below.

'Do you think this will work,' said Sue.

Lee looked out over the moonpool and thought about it.

'We can still keep track of it from here even if we can't control it,' he said. 'We shall monitor the situation as it evolves and report back to GlobeCorpMining.'

Lee and Sue continued watching as the Skimmer was released. It settled in the moonpool, submerged itself and disappeared from view.

At a depth of a hundred metres it stopped. It was stationary and motionless. Suspended like a puppet on a string it was waiting for the sim team at Xed Academy to tell its SAI what to do.

***

At Xed Academy Jonah was in the instructor area at the sim centre. She was watching the team inside the Skimmer simulator. Confirmation had come through from the Harvester that their Skimmer was in position and waiting.

'Right,' said Jonah as she talked to them over comms. 'Our sim centre SAI is synched with the Harvesters Skimmer SAI. Everything you tell SAI to do in the sim will now be mimicked by the launched Skimmer SAI. You have the location of Ngarra's Skimmer. Tell SAI to close them at maximum speed, depth a hundred metres.'

The sim team did as Jonah requested. Jonah watched them and thought about the implications remotely monitored Skimmers had for the Academy.

'Apparently,' said Jonah over the comms link, 'GlobeCorpMining has been working on this technology for a while. Rumours also exist that they are developing something called mimic drone technology.'

'Mimic drones,' said the sim team leader. 'Doesn't sound like anything good will come of that. What exactly is a mimic drone anyway? 'It's exactly what it sounds like,' said Jonah. 'Drones that mimic what goes on around them, animal and people's behaviours and actions and learn from it. Come to think of it maybe you are right. Nothing good will come of it.'

'Next we will be making drones that replicate and repair themselves,' said the sim team leader as they laughed and looked at each other.

'That's not a joke!' exclaimed Jonah. 'God forbid the day someone solves the autonomous artificial intelligence puzzle and works that one out. Anyway, let's get on with this mission.'

Jonah watched from the instructor area as the sim team worked with their SAI, which was now synced with the Harvesters Skimmer SAI.

Some of the team stood around the SAI console in the Skimmer simulator. The rest were either in the information hub or Xtract bay. It was as if they were at sea and moving along a hundred metres below sea level.

'While this remote monitored Skimmer transits to Ngarra's location,' said Jonah, 'I want you to continue to run crew recovery scenarios based on Connor's carrier signal hack and vector calculation.'

For a while Jonah continued to watch them. There was a discussion amongst the Skimmer sim team and a few chuckles. Probably a private joke thought Jonah.

The sim team leader looked over and said to Jonah over the comms link, 'Ngarra's Skimmer should be getting close to the area this off-grid Skimmer is in.'

One of the sim team at the information hub was looking over the vector calculations. While doing so, the sim team information officer caught sight of a small red flashing icon.

'The data synch with Connor and his work is showing a red flashing icon, they said to Jonah. 'It shows a file path in a subroutine not related to the hack.'

'That's strange,' said Jonah. 'Project what you see onto my screen in here.'

With a swipe of their hand the sim team leader synced with the display in the instructor area. Jonah looked at it and thought about her comments earlier to Jesse and Ngarra that there was a security breach at the Academy.

'The code in the sub routine has the word SAITech,' she said. 'It has a time stamp. I want you to contact Jesse. Get her to confirm the location of each crew member for that time stamp.'

'Sure,' said the information officer. 'SAI, communication request with Ngarra's Skimmer.'

'Confirmed,' said SAI. 'Eel drone and grid buoy proximity sub-optimal. Message only.'

The sim team leader sent a recorded video message.

'Jesse, this is urgent. The security breach we talked about. Ask SAI to confirm the whereabouts of all crew when this time stamp you can see occurred. We need to find out if someone was in the information hub at that time and whether Connor was there or not. End message.'

They waited for Jesse to receive and respond to the recorded message.

A message was sent back saying, 'the only person in the information hub at the time of the breach was Chang. Are you saying he has accessed and copied all the data? End message.'

Again, the sim team leader recorded and sent a response for Jonah.

'Could be. Confront him about it but not in front of everyone. He will not want to lose face. We may be able to do something about it. We need to know what he intended to do. Let us know as soon as possible. End message.'

***

On the Skimmer, Chang was now at the SAI console. No one else was there. He set about uploading a message to his contact containing the information he had copied. They would be able to access and download the information he had loaded to a grid buoy node.

He heard someone coming and tried to finish what he was doing but couldn't close the link in time. Jesse and Ngarra walked in.

Chang appeared nervous and a bit angry. They both looked at Chang and saw the smartwatch image with the link open to a grid buoy node.

'What's going on,' said Chang in a grumpy tone. 'I have things to do.'

With that he casually walked forward to leave and Ngarra grabbed his shoulder. Chang turned sharply, grabbed Ngarra's hand with his and stepped inside Ngarra's leg and pushed out against the inside of Ngarra's knee. He dropped to the ground.

'Leave me alone!' yelled Chang and he took off.

Jonny heard the commotion and ran up to the SAI console. At the same time Chang was running down towards him, looking back at Jesse. He didn't see Jonny put his foot out. Chang tripped and went for a skid along the deck, tumbling forward onto his back.

Jonny leapt on him, but Chang was quick. His knee came up on the inside of Johnny's thigh and he arched his back and kicked. Jonny went over Chang's head and landed on his back with a thud.

Chang got up and ran off. He headed down to the rec area and then down towards the Xtract bay. He did not get far. Ngarra raced after Chang and in the rec area tackled Chang to the floor.

Jonny raced back down the stairs behind them, and they both held him down. Jesse was not far behind, paused and grabbed something from her belt. It was a syringe with a sedative in it. The last thing Chang remembered was struggling on the floor.

'Help me get him to the recovery bay,' said Jesse.

Jonny and Ngarra grabbed him and together they got him to the recovery bay, the med bay towards the rear of the rec area. He wasn't that heavy. They moved past the gaming room and accommodation and into the recovery bay.

The others had heard the commotion and came to the recovery bay as well to find out what had happened.

Stella was watching Chang as he came to and panicked. She was usually the one joking around about most things that happened onboard but not this time.

'I can't move!' said Chang as he struggled against the restraints. 'Get these things off me!'

Chang was in a very emotional state and had a look of desperation on his face. Ngarra and Jesse had been talking quietly outside about what had happened and walked back in. Stella got up to leave them alone to talk with Chang.

'Chang, what the hell is going on!' exclaimed Ngarra. 'We are a team. If something is happening, you need to tell us. SAI has confirmed that you were the only one in the information hub at the time of a data security breach on the Skimmer.'

'I, I didn't mean to,' Chang said as he stuttered nervously. 'They said I would get a great role. My family would be so proud, and it would help my mother's situation. It was easy and no one would get hurt. I just had to get hold of all Connor's work. They would do the rest.'

Chang slumped back exhausted, angry and upset.

'Have you given anyone access to the data you uploaded to your grid node yet,' said Jesse sternly.

'No,' said Chang as he continued to plead his case. 'I was going to. That's what I was doing. I'm so sorry. I need to fix this. My father will be so ashamed of me and I'll never get into GlobeCorpMining.'

'Your father will not be impressed at all,' said Jesse.

'Don't tell him,' said Chang as he pleaded with them. 'Nothing must go further about this. Don't tell Jonah.'

'Great,' said Ngarra sarcastically. 'How is Jonah supposed to talk with your father knowing what you have done!'

'I can help,' said Chang. 'Honest I know what to do. Don't ruin my life!'

'You were about to get us all in a world of trouble,' said Ngarra.

'Let me make it right,' said Chang. 'If I corrupt the data loaded to the grid buoy node then Connor's work will be of no use to anyone.'

The others stood back and discussed Chang's suggestion briefly amongst themselves. Jesse came back over to Chang, determined find out how genuine he was about actually helping to make things right.

'We could use this situation to our advantage,' she said. 'If whoever is involved in this security breach is tied up accessing the corrupted files then they will be distracted.'

'Let's give it a go,' said Ngarra. 'What to do with you Chang though.'

'You can assist Jonny for a few days Chang,' said Jesse.

'No! Anyone but him,' said Chang groaning. The guy's a jerk, besides he hit me!'

'Probably well deserved,' said Ngarra as he glared at Chang. 'Besides, there is nothing we can do about you now. That will be up to Xed Ocean Academy and the Council.'

Chang looked utterly dismayed. He had waited his whole life to do something his family would be proud of. The contact that wanted all Connor's work had promised a role with GlobeCorpMining. His father would have been proud and now it was all slipping away.

Stella, Connor and Aamir sat with him for a while and talked about what had happened.

'I would have expected more of you Chang,' said Aamir. 'I see no honour for yourself or your family.'

Jesse took the restraints off. She got Jonny to supervise him for the next forty-eight hours.

'Let's not dwell on it,' said Jesse. 'Jonny, Chang is yours for the next few days. His attempt to secure Connor's work for someone else puts us all at great risk.'

Chang did not say a word. He hung his head low regretting that he had been caught. Now how was he going to save face and help his mother's situation.

'I'm going back to the SAI console,' said Jesse. All this may play into our hands. I need to talk to Jonah about it.'

The others nodded as she walked off. Jonny motioned for Chang to sit down. He was now pacing up and down.

'I was only trying to prove my worth to my family,' he said pleading his case to the others.

'I don't think that is the way to go about it,' said Aamir. 'What about us, the team.'

'Exactly,' said Stella. 'Come on guys we can still get the job done.'

Connor had been quietly listening. He got up and walked off looking pretty upset that Chang had attempted to take all his work from him and give it to someone else.

***

Ngarra and Jesse returned to the SAI console and were discussing how to report to Jonah what had happened.

SAI interrupted them. 'Laser signal communication from Xed Academy. Eel drone and grid buoy proximity nominal, live feed available.'

Jonah's image appeared.

'The sim team's remotely monitored Skimmer is closing on your location at maximum speed,' she said. 'The Sea Hunters will track the remote-controlled Skimmer. It should keep them distracted for a time.'

'Great,' said Ngarra. 'We have confronted Chang about trying to take Connor's work and load it to a grid buoy node. He called it SAITech. His contact has not accessed it yet. Chang agreed to corrupt the data.'

'OK,' said Jonah. 'Between that and the sim team leading the Sea Hunters astray we should be able to get to the off-grid Skimmer and get the rogue crew off before they realise what is going on.'

'What about Chang,' said Jesse.

'If he has admitted doing the wrong thing and agreed to help then let's deal with the consequences of his actions later when you are all safe and sound back here at Xed Ocean Academy,' said Jonah. 'I have to contact GlobeCorpMining with an update anyway. I will brief his father on the situation but not say it has anything to do with his son. I know what Chang is like and the last thing he needs is the humiliation this will cause him. Loosing face with his family would be devastating. Let's give him the benefit of the doubt. If he has been coerced, let's find out by who and why. Maybe Chang is not telling us something.'

Jonah's image disappeared. They moved off quickly to get Chang. They wanted to ask him further questions, but they would have to wait for a more opportune time. At least the situation was salvageable. They just had to corrupt the data that had been loaded to grid buoy node.

Chang of course was a willing participant. He hoped to save face by being seen to do the right thing. He hoped that by pleading his case about his family and the opportunity dangled in front of him that it was enough to convince everyone he was genuinely sorry.

They walked into the rec area where everyone had now gathered, waiting to see what the next step was.

'Chang, come with me,' said Jesse. 'Let's get this done before whoever you have given access to attempts to download all Connor's work.'

'OK,' said Chang as he followed Jesse up to the SAI console.

They moved off. The others quietly discussed what had happened. It seemed like they were at a turning point. Should they continue or abort the rescue attempt and get re-assigned to another mining run. They would still have to deal with the Sea Hunters though. The situation seemed hopeless.

At the SAI console Chang used his smartwatch and through SAI linked with an Eel drone and grid buoy node he had been using. As Jesse watched on, Chang used a short hack to load a virus onto the node and corrupt all the information. He showed Jesse, and she nodded her head.

'Great,' she said. 'Now, let's get on with recovering our rogue crew.'

They went back down to the rec area. Jesse debriefed them on what had happened and what they were going to do about it.

Chapter 20

At Xed Academy Jonah had spent most of the day communicating on and off with Ngarra and Jesse on their Skimmer. Sometimes it was only by message board. Other times she had a live feed. After six days of dealing with the situation unfolding out in the Pacific Ocean, she was tired. She almost thought it better to abort the rescue mission and let the Sea Hunters deal with it all.

The Council was going to meet yet again for an update. She needed to think about what to say. Rick would be there to. She was worried about him. Something just didn't seem right with all of this.

'I would rather be sitting on my deck with a wine in hand and overlooking the coast than dealing with this right now,' she thought out loud. 'Anyway, I had better get ready for this council meeting.'

While Jonah looked over her notes for the Council meeting Rick arrived. He had been at the crew monitoring centre.

'Afternoon Jonah,' he said as he walked into the meeting room. 'Let's hope the Council still sees things the way we do.'

'Yes, let's hope,' she said. 'I want to move on from all this but somehow I don't think that is going to happen.'

'What do you mean?' said Rick cautiously.

'It's nothing really,' said Jonah. 'Just a feeling.'

It was time so Jonah put her notes down. Rick wondered what was going through her mind. It would have to wait. The images of the other Council members appeared.

Jonah got straight into it. 'Here we are again everyone,' she said with a sigh.

They all nodded and exchanged greetings. Time was short so Jonah got straight to the point.

'Someone on the Skimmer has tried to access all of the information hub officers work and load it to a grid node. That person has been identified and questioned. We know it was done on the promise of a key position in

GlobeCorpMining,' said Jonah. 'I still think there is a lot this person is not telling us or even aware of though. They may have been coerced but I am not sure.'

'Who is it then?' said one of the Council members.

It's Chang,' said Rick. 'He's the son of GlobecorpMining's Chief Operations Officer.'

Jonah frowned at him. She didn't want his name mentioned at this stage. Now the Council knew it was the son of the GlobeCorpMining chief operations officer.

Rick shrugged his shoulders and carried on.

'If GlobeCorpMining gets hold of Connor's work it could end the Skimmer programme and what Xed has achieved.'

Jonah frowned again and with a facial expression mouthed 'what the hell are you doing.'

It could just be coincidence. It could be someone else entirely that wanted the technology. Rick motioned that he would tell her later. He carried on talking.

'We should let the Sea Hunters do their job and hand Connor's work over to them for safe keeping.'

Jonah was now angry as Rick had flipped and done the opposite of what they agreed. She quickly responded before Rick could carry on.

'No!' said Jonah. 'How is that going to help our rogue crew and keep Ngarra's team out of harm's way. What's more, we can't just give up what could be some significant technology if developed further. We have something others want so let's keep it that way.'

Rick thought for a while and considered his options. Jonah was a smart woman and had Xed and the Academy interests at heart. Rick still thought he could convince the Council they needed to change their business model. This potential technology could be just what he and the people he reported to needed.

A Council member spoke up. 'Maybe it should just go to GlobeCorpMining, they are a major funder of the Academy and Skimmer crew programme.'

'No, we should keep it all,' said Jonah. 'The potential benefits of its further development are undetermined, and we could leverage that into the future. If we just give it away it could be used to eliminate the need for Skimmer crews. We will no longer have a funded crew programme.'

'If its potential is that big,' said Rick, 'maybe in the process of detaining the crews the Sea Hunters will just take what Connor has come up with.'

'Why would the Sea Hunters know about this in the first place,' said one of the Council members.

Jonah kept her expression emotionless. Interesting point, she thought to herself. Rick has slipped up. Something is going on and he knows a lot more about it than he is letting on. Why is he keeping it to himself?

'I'm just saying,' said Rick flippantly. 'If they did happen to know, they would want to discredit the people that worked on it. Using the guise of carrying out emergency administrative orders issued by "the Authority" is a perfect cover.'

'I will talk with the Chief Operating Officer at GlobeCorpMining,' said Jonah. 'Maybe it was they who informed the Sea Hunters about this technology. We need to keep GlobeCorpMining onside, given that they are funding our Academy simulator training and crew programme.'

'Good point,' said a Council member. 'We will all wait to hear back from you Jonah.'

Everyone nodded and their images disappeared. Jonah and Rick were left standing there.

Jonah was frustrated. They still had no idea if Chang had been coerced, why if at all the Sea Hunters knew about the technology being developed and its potential, what was in it for them and how much GlobeCorpMining knew about it. On top of all that they had a rogue crew running around in a stolen Skimmer full of manganese nodules. She had told Chang's father very little. Something was up with Rick and it was not good. Nor did it seem things would end well for Xed and the Academy if he got his way with the Council.

'We need to get that rogue crew and Ngarra's crew back here,' said Rick.

He wanted to keep Jonah confused about what his intentions really were.

'If Connor's work is that important maybe as you said it should take priority. Maybe we should abort chasing down the rogue crew in a contractors Skimmer. Let the Sea Hunters deal with them. We can focus on getting Ngarra's crew back here with Connor's work.'

Rick could be very persuasive, so Jonah paused and thought.

'It's something we should consider,' she replied.

They walked off, moving through the administration building and deep in thought about what the best way forward was.

'Anyway,' said Rick. 'I have to catch up with a few people so I will meet you back in the sim centre later.'

Before Jonah had a chance to ask who he was catching up with Rick walked off.

Jonah made her way to the sim centre. She wanted to get an update from the crew she had selected to monitor and control the interface with the Harvester Skimmer SAI.

She took her time walking across campus. It had to work, she thought to herself. Despite what Rick was saying, they still had to at least try.

Once at the sim centre Jonah put aside her thoughts. She had to focus on the task at hand, which was to recover the rogue crew.

'I have a plan,' said Jonah over comms to the sim crew as she walked into the instructor area and watched them through the viewing screen. 'Ngarra's crew will corrupt the copy of Connor's work loaded to the grid node. When it is accessed externally, we will trace the origin of who is using it. At least that way we will know where they are, even if we are not able to do much about it yet.'

***

Just before Jonah had got there; Rick had been able to move unseen through the sim centre.

He passed through security and entered the Skimmer crew monitoring and communication complex. He moved quietly through without anyone on duty seeing him. He passed through security again and entered 'the room.'

Using an encrypted access code, he swiped his smart watch and opened a link. The SAItech grid buoy node appeared and an icon flashed. His contact on the Skimmer had done it he thought to himself smiling. Rick walked to a communication console at the end of one of the rows of data banks.

He got hold of his other contact. They would hold the data Connor had been working on.

'The grid node data is accessible,' Rick said to Max. 'I am sending it to you now.'

'Got it,' said Max. 'Downloading all the data. We will hold it in safe keeping for you. You may not be aware but there is another Skimmer closing on Ngarra's Skimmer. It has a signature, so it is not off-grid. Its signature is unique, and it has no mining history tagged to it.'

Skimmer signatures were linked or tagged with their Xtract mining work and crew monitoring history. By identifying its signature, its history, where it had been, the assigned crew, its load rate and other data could be interrogated.

'There is not much time left,' said Max. 'We are preparing to launch an interceptor drone with a breaching pod and boarding team.'

'OK,' said Rick. 'I will look into this other Skimmer. Close on Ngarra's Skimmer. Recover the off-grid Skimmer and its rogue crew. Detain Ngarra's crew and secure their information hub officer. His name is Connor.'

'We have a better plan. Wait for both crews to be on the one Skimmer. GlobeCorpMining is aware of the potential of this person's work,' said Max. 'We will separate him.'

'OK,' said Rick. 'Hold him onboard your vessel until you hear from me. I have to go.'

With that Rick swiped the smartwatch and their images disappeared. He disconnected from the grid buoy node and logged out of the system. It would just look like he was running a system check. He made his way back through to the sim centre.

Chapter 21

The next morning on Ngarra's Skimmer, seven days since they had finished their last mining run, Connor's mind was racing as he ran up to the information hub. Connor had been up late the night before. Tired, he had slept in and was eating in the rec area by himself. His smartwatch snapped him out of his thoughts as the alarm on it activated. Something was happening with the vector signal. Pushing his chair back quickly, he almost tripped over himself as he raced off. He passed Aamir and Stella as they came into the rec area. They saw the look on his face and raced after him.

'Must be something going on,' said Stella. I haven't seen our Connor move so fast.'

'Probably the change in direction from the off-grid Skimmer,' said Aamir. 'We must be close.'

Aamir raced after Stella. She was fit. One of the fittest on the crew.

Since yesterday the Xtract vector had been changing rapidly. Since yesterday Connor had thought the off-grid Skimmer might be moving towards them, unaware of closing on them. If Ngarra's Skimmer was picked up on long-range sonar it would be all on.

'We are in the vicinity of the off-grid Skimmer,' yelled Connor as they passed through the SAI console and raced to the information hub. 'I think it's moving towards us. They don't know we are here. Once it gets within range our long-range sonar should pick it up. They will pick us up as well.'

Jonny was in the SAI console checking over navigation projections as they raced past. He looked across at Stella.

'What's going on?' he said moving around the projection towards them.

'Party time,' said Stella.

'Boys and girls this it,' he said turning back to the navigation projection. 'Let's go get our rogue crew.'

He looked at the SAI console and the vector display. 'SAI, open Skimmer wide communication.'

'Confirmed.' said SAI.

'Ngarra, Jesse, Chang, come to the SAI console, it's all on folks.'

He rotated the navigation projection and focussed in on the area they expected the off-grid Skimmer to be in.

'Dead right Connor,' he said over open comms. 'What if they are coming this way because they know we are here? SAI has boxed in the area they are most likely to be in. SAI has created what the military used to call an outhouse.'

Chang arrived at the SAI console with Ngarra and Jesse and they raced around to where Jonny was standing.

'Those Xtracts on the off-grid Skimmer must be going nuts,' said Jonny as the others took in what they could see.

'What's the purpose of an outhouse anyway,' said Chang. 'What is it?'

'No time to explain,' said Jonny. 'Got one up on you there ay. Will explain later.'

Jonny's father was in the Navy and had said to him an outhouse was a forward projection of speed and direction on a chart using dead reckoning. At any given time, given a constant speed a vessel would be at point on that course. It was used to meet other assets when communication silence was required.

Chang was a little irritated that Jonny didn't explain what it was. His expression was a dead giveaway.

'Why would I listen to you anyway,' he said aggressively. He made sure Jonny was watching as he rubbed his jaw. 'Better to figure it out myself.'

'That's the trouble with you Chang my boy,' said Jonny. 'It's all about me me me and your troubles are everyone else's fault except your own.'

Chang's face went a little red and he clenched his fists. It was easy to get Chang wound up.

'Cut it out you two,' said Ngarra. 'No time for that rubbish. Let's get on with it. Do we have a confirmed sonar target yet? SAI confirm off-grid Skimmer detection by long-range sonar.'

'Confirmed,' said SAI. 'Off-grid Skimmer detected.'

Ngarra looked at everyone assembled at the SAI console. Jonny was good but when the pressure was on, he could get anxious and forget the obvious. Like confirming the sonar target.

They all looked to him for direction now.

In the information hub Connor was listening in on the conversation over open comms with Stella and Amir. He was distracted by Jonny and Chang's bickering and had a blank look on his face. Momentarily his mind was somewhere else. The bickering reminded him of the incident that had happened previously. Stella and Aamir watched as he had started pacing and muttering to himself. He snapped out of it when he heard Ngarra's voice over top of the other two.

'It's more than that!' said Connor excitedly. 'There's an unusual spread in the vector calculations.

Jonny, zoom right in on the projection you have,' said Jesse. 'If you look closely there are multiple vectors now. Like a scatter gun.'

'SAI,' said Ngarra. 'Zoom in on navigation projection, fine scale.'

SAI re-orientated the navigation hologram and expanded it outwards.

It was weird, thought Jesse. It almost felt like the projection was going to swallow the crew around it.

'Shit,' said Jesse. Standing back, she had been thinking about what to do and was growing a little concerned about whether her crew were capable of doing this.

'What is that?' she said stepping forward and pointing.

In the information hub Stella was getting excited about the whole situation.

'Come on guys this is it, she said over open comms. We need to get ready. Stop stuffing around. If the rogue crew has detected our presence, we don't know how they are going to react. It's likely they will use their ARC array or even their ARC torpedoes.'

Her enthusiasm to get on with things bubbled over.

Connor looked at Stella and Aamir. He could see their expressions. Was it excitement or concern or both, he thought to himself.

Jonny looked at the navigation hologram. Three points separated out.

SAI interrupted everyone. 'ARC torpedo array detected; cavitation impact imminent.'

'Spot on Stella,' Jonny cried out. 'Boy, they crept up on us quick!'

'You should have been watching,' said Chang. 'Not up for the task I say.'

'You should keep your mouth shut before I come in there and shut it for you boy,' said Jonny.

The bickering over open comms was getting heated. Jesse watched, thinking how close she was to pulling the pin on all this and letting it go.

'Come on guys, this isn't the time or place,' said Stella.

For the next few minutes an argument ensued over open comms which distracted everyone from what was going on.

Aamir watched on with a frown on his face. Not good enough he thought to himself.

Ngarra had to step in eventually and get them back on task and focussed.

'Cut it out! All of you,' said Ngarra yelling over open comms. 'Jonny make sure our ARC array and torpedo array are still armed. SAI calculate and execute optimal escape route to deflect any direct impact from cavitation bubbles.'

It was at that moment there was a shudder, then a sequence of further shudders from the rear to the front through the Skimmer.

The SAI alarms for propulsion and power were flashing. The status of systems displayed around the SAI console updated.

'Propulsion and power system interrupted, at 90% recovery,' said SAI.

The propulsion and power system on the Skimmer could resist repeated disruption. It would only go offline and reboot if the Skimmer took a direct hit from a cavitation bubble. However, with repeated impacts, percentage recovery would continue to diminish. It was only a matter of time before they would be suspended in the ocean and unable to move.

Another shudder went through the Skimmer and SAI said, 'interruption to propulsion and power system, recovery at 80%.'

'Shit! That was quick.' said Ngarra. 'Come on people let's get onto this damn it. Jonny, put your interface lenses on. Synch with SAI, evade and respond.'

Jonny grabbed the lenses and said, 'SAI activate operator interface for defensive tactics.'

'Confirmed,' said SAI. 'Interface defensive tactics available.'

His lenses displayed virtual reality imaging and real time sensor feeds of the surrounding water column.

'I've only ever done this in simulation,' he said.

Jonny was now in a gamer's world of augmented reality. It was like being in a giant simulation within which you could move around, change views and angles, call up status reports, use sensor information and select defensive weapons and targets. Through it all SAI calculated and advised Jonny on the best possible outcomes for the Skimmer and its crew, the preservation of life.

Jesse had been largely silent, contemplating their course of action.

'Obviously, this rogue crew don't want to talk,' she said. 'We will have to disable their Skimmer and then establish communication.'

'Agree,' said Ngarra as Jonny got SAI to alter the propulsion drives and the Skimmer veered sharply, a shudder was felt but it was minor.

Jonny burst out with his voice, 'like being taken on a roller coaster ride isn't it!'

With his interface lenses on and being synched with SAI he thought about the old Robocop or Terminator movies from decades ago. Jonny liked watching old movies. He snapped back to the task at hand.

'The off-grid skimmer is closing fast,' he said. 'SAI, calculate time to be in range for use of close quarters ARC array.'

'Estimated time is five minutes,' said SAI.

'Cutting it close,' said Jonny. 'But we like a tight game. Down to the wire with being disabled boys and girls.'

Once within range it would only take a few direct hits by the off-grid Skimmer to disrupt propulsion and power and shut down the Skimmer. They would be dead in the water and require a complete system reboot. They would be vulnerable and exposed.

They were now to close to use an ARC torpedo array. It would take too long for the torpedo to deploy the array and triangulate the cavitation bubble.

In the information hub everyone was listening intently to what was being said at the SAI console.

'Might I suggest,' said Aamir, 'that we think about getting their Xtracts to launch and head to the coordinates you set Connor.'

'Exactly,' said Ngarra. 'We need a direct hit on this off-grid Skimmer to disable it,' said Ngarra. 'Why not use their Xtracts and ours to distract them so we can get close enough?'

'Connor is onto it now,' said Stella over open comms. 'We have their exact location. He should be able to get SAI to make them launch using a laser communication signal. They are designed so that one Skimmer can take control of another Skimmers Xtracts if needed.'

'Do it and quickly!' said Ngarra. 'SAI, launch our Xtracts, proceed with Xtracts to set coordinates. Skimmer to match Xtract speed. Position all Xtracts in front of Skimmer.

'Confirmed,' said SAI.

Along each recess Xtracts activated and one by one the docking clamps released them.

'Jonny,' said Ngarra. 'When we get close enough work with SAI and use the ARC array to disable the off-grid Skimmer. Connor get SAI to use your ocean bubble hologram simulation to link with the Xtracts and take control.'

There was another shudder and SAI said, 'impact recovery at 70%.'

'We need to end this fast,' said Ngarra. 'The Sea Hunters are approaching and will deploy an interceptor drone and breaching pod.'

Ngarra continued to watch the navigation, propulsion and power displays as SAI compensated for the impact of the cavitation bubbles.

In the information hub Connor had got SAI to use a laser communication signal to get the off-grid Xtracts to launch. They were also now moving towards the set coordinates. But how could he get all those launched Xtracts to do something they would not otherwise do? They would all be individually controlled. Connor needed them to be in some sort of responsive group formation.

He thought quickly, in his ocean bubble hologram, he had got his own group of simulated Xtracts to respond much like a group of schooling fish. However, the simulation always fell apart. He thought about nature. Nature had many examples of group behaviour in response to a stimulus, event or threat.

Connor looked over at Stella and Aamir and thought to himself out loud, 'what populations in nature act in unison to provide a barrier either for their home or to protect everyone else? Ants will swarm over another organism to protect the colony at the expense of themselves but that is not a barrier. For bait balls of fish, the outer and inner ones rotate their positions trying to protect both themselves and the rest. They sense a change in an adjacent fish position and adjust accordingly.'

Stella and Aamir watched on as Connor carried on thinking to himself.

'So,' he continued. 'Any hack would have to command the Xtracts in our simulation, which is now linked to the ones outside to stay together and move when we actually move.'

Connor looked at the ocean bubble for a few minutes and then his eyes lit up.

'I know!' he said excitedly, talking to his ocean bubble Xtracts. 'The Skimmer needs to be thought of as one of the Xtracts, not another object. So, we just need to make their Xtracts and ours think that we are also an Xtract. Then in the simulation when we move our Skimmer, all Xtracts will adjust their positions relative to us.'

It was like being in a bait ball. Not direct communication but sensing through vibration in the water a change relative to each other and adjusting position accordingly.

With the help of SAI Connor inserted a simulated Skimmer into the hologram. He trialled several hacks to the layered algorithms and source code for his ocean bubble hologram that now represented all the off-grid Skimmer Xtracts that had been launched and their own Skimmer.

Through test sets of data, he made the Xtracts learn to gather around and protect the Skimmer from being pounded by ARC arrays. Like the giant squid scenario, he had used previously. It seemed to work and got better the more iterations it did. He then got SAI to link the simulated Skimmer with their Skimmer.

'It will work long enough,' he thought to himself.

'Ngarra,' he said over open comms. 'I have it. I have linked the simulation to all the Xtracts outside. They will react to our movements and will adjust their positions relative to us. It will work for a short time. They will provide a barrier. Every time Jonny moves the Skimmer, they will adjust position relative to us. Like being in a bait ball of fish.

'Great stuff!' said Ngarra. 'We are onto it.'

Jonny smiled and pointed both fingers at the SAI console saying, 'it's you and me babe.' He carried on working with SAI to position the Skimmer.

Chapter 22

The sim team at Xed Academy were using the Harvester Skimmer they had control of to distract the approaching Sea Hunters.

'SAI, prepare to launch ARC torpedo array at the off-grid Skimmer,' said the sim team leader.'

The simulator SAI responded, 'confirmed, ARC torpedo array armed, coordinates locked.'

'SAI, launch torpedo array,' he said.

Onboard the Harvester Skimmer the torpedo array exited the breach and disappeared into the depths of the ocean. Once within range it would release its array. The array would triangulate and focus the release of cavitation waves to form a bubble targeting the propulsion and power system of the off-grid Skimmer.

Jonah watched the sim team from the instructor area. They were just as nervous as everyone else. If they didn't pull this off the fallout from what was going on could cost them their jobs. The Council would demand they step down and GlobeCorpMining would deny any involvement. If this all goes south, we need a plan to protect Xed and ourselves she thought to herself. Whoever is behind all this has a lot of influence. She watched on as the sim team did what they could to delay the Sea Hunters while also assisting with recovery of the rogue crew.

***

On Ngarra's Skimmer SAI picked up the signature of the ARC torpedo array.

'ARC torpedo array launched,' said SAI.

'SAI, confirm target,' said Ngarra.

'Torpedo array launched from Harvester Skimmer at off-grid Skimmer,' said SAI.

SAI received an incoming message request from the sim team leader at Xed Academy.

'Laser communication signal,' said SAI. 'Eel drone and grid buoy proximity sub-optimal, message only.'

'Ngarra,' said the sim team leader as their image appeared on screen and relayed the message. 'We are within range of the off-grid Skimmer and have released an ARC torpedo array. That should keep them busy long enough for you to get organised. '

Ngarra recorded his message in response for SAI to send to the sim team leader.

'We know,' said Ngarra. 'Connor has also been able to get SAI to take control of their Xtracts and group them with ours. We have them formed up between us. They adjust themselves relative to each other and to us. Like a bait ball of fish. Now we just need to disable the off-grid Skimmer and get the crew off before the Sea Hunters show up.'

SAI sent the recorded message and they waited for a response. It wasn't long before they got a reply message.

'The rogue crew can't use their ARC array on both our Skimmers at once,' said the sim team leader. 'From our end we should be able to disable them using the ARC torpedo array while also standing off far enough to distract the Sea Hunters.'

***

At that moment the Harvester Skimmer SAI the sim team were monitoring and controlling detected another signature closing its position.

'SAI confirm identity of new signature,' said the sim team leader.

'Confirmed,' said SAI. 'Signature is from a Sea Hunter interceptor drone.'

'Damn!' said the sim team leader. 'The Sea Hunters have launched an interceptor drone.'

Once the drone was close its breaching pod would be deployed and attempt to couple with the Skimmers topside hatch and airlock, board them and detain the crew. The interceptor drone could also launch an ARC torpedo array.

The sim team leader sent another recorded message to Ngarra.

'I am not sure how long we will last until the Sea Hunters disable our Harvester Skimmer,' said the sim team leader. 'We will not be able to help you after that. You have to get the rogue crew and get out of there.'

A pause followed and the sim team received a reply message from Ngarra.

'Go,' said Ngarra. 'Do your thing, we will be OK.'

The sim team carried on knowing that sooner or later the Skimmer they were controlling would be disabled and they would no longer be able to assist.

***

Travelling just below the ocean surface the interceptor drone launched by the Sea hunters was approaching the three Skimmers fast. The breaching team were strapped into the pod. When the pod was released, it would approach and clamp onto the Skimmer hull topside entry hatch and airlock.

On the Sea Hunter vessel Alex and Max were overseeing operations. They were tracking the interceptor drone and its breaching pod and boarding team.

'If we can disable the Harvester Skimmer that will be one less thing to deal with,' said Max.

The Sea Hunter SAI had been tracking the interceptor drone and interrupted Alex and Max.

'Interceptor torpedo array launched,' said SAI.' Cavitation bubble impact with Harvester Skimmer confirmed. Propulsion system interrupted.'

The crew aboard the breaching pod had launched an interceptor torpedo array.

'Good,' said Alex. 'SAI, launch a Sea Hunter ARC torpedo array at Harvester Skimmer.'

'Confirmed,' said SAI. 'ARC torpedo array launched.'

'Another direct hit by us should stop the Harvester Skimmer dead in the water,' said Max. 'Then we can close the other Skimmer, wait for them to recover the rogue crew from the off-grid one, disable it and then get that breaching pod deployed from the interceptor for a boarding.'

The duty operations officer swiped his hand across the screen on the SAI console, He pulled up a navigation hologram of the situation unfolding around them. He used the icons to touch and drag assets, directing them where to go.

'Either this Harvester Skimmer crew has little experience in defensive tactics and deploying ARC arrays or there is no one on board,' he said.

The ARC torpedo array they had launched closed on the Harvester Skimmer and activated.

'ARC torpedo cavitation bubble impact confirmed,' said SAI. 'Propulsion system interrupted. Harvester Skimmer has reduced speed.'

The Sea Hunters closed the Harvester Skimmer. 'Right,' said Alex. 'Let's use our close quarters ARC array and finish it off.'

Max commanded SAI to target the Harvester Skimmer, which had turned to port and was slowly ascending. The Sea Hunter vessel also turned sharply to Port, keeping adjacent to the direction it was moving in under water.

The schematics of the ARC array appeared on screen and Alex and Max watched as it initialised, powered up and released its triangulated cavitation waves. There was no escaping the resulting cavitation bubble aimed at the Skimmers propulsion and power systems.

'It's stopped dead in the water now,' said the duty operations officer.

'Leave it and let's move on to the other Skimmer,' said Max. 'It will surface anyway. How is our interceptor drone and breaching pod doing?'

They turned their attention to Ngarra's Skimmer. Both Alex and Max were hoping Ngarra's Skimmer was now close to the off-grid one.

***

The off-grid Skimmer was continuously altering its position and using its close quarters ARC array to try and disable Ngarra's Skimmer. The off-grid Skimmer Xtracts between them were taking the brunt of the cavitation bubbles.

'Come on Jonny,' said Ngarra. 'We need a good line through all these Xtracts to the off-grid Skimmer so we can disable it.

'The problem is,' said Jonny, 'that the Xtracts now react to our every move. If we try to move out of the group, they adjust accordingly like a bait ball of fish.'

In the information hub Connor heard the discussion coming from the SAI console.

'Listen, listen guys. To overcome the problem,' he said, 'we need to change position fast. As if a predator has moved in on the group. We will then briefly be on the outer edge. Just move straight through and they will part briefly. That's your chance before they close around us again.'

'If it doesn't work,' said Chang over comms from the SAI console, 'we are screwed.'

'That is one way to put it,' said Aamir from the information hub as both he and Stella watched what Connor was up to. 'But I trust Connor's work.'

'Right, Connor good work with the Xtracts,' said Ngarra. 'Jonny, take us straight through those Xtracts.'

'On to it,' said Jonny.

'Get ready on my count,' said Ngarra. 'Three, two, one, now.'

Jonny got SAI to move the Skimmer at maximum speed through the Xtracts.

'Now,' said Ngarra just as they broke through to the outer perimeter of the Xtracts surrounding them.

Everyone was on edge. In the SAI console Chang, Ngarra and Jesse watched on as Jonny coordinated with SAI to disable the off-grid Skimmer using the ARC array. In the information hub Connor, Aamir and Stella watched as the ARC array was used. It had to work. Time was short.

At the SAI console they watched the navigation hologram. To the rear of the off-grid Skimmer the main propulsion system took a direct hit. The off-grid Skimmer shuddered, and the propulsion drive went offline. The Skimmer slowed to a halt, suspended in mid water, not moving.

'It worked,' said Stella jumping around in the information hub. The ocean bubble hologram showed the off-grid Skimmer as motionless and suspended in the water. The Xtracts in the simulation had moved back around their Skimmer. Outside, their Xtracts were now back in position, like a bait ball of fish they had parted and then closed around them again. Stella went to hug Connor and Aamir and thought better of it.

'Awesome,' said Jonny from the SAI console and followed up with a little fist pump. He stood up and did a little warrior dance.

'I like your work Jonny boy,' said Stella over comms. She smiled and winked at Aamir and Connor.

The rogue crew used a laser communication signal to communicate with Ngarra's Skimmer. Being stopped in the water and close to each other it was easy to transmit directly.

SAI received the signal and an image appeared on screen.

'You have us,' one of them said. 'You don't understand what you have done but you have us all the same. Our long-range sonar has picked up the interceptor drone. Get us off here before we are boarded and detained by the Sea Hunters.'

Part of the plan was for the Sea Hunters to board the off-grid Skimmer after they had disabled Ngarra's Skimmer. Plans had now changed.

'Use one of the escape pods and fast,' said Jesse. 'Time is short and yes the Sea Hunters are not far off. Our moon pool will be open.'

The laser communication signal link went silent.

Ngarra's crew looked at each other. A silent pause followed. For a moment you could have heard a pin drop.

'Incoming laser communication signal,' said SAI. 'Eel drone and grid buoy proximity nominal, live feed available.'

Their Skimmer was stopped in the water and surrounded by their Xtracts. The sim team at the Xed Academy had been waiting to hear what was going on. They tried to contact Ngarra.

'Open message board,' said Ngarra.

The sim team leader's image appeared.

'Ngarra, the Sea Hunters have disabled the Harvester Skimmer we were controlling. It's offline and going through a system reboot. You have an interceptor coming your way fast with a breaching pod and boarding crew.'

'We know,' said Ngarra. 'SAI is tracking it. The off-grid Skimmer is now also shut down and going through a system reboot. We are recovering the rogue crew. We are at 60% system recovery ourselves. At 30% we will start losing propulsion. It will be almost impossible to outrun the Sea Hunters by then. SAI will not compromise our life support system. Power will be diverted from propulsion and we will start slowing down.'

Jonah was also watching and listening in on what was unfolding.

'You have to go-off grid,' she said over comms to the sim team. Ngarra would be able to hear her voice 'Jesse knows what to do. Get the rogue crew on board and get out of there.'

'And go where!' exclaimed Chang listening in. 'We are in the middle of the Pacific Ocean!'

They will still in Skimmer wide comms mode so between the SAI console, the Xtract bay and the information hub everyone could hear and see what everyone else was saying.

Connor and Aamir looked at him and nodded their heads. He was right, they would have to disappear. In no way would they be able to outrun the Sea Hunters.

At the sim centre Jonah discussed this with the sim team. They got their SAI to project in hologram a map of the closest Island groups.

'Head towards the southern-most group of Cook Islands,' said Jonah. 'Most are now uninhabited Islands with low lying areas flooded by sea level rise. The shallow coral reefs are pretty much dead as well. Deeper parts of the reef are fine though. Find a deep lagoon to shelter in and wait. I will talk with GlobeCorpMining. Wait to hear from me.'

'GlobeCorpMining,' grumbled Chang. 'Out of the frying pan and into the fire.'

Chang didn't think telling his father what was going on in the hope they might get them out of trouble was a good idea at all. It was embarrassing enough that he was caught up in all this and if his father found out what he had done he would disown him. I will prove my value to him yet, he thought to himself.

'It's not what you think,' said Jonah. 'Jesse and Ngarra get your Skimmer out of their as soon as you can. Don't let the Sea Hunters board you. Don't trust anything they say. Someone may be working with them to get hold of Connor's work.'

'OK,' said Jesse.

They once more faced with situation unfolding in the surrounding ocean.

***

At the sim centre Jonah stood looking out at the Skimmer simulator and the sim team. She was worried. What if the crews were detained by the Sea Hunters? Or worse, what if they got hurt or injured when their Skimmers were disabled.

She was thinking about this and what to say to GlobeCorpMining when Rick came in. He suddenly realised they had been monitoring and controlling a Skimmer remotely.

'I didn't know they were synched with and monitoring another Skimmer. Who's on it,' he said to Jonah.

'I didn't tell anyone,' said Jonah. 'But GlobeCorpMining has let us synch with and monitor one of their next generation Skimmers they have been working on at the Harvester. They have been trialling unmanned and remotely monitored Skimmers.'

'You could have told me,' said Rick with a sigh. 'I had better go and chase up our Sea Hunter liaison officer here on campus about all this.'

With a frustrated look on his face, he frowned at Jonah and walked off. On the way out he said to her, 'let's hope the Sea Hunters do not catch up with either crew, and that they get out of there in one piece.'

He wanted Jonah to think he looked disappointed. He wanted Jonah to think he cared about what was going on; to think he was disappointed about not being told what was going on.

Ricks mind was someone else though. He had overheard the end of the conversation between the sim team leader and Ngarra's crew. He had to contact the Sea Hunters and tell them to secure Ngarra's Skimmer before they went off-grid.

Rick made sure Jonah didn't notice and walked through the instructor area between the two large Skimmer simulators. At the rear he passed security and entered the crew monitoring and communications area. Once inside he could see a few people on duty watching and monitoring Skimmer crews. They had all gathered around the monitoring station that had Ngarra's crew vitals on it. Rick walked past them and briefly said hello, trying to look casual. He passed through security again and into "the room".

He was making a habit of popping into "the room" lately and hoped no one noticed too much. He swiped his smartwatch and used his secure communication link to get hold of Max. He waited and then his image appeared.

'Max,' he said. 'I do not have much time, Ngarra's Skimmer will go off-grid soon and you will not be able to track them. You need to disable it and board them.'

'It's organised chaos out here,' said Max. 'I have Xtracts everywhere, two disabled Skimmers and another one trying to do God knows what. Our interceptor and breaching pod are about to attempt a boarding. We will focus on Ngarra's Skimmer.'

'OK,' said Rick. 'Talk soon.' Max's image flickered, and his image disappeared.

Rick rushed off and exited the secure area before people became suspicious. He walked back through the crew communications and monitoring area. No one was looking his way.

His concern was growing. Was there any chance of getting hold of all the work that had been developed on that Skimmer or even Connor, the person that had come up with it.

He thought about it some more. Chang's sister was on the Harvester and part of the laboratory team developing next generation remotely monitored Skimmers. Just one step away from autonomous mining operations.

Their father was senior in GlobeCorpMining so detaining Chang on the pretence of collusion with his sister and the Chinese made sense and would force their hand in all this.

Where was that Sea Hunter liaison officer, he thought to himself? Always so hard to track him down on campus.

***

On Ngarra's Skimmer Connor was looking at the ocean bubble hologram. In it was now a simulation of their own Skimmer in amongst all the Xtracts in the ocean around them. The Xtracts were keeping their group positions relative to each other and the Skimmer.

The trouble was, he thought to himself that in the previous simulations when he introduced a foreign object for them to surround if it threatened one of them it all broke down. The Xtracts eventually wandered off randomly. He had not been able to get them to learn. Connor tagged the Sea Hunter vessel in the ocean bubble hologram. He also tagged the interceptor that had been launched and was heading towards them.

He wanted the off-grid Xtracts to see the object as a threat and not just something in their surroundings to avoid. They would then move around it if it got too close to any one of them. He needed them to do it just long enough for SAI to shut down the simulation link. The off-grid Xtracts would then stay in position and they could recover theirs.

'Ngarra,' said Connor from the Information hub over the open comms link.

'Yes Connor,' said Ngarra.

'The only way to get our own Xtracts back is to shut down the simulation link and turn and run. The off-grid Xtracts will then hold position and provide a barrier while we recover ours. Then we move off as fast as we can and go off-grid. The tricky part will be moving beyond sonar detection range.'

'That will be risky,' said Ngarra. 'We are at 60% recovery. If we take any more hits we will start to slow down. There will not be enough power for propulsion without compromising other systems.'

Stella was with Connor, listening with Aamir and said, 'SAI has recovered Xtracts underway before, it's not hard. It's only when using the moon pool that we must be stopped. We must be stopped to recover the escape pod from the off-grid Skimmer.'

'Make it happen Stella,' said Ngarra urgently. 'Tell us when you are ready. We don't have much time.'

'OK,' said Stella. 'Come with me Aamir.' They left Connor to it and raced off to the Xtract bay to coordinate the recovery operation.

Chapter 23

In the escape pod the rogue crew were heading straight for Ngarra's Skimmer. They were nervous. The situation was out of their control. Threats had been made against their families if they didn't comply with the demands of the people that had made them take their Skimmer off-grid.

Under the guise of stealing nodules, they had been coerced into causing havoc in "the Area". They were meant to disable Ngarra's Skimmer and wait to be boarded themselves. It had all gone wrong. Worried and anxious, they approached the group of Xtracts and Ngarra's Skimmer.

Connor was in the information hub looking at the ocean bubble hologram. SAI had shut down the link to the Xtracts. Connor could no longer control them. The Xtracts from the off-grid Skimmer were stationary and positioned not far from their Skimmer. Connor felt strange, like a part of him was not working. He had become so connected to the ocean bubble hologram and his work. He stood in silence looking into the hologram.

Meanwhile in the Xtract bay it couldn't be more different. Stella, Aamir and Chang were preparing to recover the escape pod and their own Xtracts. In a flurry of activity, they had got SAI to pressurise the airlock and moon pool. The moon pool entrance was open, waiting to receive the escape pod. Outside along each recess the docking clamps were open, waiting to receive the Xtracts.

'Stella,' said Ngarra over comms from the navigation console. 'We are at full stop and ready. The escape pod is inbound. Will the Xtracts get in the way?'

'No,' said Stella in reply. 'Connor has shut down the simulation and its link to the Xtracts. Ours are being recovered. The escape pod can move straight through.'

'Great,' said Ngarra. 'Standby to receive the pod and crew.'

Escape pods were designed to do three things; go to the surface, dock with the topside hatch of a Skimmer or submarine and lastly use a moon pool of a Skimmer or Harvester.

'SAI confirm moon pool is ready to receive off-grid Skimmer escape pod,' said Stella.

'Confirmed,' said SAI. 'Moonpool is ready.'

'How do we know they will not be aggressive and make demands or do something worse,' said Chang.

'It doesn't matter,' said Stella. 'They will be stuck in the maintenance bay. They are not going anywhere until we get out of this mess.'

'That will do it,' said Chang as he looked at Aamir and managed a smile.

Chang seemed a have got over himself, Stella thought to herself. He had gone out of his way to help them out of the situation they were in.

At the SAI console Jonny, Jesse and Ngarra were ready to escape the mayhem. Between the information hub, the Xtract bay and the SAI console everyone was closed up and ready.

Jonny was tense. Time was running out. If they didn't get it right, they were screwed.

Ngarra!' exclaimed Jonny. 'Those off-grid Skimmer Xtracts will not distract the Sea Hunter vessel and Interceptor for long.'

Jonny still had his interface lenses on and was monitoring the status of the Xtracts on the tactical display. He used his hands to zoom in and out and rotate the projections.

Ngarra looked at the projections Jonny was rotating.

'Stella,' he said over comms. 'Get our Xtracts docked. Once the Interceptor drone is in range, they will finish us off, deploy the breaching pod and board us. We need to get out of here and fast. Let's go, hurry up!'

Jesse watched on hoping her crew would hold it together long enough for them to get out of there.

In the Xtract bay Stella, Aamir and Chang watched as the escape pod surfaced in the moon pool. A robotic arm secured it and lifted it up and out of the water and into the adjacent airlock. The moon pool entrance closed, armed itself and the area returned to one atmosphere of breathable air. The airlock closed and then also adjusted to one atmosphere. The other side then opened into the maintenance bay. The escape pod was moved through and the airlock closed behind them. The robotic arm lowered it to the deck where a docking clamp secured it.

'Escape pod retrieved,' said SAI.

A hatch opened and the rogue crew stepped out of the escape pod. Stella, Aamir and Chang watched them. They looked exhausted and a little scared.

'You have some explaining to do,' said Stella. 'You lot will have to stay in there until we get safely away from here. We will talk later. An interceptor drone and breaching pod is about to engage us.'

'What's with all those Xtracts out there and how on earth did you get ours to launch,' said one of them in a weary voice.

'Don't worry about that,' said Chang, 'it's part of the reason we haven't been disabled.'

'OK,' he said sighing and sitting on the deck.

They all sat down on the maintenance bay deck and looked back at the airlock. A look of worry, as if they half expected it to open.

Maybe they wished the ocean would just take them Aamir thought to himself.

'I will keep an eye on them,' said Aamir. 'You two can get on with recovering the Xtracts.'

'OK Chang,' said Stella. 'Would you like to get this done.'

'Onto it,' said Chang. 'You lot need all the help you can get to get out of this mess.'

Stella and Chang monitored the recovery of the rest of their Xtracts. Chang moved off and raced down each side of the Skimmer to check the docking displays.

With all the activity going on the others had not noticed how close the interceptor drone and breaching pod were. At the SAI console a sense of panic was growing. Jesse had removed herself from it. Taking it all in and tapping her fingers on the bulkhead. Her role was one she didn't want to have to do; to step in and prepare the crew for a boarding under such circumstances was a hard ask.

'Ngarra,' said Jonny as he looked at the situation unfolding. We do not have much time.'

The interceptor drone was closing fast. Once they were disabled the breaching pod would be released. It would dock with the Skimmer, creating a watertight airlock through which to enter and board.

'Shit!' said Ngarra as he looked at the navigation hologram and the approaching pod. 'Hurry up Stella,' he said over comms. 'Jonny, get SAI to launch an ARC torpedo at the interceptor.'

SAI said, 'confirm command statement.'

Jesse had been watching. Contemplation of her next move was interrupting by what Ngarra had just said.

'No!' she shouted. 'We can't come back from that. So far, we are just on the run. An act of aggression is a whole other level.'

SAI did not execute statements that did not start with SAI.

In the Xtract bay they could all hear through open comms what was going on. Aamir was still watching the rogue crew locked in the maintenance bay. Aamir was listening to everything being said and suddenly had a great idea.

'Ngarra, I suggest using our ARC array on the off-grid Xtracts stuck in position out there. The pressure wave from the cavitation bubbles will send them backwards. The interceptor drone will have to take evasive action. It will slow them down a little. We just have to position ourselves broadside to do it while we also finish recovering the Xtracts and then move off.'

'All of the above, now!' yelled Ngarra over comms. 'SAI, position Skimmer to use ARC array. Target remaining off-grid Skimmer Xtracts.'

'Confirmed,' said SAI. 'Moving into position. ARC array armed.'

Jonny worked with SAI to coordinate the positioning of the Skimmer and deployment of the ARC array.

In the Xtract bay Stella updated everyone on the status of recovering Xtracts. As each one docked Chang checked their display, moving along the inside of each recess.

'We have four more Xtracts to dock on their clamps,' he said.

Stella watched them on the camera system from the main console as one by one they proceeded towards the Skimmer and onto docking clamps. She wished it was faster. They were cutting it close with getting away.

At the SAI console Jonny targeted cavitation bubbles at the remaining off-grid Xtracts from the other Skimmer. The array powered up.

Ngarra and Jesse viewed the navigation display. Jonny was excited. It was amusing to watch.

'Watch this!' said Jonny to the crew. 'Batter up and going for a home run.'

He laughed at himself. There were nervous smiles from Jesse and Ngarra. A nervous chuckle could be head over open comms from the others in the Xtract bay.

Like a game of chess, it all had to come together thought Jesse. So far, it looked like they would pull it all off. The Xtracts were just about recovered, the remaining ones from the off-grid Skimmer were being sent backwards into the path of the interceptor drone.

In the Xtract bay Chang finished checking each docking display. All the Xtract docking clamps were engaged. He then checked the power and control system status of each one.

'All Xtracts recovered,' said Chang as he raced back to the Xtract bay console.

'We are ready,' said Stella over comms.

'SAI,' said Ngarra. 'Turn 90 degrees to Port, head due North at maximum speed.'

'Confirmed,' said SAI.

The Skimmer turned in a wide arc and gathering speed started moved off.

'Once we move off,' said Jonny, 'we can no longer triangulate the ARC array. Everything will be behind us. The disabled Xtracts will not delay them for long. The Interceptor drone and breaching pod will move around them and close us.'

They watched the navigation projection as the Sea Hunter interceptor drone and its breaching pod approached the disabled Xtracts that had been sent flying backwards in the water.

'We need to go offline now!' said Jesse as she came over to where Jonny was sitting and stood behind him.

'We are not far enough away, there's no point, it won't work damn it!' exclaimed Ngarra. 'They will be able to track us on sonar. Get us out of here Jonny max speed.'

'Got that,' Jonny said as he swiped propulsion icons and SAI took control.

'SAI, divert all power to propulsion and engage overspeed,' said Ngarra.

'Confirmed, power diverted and overspeed engaged,' said SAI.

'We will have to try and outrun them,' said Jesse.

The Skimmer picked up speed. Everyone turned and watched the navigation hologram as the interceptor drone negotiated its way through the Xtracts. It slowed them down but not for long.

In the Xtract bay Aamir was watching the rogue crew in the maintenance bay and thinking intensely. He had a furrow on his forehead and was deep in thought.

'Our crush depth is 200 metres,' he said over open comms. 'A breaching pod crush deep is the same. What if we descend to our depth limit? The interceptor will follow and gain on us. As we ascend, they will be directly behind us and closing fast. On ascent we override the Xtract safety protocols. We release their loading buckets one at a time from the rear to the front. They will be dragged into our wake. Our propulsion system will push them straight at the interceptor drone. They will have to take evasive action and will likely take several hits. They will have to surface. That will give us the time we need to disappear.'

Over open comms everyone heard what Aamir had said. They all considered the idea. The discussion started to get a little heated. Jonny was usually the go in 'all guns blazing' type. However, this time he was not impressed at all. Jesse didn't like it either but for her, their options were running out.

'That is a breach of mining protocols!' exclaimed Jonny. 'Imagine the trouble we will be in not to mention one expensive contractor bill to pay.'

Jonny stood up and started pointing his finger at the others. Jesse could see the crew was at breaking point.

'We are just a bunch of youth monitoring a Skimmer,' said Jonny as he yelled at them. 'Geeze, I didn't sign up to knock out Sea Hunter drones.' Jonny was getting pretty wound up and aggressive.

Jesse's hand moved towards her belt. Reassuringly she rested her hand on the stun rod and pouch containing a syringe filled with sedative.

'Come on,' said Chang jokingly. 'We are already in a world of trouble. You're supposed to be the cowboy in this posse.'

Jesse jumped in before the argument turned into something more. 'Do you want to be detained by the Sea Hunters!' she exclaimed. 'Who knows what their agenda is now. We have no idea.'

Jonny backed off a bit. He was still fuming about the whole situation. He was over it.

'True,' said Ngarra as he raised his voice. 'We have no time to debate this! Take our chances after being caught by the Sea Hunters and detained or do what Aamir said. Jonah was quite clear that we need to avoid being detained.'

'I do not like this!' yelled Jonny. 'We are about to do something that could get us in a lot of troubled. I didn't sign up for that!'

Jonny took off his interface lenses and stormed off waving them off dismissively.

They were just that thought Jesse. A bunch of youth monitoring a sub-surface mining skiff.

'Get back here and get a grip!' said Ngarra yelling at Jonny as he stormed out. 'We are a team and we will stay a team! Time to grow up everyone one and live another day.'

'Good one Bruce,' said Stella over comms and with a chuckle. She was thinking about the old Die-Hard movies starring Bruce Willis. In the Xtract bay they heard everything going on. Looking at each other they shrugged their shoulders, not knowing what to do.

'Rubbish!' said Jonny as he left them to it.

'Do it!' yelled Jesse. 'I am responsible for the safety and security of this Skimmer and its crew! Something else is going on here. If Jonah thinks someone has another agenda, then I trust her judgement. It's my call so do it now!'

Jesse nodded at Ngarra. If they did not take control of the situation the team would fall apart.

'SAI, descend to two hundred metres,' said Ngarra. 'Angle ten degrees down.'

'Confirmed,' said SAI. 'Descend to two hundred metres, angle ten degrees down.'

As the Skimmer descended the interceptor drone and breaching pod continued to close on them and fast. It was within ARC array range now. The interceptor moved away from them exposing its port side to create an angle to triangulate a cavitation bubble.

'ARC array detected,' said SAI. 'Cavitation bubble impact imminent.'

The Skimmer shuddered and system displays faltered but carried on.

'Skimmer at 50% recovery,' said SAI. 'Diverting non-essential power to propulsion.'

'That's low,' said Chang over comms from the Xtract bay. 'We should turn out on an angle ourselves and use the ARC array. No point releasing the loading bins. They need to be behind us.'

In the Xtract bay Stella was trying to keep calm. Chang was getting anxious, moving around, muttering and waving his hand at thin air as if he was trying to tell the Skimmer what to do. Aamir was watching him. He looked at Stella. She was trying to keep it together as well. So much for a quite ride monitoring mining operations he thought to himself.

At the SAI console Ngarra thought quickly. Time was running short. If he did not act now, it would all be over. They would be disabled, boarded and detained. He looked at the Skimmer monitoring systems status.

'SAI will tolerate 40% recovery guys,' he said looking at the Skimmer monitoring system status. 'But it's damn close to the critical 30% recovery before emergency life support systems are prioritised over propulsion. Remember if not disabled, at 10% recovery SAI will surface the Skimmer no matter what.'

SAI always prioritised human life over everything else. It was a default that was built into its primary protocols.

'At two hundred metres and levelling off,' said SAI. 'Starting ascent to a hundred metres.

'No!' said Ngarra. 'SAI, descend to two hundred and fifty metres, angle ten degrees down. Then ascend to a hundred metres, angle ten degrees up.'

'Deny,' said SAI. 'Require Skimmer depth limit override to go beyond crush depth.'

'SAI, command override,' said Jesse. 'SAI, override crush depth.'

SAI would go to the limit of the safety margin and no more. Only Jesse could override Skimmer life support protocols. She said, 'A Skimmer will go deeper, there is a safety margin built in.'

'SAI descend to two hundred and fifty metres, angle ten degrees down then ascend to a hundred metres, angle ten degrees up,' said Ngarra.

'Confirmed,' said SAI. 'Descend to two hundred and fifty metres, angle ten degrees down, then ascend to a hundred metres, angle ten degrees up.'

'An interceptor drone will not go beyond its crush depth,' said Ngarra. 'They will level off and try to come over top of us and end up right behind us.'

The whole crew were now hoping they would pull all this off and get away.

Amongst all the hype and tension Jonny had come back to the SAI console. Jonny looked around at them all and held his hands in the air with fingers crossed.

'Sorry folks,' he said. 'A momentary lapse of reason.'

Stella heard what he said over open comms from the Xtract bay.

'So, so you think you can tell, heaven from hell then,' she said laughing nervously.

'What is it with you two!' said Ngarra with a frustrated look.

'Pink Floyd bro,' said Jonny. Can't you tell.'

'Cut it out,' said Jesse. 'Focus, this isn't a game!'

Stella and Jonny tended to joke around when it all got too much for them. It was their way of calming themselves. Jonny returned to his station and put the interface lenses back on. The SAI console now looked like a giant video game again.

'What do you mean this isn't a game,' said Jonny. 'It sure looks like it now boys and girls.'

There was a laugh from the whole crew. A strained laugh but a laugh none the same. Luckily, the comms link to the maintenance bay was inactive. The rogue crew had no idea what was going on.

At the SAI console Jesse overrode the Skimmer safety protocols to enable the Xtract loading buckets to be decoupled. Once this was done, they were good to go.

In the Xtract bay Stella and Chang were ready for action. They had got SAI to display all the Xtracts and their docking schematics.

'Stella release the Xtract loading bins,' said Ngarra.

'SAI,' said Stella. 'Decouple Xtract loading bins from front to rear at ten second intervals.'

On the screen in front of her was the coupling icon for the Xtract bins. She located the locking mechanism for each bin. Chang moved quickly, running along each recess swiping each lock on the displays.

Stella then swiped the master icon and watched as SAI controlled their release. The rear ones first followed by all the others; It minimised the chance of colliding bins causing any damage to the Skimmer.

At the SAI console the others watched through the camera system. The released bins entered the wake of the Skimmer. In overspeed mode they got a boost from the rim driven propulsion and as they rose and came in front of the interceptor drone.

It was now right behind them. It took evasive action but there were to many bins caught in the wake of the Skimmer. Despite repeated efforts to avoid being hit it started to take glancing blows. It slowed and changed direction, moving away from their Skimmer.

'It's falling behind,' said Ngarra.

As it slowed and turned away it took a glancing blow to its propulsion system. It stopped, then slowly scended to the surface.

SAI continued returning the Skimmer to its original course, depth and speed.

'Oh my god we did it, we did it!' shrieked Stella as she jumped up and down. 'We did it, we did it.' She grabbed Chang.

He winced as Stella gave him a bear hug. Not being one for showing much affection he was a little more than embarrassed.

'Get away woman!' he said.

He was of course relieved but still thought it stupid that they had not just stopped and let them board. In the back of his mind, he still had another agenda. It would have been the perfect opportunity.

Stella was going to hug Aamir as well. He was quick to avoid it. Forgetting cultural protocols, she was a little embarrassed and flushed red in the face.

At the SAI console Jonny was more than a little concerned about what they had just done.

'We are in serious trouble,' he said regretfully. 'Can't say I'm overly enthusiastic about it.'

'Maybe,' said Jesse. 'Let's deal with that later.'

Ngarra looked at Jonny. His shoulders were slumped forward. He had not seen him like this before. The warrior; always staunch and standing tall. Time to get Jonny back on side he thought to himself and forget about his little outburst. It was understandable, given the fact that none of them except Jesse and himself were expected to make such drastic decisions. After all, they were all meant to be monitoring mining operations. They were not rescuers or meant to be fugitives running from the Sea Hunters.

Despite this, everyone was relieved that they had pulled it off and recovered the rogue crew. They now had to find a place to hide and wait to be picked up and returned to Xed and the Academy.

'SAI take us off grid,' said Ngarra. 'Head due North.'

SAI responded, 'confirm command override protocol to go off grid.'

'SAI, command override, go off-grid,' said Jesse.

'Confirmed, preparing to go off-grid,' said SAI.

'I thought we were not to use that without Xed Academy approval,' said Jonny.'

'Nothing to worry about,' said Jesse.

Only Communication and Security officers could execute a command override to go off grid. Jesse was the only one that could give such a command to SAI.

'This is a unique situation and I will take full responsibility for the consequences. Jonny, monitor the situation and keep an eye on things out there.'

Jonny swiped the display in front of him and updated the navigation hologram. They would have to chart their way to wherever they were going. While he was doing this a threat detection alarm activated.

'ARC torpedo array detected,' said SAI.

'Bugger, the Sea Hunters,' said Jonny. 'They have anticipated our position. An ARC torpedo array is coming our way. Any impact and we will lose propulsion speed.

'They may not have our exact position,' said Ngarra as he quickly thought about what to do.

Stella and Chang were still in the Xtract Bay and heard what was going on. Chang had been looking at the rogue crew in the maintenance bay.

'What about the escape pod from the rogue crew we recovered,' he said. 'We can launch that as a decoy.'

Stella and Aamir thought it was worth a go and gave him the thumbs up.

'Great idea,' said Ngarra over the comms link. 'Stella, get that rogue crew out of the way. Get SAI to move the escape pod back into the air lock, pressurise and open the moon pool.'

He then turned to Jonny. 'Jonny, can you work with SAI to control the pod remotely?'

'Sure,' he said. 'Escape pod control systems are designed to interface directly with a Skimmer. SAI, link and display the control systems for the escape pod.'

'Confirmed, escape pod control systems accessed,' said SAI as the schematics appeared in a virtual dashboard in front of Jonny.

'Got it,' said Jonny.

In the Xtract bay Stella told the rogue crew to move to the rear of the maintenance bay. The rogue crew were tired and a little apprehensive. Reluctantly, they shuffled to the rear. Stella tried to keep them calm.

'When we get out of this sticky mess you have gotten us into,' she said, 'we can arrange more comfortable surroundings. Just sit tight.'

They moaned, and their security and communications officer pressed the comms link and asked about how they intended to get back to Xed and the Academy.

'Not your concern right now,' said Chang as he pressed the link and replied. 'You're the ones that got us into this damn mess!'

'Not now,' said Stella. 'Just leave it!'

'Why, why should I,' said Chang. 'Those little shits had a lot to answer for!'

'And they will,' said Aamir. 'We need you Chang, so let's get this done.'

Aamir was smart and could read Chang quite well. He knew how to entertain his ego. And it was a big ego.

The escape pod was picked up by the robotic arm off its docking clamp and moved into the airlock which closed behind it. The airlock and moon pool pressurised.

'SAI, open the moon pool and release the escape pod,' said Stella.

The airlock and moonpool were pressurised and the entrance to the moonpool opened. It couldn't be done at speed, so the Skimmer slowed while the escape pod was released.

'Confirmed,' said SAI. 'Reducing speed, launching escape pod.'

'We don't have much time,' said Jesse as they watched what was going on in the Xtract bay from the SAI console.

The robotic arm moved the escape pod over the moon pool and lowered it in. Propulsion system activated. It descended into the water and the robotic arm released it. The escape pod dropped quickly out of the moon pool and behind the Skimmer.

The moon pool closed as did the air lock, which both returned to one atmosphere of breathable air.

A proximity alarm sounded.

'Remote cavitation torpedo array impact imminent,' said SAI.

'Hurry up guys!' yelled Stella over open comms 'We need to get out of here.'

Aamir could see how nervous the rogue crew were and decided to go and talk to them in the Xtract bay. He thought they might need some comfort. He entered the maintenance bay. They looked frightened to say the least.

At the SAI console, Jonny watched as the escape pod was launched. It exited the moon pool. Once clear, SAI positioned it directly behind the Skimmer.

'SAI match the escape pod depth, course and speed to ours,' said Jonny.

'Confirmed,' said SAI.

SAI announced that final preparations to go off grid had been completed.

'Shutdown imminent,' said SAI. 'Switching to off-grid mode.' A red glow appeared throughout the Skimmer and all systems flickered then settled.

'In manual mode and off-grid,' said Jonny. 'Altering course, depth and speed.'

The escape pod maintained its course and speed and would attract the attention of the ARC torpedo array. They all watched and waited. The escape pod signature disappeared. Then nothing.

'Must have worked,' said Jesse.

'Well, we are still moving aren't we,' said Jonny.

Ngarra looked at everyone. They were exhausted.

'Right, everyone to the rec area,' said Jesse. Let's sort out where we are going and what to do with the rogue crew.

In the Xtract bay Chang pressed the comms link and told Aamir to leave the rogue crew there and come up for a briefing in the rec area. He left the rogue crew chatting amongst themselves and went off with the others.

Chapter 24

The next day Jonny was up early and looking exhausted went to check on their guests locked in the gaming room. Jesse met him as she came out of her cabin. Yawning, she laughed at how terrible Jonny looked. The last week had been tough on them all she thought to herself.

'You look like crap,' she said as they walked to the gaming room.

'Can't say you look much better,' he said with a chuckle and pointed at her hair.

Looking at her reflection Jesse could see how untidy it now was and looked forward to getting off the Skimmer for a while.

They both stood in front of the gaming room and for a moment and wandered whether they should open it. The fight the day before was unsettling to say the least.

'SAI,' said Jesse. 'Open the gaming room entrance.'

Jesse had used her security protocol to override any manual attempt to open the entrance from either side.

The entrance opened and a tried and exhausted rouge crew looked over at them from where they had been sleeping.

'Morning everyone,' said Jonny.

A few of them muttered good morning.

'Right,' said Jesse. 'Get yourselves dressed and tidied up and meet us in the rec area in half an hour. And no more of the nonsense we had yesterday guys!'

'Hi,' said a few of them.

Jesse had a brief conversation with their security and communications officer and then they left them to get ready. Jonny walked out behind her and couldn't resist quickly turned and doing his warrior facial expression.

The rogue crewed didn't know whether to smile, laugh or jump back. Not that they were in any state for humour, but Jonny tried non the less.

Jonny and Jesse walked into the rec area. Aamir, Connor and Ngarra were sitting quietly at the main table having something to eat.

'Morning,' said Ngarra as they walked in, got some food and sat down.

'You all look like shit,' said Jonny laughing.

'Right back at you,' said Ngarra.

Stella and Chang came in. They had been down in the Xtract bay console.

'What a bunch of grumps,' she said. 'Even Chang looks better than you lot and that's saying something,' she said winking at Chang.

He shrugged his shoulders and went and got something to eat.

'You lot need a cup of harden up,' he said sitting down.

'Chang, you're not actually trying to be humorous are you,' said Jonny.

Chang gave him a smirk and carried on eating.

A short time later the rogue crew wandered in and got something to eat. Everyone was now assembled in the recreation area. It had been quite a commotion the night before.

Aamir had briefed the rogue crew on what was going to happen and then let them into the Xtract bay monitoring area. He was going to take them up to the rec area for some food and a chance to clean up and rest. They had tried to take control of the entire level. Jesse had to seal it off with Stella, Aamir and Chang stuck there.

Chang had punched and knocked out their Security and Communications Officer. The others quickly submitted when Aamir also put their Skimmer operator in a head lock. Stella had kicked him between the legs, and he had gone down like a sack of potatoes.

The rogue crew were now apologetic and calm. They had been given food and water and locked in the gaming room overnight with bedding and a couple of tables and chairs.

Ngarra looked at them and then at his own crew. Nothing like a crisis to bring a team together he thought to himself.

Jesse stood up and everyone stopped eating and talking.

'First things first,' she said looking intently at the rogue crew they had recovered. 'I oversee the Skimmer Communications and Security protocols. Why were you off-grid and why threaten us and risk damaging both your Skimmer and ours?'

'You don't understand,' said their Security and Communications Officer.

'And why would that be?' asked Ngarra.

He carried on. 'We had no choice. It was meant to be about skimming nodules and selling them. Our contact had a buyer and said he would look after us. Then it became about your crew and something about some technology they wanted to get hold of. If we didn't do it, well he sent us personal details of all our families and asked if we would miss them. We were the decoy. You were meant to be so tied up with us that you wouldn't realise the Sea Hunters were here for you.'

Ngarra could tell he was getting pretty upset and worked up about it all. He glanced at Jesse, stood up and then looked back at the rogue crew. 'How did they access all that personal family information on us. Only senior staff in the crew monitoring and communication centre at the Academy have access to that data.'

'Exactly,' said Jesse. 'That confirms something that has come up. Jonah said there was a security breach and they are working on how it happened. Also, why would the Sea Hunters want to get hold of this supposed technology we have on our Skimmer.'

'We don't know,' said their Skimmer operator. 'We were just told to engage you and to try and distract or disable your Skimmer as quickly as possible. After that we were told to wait to be boarded by the Sea Hunters. That's all we know. It didn't make sense at all.'

Jesse thought about it. None of it made sense and it seemed there was a very convoluted trail of deception going on. She decided to tell them a little about Chang and what he was made to do and to tell them a little about Connor's work.

'You've met Chang,' said Jesse as she thought about the scuffle the night before. 'It seems we have something in common here. Chang was manipulated as well. His sister works in the Harvester research laboratory. Chang like you was also asked to secure all of Connor's work. But rather than his family being threatened, an opportunity was dangled in front of him.'

'What is so valuable about this work,' one of them asked.

'And you are?' said Connor with a threatening grimace. 'You can't have it.'

Connor was very protective of his work. It had taken him a year or more to build up the systems he needed for SAI to generate the technology he was now working on.

'I am our information officer, same role as you Connor. I spend my days in the information hub.'

Jesse jumped in before Connor got to emotional. He wasn't good at reading people.

'Connor's work could change a lot of things about deep sea mining if developed further. That is all I can say at present. Jonah knows about it and GlobeCorpMining keeps asking if we need their help to develop it further.'

Jesse again paused and thought how bizarre this was all getting. Who was doing what for whom and why all the fuss? Connor must have come across something significant for it to be perceived as a threat to everyone else.

Looking around she could see that the rogue crew looked shattered, but she needed to push on and try and make some sense of all this.

'So,' said one of the rogue crew as they stood up. 'The person who got hold of the details of our families and backgrounds is the same person that was able to get the Sea Hunters to try and board both our Skimmers. 'What is so important about this work?'

'OK, and who are you,' said Connor again. He was getting very worked up about everyone asking questions.

He stood up and walked over in a threatening manner.

'Connor, it's OK,' said Jesse. 'They can't do anything now. We are just trying to find out what on earth has been going on.'

Aamir had been watching things as they got tense. He got up and moved towards Connor. 'It seems as if we are all being set against each other,' he said moving to Connor's side.'

'Seems so,' said Ngarra. 'My guess is this is not over. Someone knows a lot about us all. We may be safe and sound for now, but Chang's sister is not. Would they threaten our families if we are no longer able to give these people what they want?'

The conversation continued for a while, but no solution was reached. Eventually Ngarra's crew moved off to carry out their daily routines. The rogue crew stayed in the rec area. Ngarra, Jesse and Jonny made their way up to the SAI console.

'I still don't trust that crew,' said Jonny as they walked into the SAI console. 'Nor do I think Chang will stop trying to get hold of Connor's work. I smell a rat somewhere.'

'You may well be right,' said Jesse. 'But until we know more, we just have to keep looking out for any signs of trouble.'

'Besides,' said Ngarra. 'Once back at the Academy we will have their protection.'.

***

Late in the day they arrived at a sheltered reef off one of the southern-most Cook Islands. The Sea Hunters were nowhere to be seen and they had not been picked up by any military submarines or other defence force assets in the region. They had managed to slip quietly through "the Area" and into the Cook Island's EEZ unseen and unheard.

Everyone was in position and on watch for final approach. The outer hull shields were closed, and the camera system was on. They moved along next to the reef in deep water. Silently they passed species of coral and fish that had either adapted to the devastating impact of climate change or existed survived its onslaught due to living in deeper parts of the reef.

In front and to the side there was a large gap in the reef that led to a deep lagoon. It opened out and they slowly turned into it moving into a deep lagoon. The corals on the tops and slopes of the surrounding reef had long since died off. The ocean had a warmed and bleaching combined with the impact of the intensity of super cells that raged across the region meant there was little to look at.

They surfaced in the lagoon and moved in close to the edge of a steep cliff face. The cliffs around them were draped in tropical plants, a good place to hide for a while. Like something out of a movie set, the deep clear blue water met the rocky cliff face as it rose green above and around them.

'SAI secure Skimmer and open the main entrance, port side,' said Ngarra.

'Confirmed,' said SAI. 'Skimmer secure and port side entrance opened.'

In the rec area the rogue crew watched as the entrance opened. They stepped out onto the Skimmer wing above the Xtract recess and adjacent to the mineral trays. The others came out after them and for a moment everyone forgot about the events of the last week. Silently, they looked at the beauty of their surroundings.

The plan was to bring the Skimmer back online and make contact with Academy crew monitoring so they could be picked up. They would leave the Skimmer where it was. Its signature would be detected by the Sea Hunters. They would arrive to find it empty.

It was easy enough for GlobeCorpMining to assign a transport drone to pick them up and do a crew transfer to New Caledonia. Their drone operators were good, and they would go to manual mode for the detour so they could not be tracked easily. Jonah had arranged with GlobeCorpMining for one of their crew transfer drones to be in the general area. However, if the Sea Hunters caught up with them before then, they would deny any involvement.

As the afternoon wore on everyone except Ngarra and Jesse were back in the rec area. At the SAI console Jesse had re-instigated the mining protocols and got the Skimmer back online. They were outside "the Area" grid communications network now. At the surface and using a satellite communications link, she contacted Jonah. Her image appeared in the centre of the SAI console.

It had been a nervous wait for Jonah, Rick and everyone at the Academy involved in what had unfolded over the last week.

'It's so great to see you all in one piece,' said Jonah. 'I was so worried. Let's get you all back to Xed Academy as fast as possible before anyone else gets hold of you. More importantly, what Connor has developed needs to be kept at Xed Academy so we can work on it further. It's crucial. GlobeCorpMining may support us for now but they are poking their noses around too much. We have a security breach here as well.'

'So, you said,' said Jesse, 'The rogue crew families were threatened. The crew was told to skim nodules and hassle us as a decoy. They were also given pictures of their families and asked if they would miss them. We think it's the same people that found out about Connor's work. They also tried using Chang to secure all the work and sent the Sea Hunters after us.'

'Makes sense,' said Jonah. 'I have an idea where all this is coming from but need more proof. There has to be others involved, which puts Connor in significant danger.'

'Chang is still in danger as well,' said Ngarra. 'His sister and father may be as well. Hell, they could even be involved in all this. Anyway, his sister works in the research laboratory on the Harvester. We have no way of getting to her though. We think this person or whoever these people are will still try and use Chang to get to Connor.'

Jesse thought about what was discussed and in what way Chang's sister might be involved.

'Even the Sea Hunters can't get access to sensitive areas or even board the Harvester without consent. It's in international waters on the high seas in "the Area". I think the Sea Hunters are compromised as well. We can't trust anyone.'

'But we have easy access to the Harvester,' said Ngarra. 'We just go back to doing what we do, mining nodules and use that as cover to get onboard and get to Chang's sister.'

'We will discuss it when you get back,' said Jonah. 'Let's talk again when you reach Xed. A transport drone is inbound, so you need to get ready to go and secure that Skimmer before you leave. Take all Connor's work with you. We will deal with the contractor, State sponsor authorities and the Sea Hunters. We still have GlobeCorpMining's support on that front.'

Jonah's image disappeared and Jesse and Ngarra talked about the situation further. After their discussion Jesse and Ngarra went to tell the others what was going on. They walked into the rec area and everyone looked over at her and fell silent.

'OK listen up,' said Ngarra. 'I want the rogue crew topside for pickup. My crew secure this Skimmer, so the Sea Hunters don't find anything. Connor take all your work with you. Secure the data and get SAI to erase the Skimmer information hub data bank. Stella get SAI to shut down and reboot the mining Xtract operating systems so there is no trace left of Connor's Xtract communication signal work. Everyone else get your things and go topside for pickup. We have about two hours.'

'Everything we have done over the past week has been logged,' said Jesse. 'I will get Stella to help clear SAI's records of our movements and conversations. Crew monitoring will have copies of all of it.'

Everyone disappeared. Connor went to the information hub to get SAI to shut everything down and to copy, save then erase what he had been working on.

Chang followed Connor to the Information hub. He wanted to talk to him about his sister and the Harvester.

'So,' said Chang. 'Do you think whoever these people are will stop with all these threats to our families if they got hold of what you are developing.'

'If I were that person,' said Connor, 'I would want to get hold of whoever was developing the technology, not just their work. Even if they had the work, they would still want the person. That way they could carry on with the work. So no, I do not think they will stop.'

Chang thought about what Connor had said.

'Wouldn't they just make the person disappear once the work was done?' he said. 'It's not easy to hold a person captive when everyone knows about it though. It's hard to get to a person when all they must do is hide in plain sight.'

'The work would never be done,' said Connor. 'Unless of course you are talking about a fully autonomous AI that is able to learn by itself. For me, to achieve that we need to look more into nature. We need to understand the way organisms react both individually and collectively to each other and their surroundings.'

Connor was off again and fully into the conversation. Chang smiled thinking to himself, damn it now I must listen to all this.

'Learning about group behaviour patterning in nature is key,' said Connor. 'I then use natural language programming to get SAI to develop algorithms for me. It's like building a mesh within which deep learning occurs. You can't make a drone autonomous. You must teach it to be autonomous. It's a long-term project.'

Connor paused for a moment and thought about what he had just said. He imagined what it would be like to be a wanted person. He stared into space for a while and then refocussed on Chang.

'These people would have to be smarter than that,' he said. 'I mean getting rid of the person that came up with it. But if they kept that person, he or she would have to want to work on it and feel free to do so. Hiding in plain sight.'

'Perhaps whoever they are that is threatening us is also being played,' said Chang. 'Maybe someone else is playing all of us, including whoever is threatening us, to get the outcome they want.'

'Maybe,' said Connor. 'Time will tell. I'm just glad to be getting out of here and back to the safety of Xed and the Academy for a while so I can continue my work.'

Chang was smart, perhaps to smart but he was using Connor to bounce some thoughts around.

He thought to himself that somehow and, in some way, GlobeCorpMining was behind it and his father was involved. He would keep that to himself for now.

He walked out of the information hub and went to get his things, the few possessions they had on board that they could take with them.

An hour or so later and everyone was out on the Skimmer wing again waiting to be picked up.

'I will be glad to get out of here,' said Jonny.

'Same,' said Aamir. 'My first crew placement has been a little different to what I expected.'

'That's one way of putting it,' said Jesse smiling.

'So much for mining manganese nodules,' said Ngarra. 'It will be good to get back to some normality and routine.'

In the distance a large transport drone was approaching low over the water. They all watched as it flew towards them, a low humming sound emanating from it.

It came in low and rotated in front of them. Hovering just above the water, a stern ramp was lowered from between and below the rear two blade cowlings.

'Right let's go,' yelled Jesse over the down draft and humming of the drone.

A person was waving for them to come up the ramp and inside. They moved off the Skimmer wing and up the ramp into the transport drone.

Once inside, they all got themselves strapped in and were handed out a drink and something to eat. It would be a long flight back to Xed Academy. Jesse had made a point of sitting next to the person in charge of security and communications from the off-grid Skimmer. The drone operator from the off-grid Skimmer also sat next to them. Once underway would be able to get up and sit in the small recreation area forward.

The stern ramp closed, and the transport drone rose and angled forward and down. It moved off low over the lagoon, banking and rising. As they levelled out the crew relaxed a little and settled in for the trip back.

'So, what do you think will happen once we are back,' said Jesse.

'We will be debriefed of course. I hope we are not kicked off the programme as we really didn't have much choice about what we did,' they said.

'I want to know how security was breached,' said Jesse. 'How was it that personal information was accessed.'

'Irrespective of that,' said the off-grid Skimmer operator sitting across from Jesse, 'I'm sure your team will be sent off on another skimmer to carry on monitoring Xtract mining operations.

'I wouldn't be so sure of that,' said Jesse. 'Hopefully we will be reassigned at the Ocean Academy for a while.'

'We have been off-grid for a while,' said the off-grid Skimmer communications and security officer. 'Nothing beats being back at Xed and the Academy.'

'I miss Xed and the Academy as well,' said Jesse. 'I miss the things I like doing. Jonah will fill us in on what is happening so let's relax on this transporter until we get there.'

With that they looked around at the others. All were relieved to be away from the whole situation and in one piece. It could have been very different if the Sea Hunters had reached them.

The trip back to Noumea, New Caledonia was uneventful. Flying low over a vast open ocean was surreal and the crews spent much time looking out at the horizon and an endless sea.

***

The transport drone approached the coast. It flew in over the bay and approached the drone port at the Academy. They could see Jonah, Rick and a security team waiting for them. Once landed the stern ramp opened and they walk down.

'Thank God you are OK,' said Jonah as she approached and gave them all a hug.

'We were so worried you would be detained by the Sea Hunters,' said Rick.

'It was close but we all made back in one piece,' said Jesse with a huge sigh of relief.

'Apologies people,' said Rick as he greeted them all, 'but we have to take you all to a debrief straight away. We have the Skimmer contractor, a government agency and a Sea Hunter liaison officer wanting answers. Campus security will escort us there.'

'Right let's get this over with then,' said Chang looking wearily at everyone else.

'I'm particularly concerned about you,' said Rick. 'And Connor. There's a lot going on.'

'Let's get moving then,' said Ngarra.

The rogue crew and Ngarra's crew were taken away for a debrief. After everything that had happened, they all looked forward to some normality for a while.

They were taken to a meeting room. The Academy sim team and people from crew monitoring were also waiting for the debrief. They were in a secure area in the administration block.

Jonah sat down at a long and curved table with Rick and the head of campus security. Everyone else was seated in rows in front of them.

'For the near future,' said Jonah, 'you will all stay on campus and use the time for advanced training and study. We will put you on the duty roster for the crew monitoring and communications centre and assisting with instruction.'

They all nodded their heads in agreement.

'Some you want to take some leave and that is fine,' said Rick. 'You can use your allocated leave weeks.'

Explanations followed about how everything had unfolded at sea. The topic of discussion then turned to the security breach at Xed. Everyone wanted to know how it was related to the threats against their families.

'If we don't find out how this breach happened,' said Jesse, 'then we will end up in the same situation again on another Skimmer.'

'I'm not so sure about that, said Rick. 'We are looking into it. In the meantime, do not go off the campus grounds. A lot of this seems to be related to Chang and to Connor.'

'They were targeted and perhaps still are, said Aamir. 'Will continue his work here at the Academy?'

'Connor will be working in a secure facility,' said Rick as he looked at Connor. 'Campus security has assigned you a security detail. Do not wander around alone. As for you Chang, whoever is involved in this security breach does not know that we know you have been targeted. So, no one is to talk about any of this.'

A brief discussion followed about how the Academy might change and evolve because of what had happened. Thoughts turned to what would happen if Connor was able to apply his concepts that he had developed for learning autonomous group behaviour in mining Xtracts.

Jonah interrupted everyone. 'OK listen up, the important thing to remember is that Connor's work has the potential to transform Deepsea mining. Now that is a dangerous piece of knowledge. People want to gain the upper hand, take advantage and monopolise it.'

Everyone nodded and started talking amongst themselves again.

'Listen, listen everyone. So, this is my plan,' said Jonah looking over at Rick. 'For now, some of you will help Connor and the rest will continue your advanced training and education courses and assist with instruction and duties. I am going to talk with GlobeCorpMining about Chang's vulnerability and his sister's. Being on a Harvester she can't go anywhere and unless someone on that monolith is in on all this, she is safe for now.'

'That's it for now then,' said Rick. 'Off you lot go then.'

'What about "the Authority" and the Sea Hunters wanting to detain us,' said Stella. 'What about the contractor complaints. We could still be prosecuted.'

'Let us worry about that,' said Rick looking over at Jonah.

'What if Chang's father is vulnerable as well,' said Aamir.

'Our focus are our crews,' said Jonah. 'Secondly, our focus is protecting our programme and its funding. Lastly, looking to the future and what Connor has come up with. If that means working with GlobeCorpMining to call off these people and securing Chang's sisters safety, then that is what we will do.'

'We will talk about this more later,' said Rick. 'You lot in the rogue crew need to stay here. Our security team need to ask you some more questions to better determine your involvement in all this.'

With that everyone moved off back to their accommodation blocks to get some well-earned rest for a few days.

***

Over the following weeks Connor relished the opportunity to absorb himself in his. He was tucked away working with SAI in a secure research facility in the sim centre. He had run the source code for his giant ocean bubble hologram. Within it once again he had a group of simulated Xtracts. With different hand gestures he could now get the group to do different things, reacting to his hand as a group and learning from their own behavioural responses.

The limit of Connor's success with learning collective behaviour responses in the Xtracts was related to decisions amongst individual ones about whether to assist others directly if malfunctioning, or for an individual to protect the group from an external threat or to look after their own systems. Any learnt group behaviour that involved gathering around a threat eventually broke down, and they became disorganised and chaotic. Connor decided to turn back to nature for more answers.